THE FROST KILLER

DALTON SAVAGE

BOOK 4

L.T. RYAN

WITH

BIBA PEARCE

For information contact:

contact@ltryan.com

http://LTRyan.com

https://www.facebook.com/groups/1727449564174357

THE DALTON SAVAGE SERIES

Join the L.T. Ryan reader family & receive a free copy of the Rachel Hatch story, *Fractured*. Click the link below to get started:

https://ltryan.com/rachel-hatch-newsletter-signup-1

Love Hatch? Savage? Noble? Maddie? Get your very own L.T. Ryan merchandise today! Click the link below to find coffee mugs, t-shirts, and even signed copies of your favorite L.T. Ryan thrillers! https://ltryan.ink/EvG_

ONE

SHERIFF DALTON SAVAGE narrowed his eyes as he squinted through the windshield. Damn snow. It had been coming down for three days now with another line of storms on the way. The whole county was blanketed, roads blocked, people stranded, his team and the emergency services working around the clock.

It was pretty to look at, but that didn't make up for the inconvenience. The windshield wipers flicked back and forth, scraping over the frosted glass. He was lucky if he could see ten feet in front of him.

Savage grimaced as the tire chains bit into the icy crust that covered the roads. What with the screeching wipers and the roar of the wind, he almost didn't hear the crackle of the radio.

"Sheriff Savage, do you copy?"

Savage picked up the radio and keyed the mic. "I read you, Barb. What's up?" Barbara Wright, admin assistant at the Hawk's Landing Sheriff's Department and mother hen to the team, came back on the radio. "We got a call from the Thompson ranch. Says they heard something strange out by their barn. I was going to send Sinclair, but figured since you were closest...."

"Sure thing."

“They said it’s probably nothing, but given the recent livestock disappearances—"

"Copy that, Barb. I’m on the Durango Road now, so I’ll detour to the ranch and check it out.”

He never used to take this stretch of road home, but since he and Becca had purchased the old Apple Tree Farm, he was getting to know it pretty darn well. They’d moved in just before winter hit, but still hadn’t done much to the property. The previous owners had abandoned it when the bank had foreclosed, so it was in a pretty bad state. What with baby Connor demanding most of their spare time, and him going back to work, they hadn’t gotten around to making many improvements.

He sighed. Never mind, the renovations would keep. At least they were warm. While he was on leave, he’d installed a central heating system – and just in time too. This winter’s storms were the worst he’d seen since first arriving in Hawk’s Landing.

Adjusting his grip on the wheel, Savage made a U-turn and headed toward the Thompson property. Lone Mountain Ranch had once been a large, profitable place, but like so many businesses in the county, it had fallen on hard times. The recent icy conditions made things even worse. The blocked roads outside of town caused supply issues. Emergency services couldn’t clear them fast enough and trucks got stranded. Suppliers weren’t willing to take a chance and were waiting out the worst of the storms.

To compound the issue, the local businesses couldn’t get their stock to market. Durango was one of the few exceptions, since many people from Hawk's Landing worked in the bigger town, so it was one of the few roads they made sure was cleared regularly. Good thing too, else he wouldn’t be able to get home.

Savage wound his way up the drive to the Lone Mountain Ranch and pulled in beside a beat-up Chevy pickup blanketed in a layer of snow, its once-red paint faded and chipped. No sooner had he climbed out of the SUV than the front door opened and a stocky man wearing a cap and a checked winter jacket with fur trim nodded at him. "Sheriff, good of you to come. Wasn't sure you'd make it in this weather."

"No problem, Nate. You reported sounds coming from the barn?"

"Well, it wasn't me as such." He hesitated. "Come on in. There's someone here you gotta meet."

Savage followed Nate Thompson into a cozy living room. A crackling fire burned in the grate, but it was the man that stood in front of it that commanded his attention. Easily six-three with a barrel-like chest and a craggy face weathered by years of outdoor living, he was not the kind of man that escaped notice. Wearing a tawny fur coat almost the same color as his scraggly beard, he regarded Savage with dark, suspicious eyes. When the stranger turned to the side, Savage noticed the old scar running down his cheek.

"Sheriff, this is Jack O'Donnell, but we call him Grizzly. He lives in a cabin up in the mountains."

Savage gave a curt nod. He was still wondering what this bear of a man had to do with anything.

"Go on," Nate prompted, looking at the visitor. "Tell him what you saw."

Saw.

"I thought you'd heard signs of an animal in distress," Savage said.

"I heard something." The mountain man spoke for the first time. He had a deep, gravelly voice, and his eyes widened as he spoke, as if he were surprised by the sound of it. "Sounded like an injured animal."

Savage bet he didn't have much contact with the outside world. He'd heard of men like this. Loners, living off the land, hunting elk, fishing in ice-covered rivers, and trapping small game.

"I was bringing some elk to Nate because I know he ain't been able to get meat for a while, when I heard screeching coming from the barn."

"Screeching?"

The man nodded.

"I got a barn a mile from here, near the foothills," Nate confirmed. "Use it to store equipment and the like."

Savage turned back to Grizzly. "Go on."

"I went to see what all the fuss was about. Thought a deer had got trapped inside or something. That's when I saw the blood."

"Blood?" Savage's heart skipped a beat.

"Yeah, in the snow. Leading away from the barn."

"Did you check the barn?" His voice was low.

"No, I didn't go inside."

"Why not?" Savage studied the mountain man.

"Not a good idea when you got an elk hindquarter over your shoulder. Could be a wild animal in there. Besides, I wanted to get here before the temperature dropped any lower." It was icy outside and getting colder by the minute. In another hour or two, the temperatures would be in the teens.

Savage let out a long breath. "Okay, fair enough. It was probably a deer that got attacked by a mountain lion or a coyote or something."

"That's what I thought."

"It was my idea to call you." Nate ran a worried hand through his hair. "I mean, what if it's not an animal in there. What if someone's lying injured? They could have gone inside to shelter from the storm."

Nate had a point, although no one would be foolish enough to be out in this weather, would they? Certainly not a local. He glanced at his watch. Nearly seven o'clock. It was pitch dark outside, no lights around these parts, certainly none on the snow-covered land leading to the barn. The sensible thing would be to leave it until daylight, then they could muster a team and go up to take a look.

"How much blood?" he asked Grizzly.

"A fair bit."

Damn.

As much as he wanted to go home, he knew he wouldn't sleep until he'd checked it out. He turned to the mountain man. "You up for taking a walk?" Grizzly would be able to lead him straight to the barn.

A shrug. "Sure. It's a good mile, though, and it's getting pretty icy out there." Icy was an understatement. There were severe weather warnings in place all over the county, and up in the foothills, it would be colder still. His brown suede, fleece-lined sheriff's jacket was fairly warm, made for the cold weather. It should be okay for a mile-long hike.

"I'll join you." Nate got a couple of high-powered outdoor flashlights out of a side cabinet. "We're going to need these." He handed one to Savage, who grunted his thanks. It was more powerful than the one he had in the SUV.

Savage waited while the two men slung hunting rifles over their shoulders. He had his trusty Glock in his holster, but his pump action shotgun was still in the safe back at the office. If there was a threat from a wild animal, he'd leave that to the experts. Any human threat, and he was prepared.

"Ready?"

They both nodded.

"Let's head out."

Thick snow blanketed the terrain. Savage looked toward the mountains, but it was impossible to see where the ranchland endedended, and the hills began. Above, the slate-gray sky shot diagonal arrows of stinging snow into their faces. Every now and then the clouds parted to reveal a sliver of moon before blocking it out again.

The only sound was the creak of their boots as they trudged blindly along, and the hollow whistle of the icy wind as it howled across the terrain. Savage's eyes watered, but he blinked back the tears.

Soon, however, his blood was pumping, and he'd worked up a sweat. They were moving at a rapid pace, set by the mountain man, who was obviously used to such terrain. His long legs stomped through the snow, one arm swinging freely by his side, the other holding the shoulder strap of his rifle. He wasn't even panting, unlike Savage, who was sucking in rough gasps of frigid air. "How far?"

"Around that ridge." Nate pointed up ahead. Savage squinted but couldn't see any ridge. Everything was uniformly white. He could have been about to fall off a precipice and he'd never know it.

A short while later, they rounded a camouflaged ridge in the foothills and came across a snow-covered barn. It was so well hidden, he'd never have found it by himself.

"Where's the blood?" he asked, eyes glued to the ground.

"Over here."

Savage followed Grizzly to the front of the barn where he could see faded red indents in the snow. The heavy snowfall had almost completely covered them, but there were still dirty pink paw-sized smudges leading away from the structure.

"Whatever made these prints is long gone," Grizzly said, bending down. "These tracks lead away from the barn."

Savage didn't need a trapper to tell him that much.

"Let's take a look inside." They made their way to the wooden double doors that stood slightly ajar. Snow and ice had jammed them open.

"You usually keep this locked?" he asked Nate.

"Yeah, someone must have forced them open."

It was dark inside, and eerily quiet. No sound of animal noises now. Savage shone his flashlight through the gap and peered into the gloom.

Nothing.

He couldn't see a damn thing, but there was a rank, musky smell, and he wrinkled his nose. He knew that smell. Definitely a dead animal.

Stepping through the gap, he shone his flashlight around the interior of the barn. It was bigger than it looked from the outside. Shadowy, metallic shapes loomed out of the darkness, casting distorted shadows against the back wall.

Before Savage could advise otherwise, Nate entered behind him, throwing his flashlight beam over the assortment of farm machinery, bags of feed for the animals, and boxes of supplies. "There's nothing here."

"Over here," growled the mountain man, his deep voice hovering in the darkness. He'd somehow managed to enter behind them and move to the middle of the barn. For a big man, he was surprisingly quiet. Savage hadn't heard a sound.

Nate rounded a tractor and stared down at the darkened floor. His voice was a hollow rasp. "*That* is not an animal."

Savage joined them, following the beam cast by Nate's flashlight. His breath caught in his throat at the sight.

TWO

SHE LAY SPRAWLED across a pile of hay as if she'd been thrown there. Discarded by something larger and more powerful than she was.

Savage shone his flashlight onto her face. So pale, almost as pale as the snow outside, and her hair, once blonde, was wet and clotted with blood. Eyes closed, she looked like she was asleep, except for the wound on the side of her neck. Forcing a shallow breath, he turned his gaze away from her face, down to the gouging injury.

"Is that a bite mark?" He leaned in to get a closer look.

"Wild animal," Grizzly growled. "Too clean for a bear. I'm guessing a mountain lion by the look of those claw marks. It got her by the neck. She was mauled to death."

Savage ran the light over her body. Her woolen jumper was shredded, and there were deep gashes in her jeans where sharp claws had ravaged her. Faint pink flesh was visible through the worst of the lacerations.

"I would have expected more blood," he murmured, studying the dark smears under her head, no doubt from the artery that had been severed.

"Too cold to bleed for long," Grizzly replied.

"She wouldn't have stood a chance with injuries like that." Nate cringed, visibly shaken. "Poor girl probably came inside to shelter from the storm and something must've followed."

That seemed to be the most likely scenario. It was a horrific way to go. Savage avoided her face and focused on the neck wound. A large chunk of flesh was missing.

"Not too common for a mountain lion to attack like that," remarked Nick.

"Not if she startled a mama protecting her cubs." Grizzly shrugged. "It would have ambushed her, taken her by surprise."

"I'm going to need to seal this area off and get my people to come run the crime scene."

"You really think all that's necessary?" Nate cocked an eyebrow.

"I'm not saying it isn't an animal attack. But it's standard protocol in an unexplained death. And in my experience, you don't know the answer until you do." Savage searched her pockets and the area around her body for any identification. Nothing. He straightened up, his knees clicking. "Either of you recognize her?"

Neither man spoke, each offering only a solemn shake of their head. Savage exhaled, the air fogging in front of his face.

"It's still coming down." Grizzly motioned to the driving snow outside the door. "Gonna be hell tryin' to make it up here now. Might be safer to wait until daybreak."

"I can't just leave her here." Savage looked around. The barn was unprotected, snow was blowing inside the door in little flurries, the frozen hinges creaking in protest. "We'll be digging her out by morning. That is, if something doesn't come in and haul away what's left of her."

"What about Search and Rescue?" asked Nate. "They could take her body away in a chopper."

"A chopper's not going to take off in this, but they might be able to get here on a snowcat or something." He keyed the mic on his lapel. A buzz sounded. He looked down at his radio. The red indicator light was activated, letting him know he was out of range. Savage pulled out his cellphone, but there was no reception.

"Dammit." Holding it in the air, he scowled at the lack of signal.

"We'll have to hike back to the ranch," Nate reasoned. "Land line should be working. We can call from there."

"I'll wait with her," Savage said. "You two go."

"You sure?" Nate frowned. "There's no heating in here, and the temperatures are still dropping."

"I can wait with you," Grizzly offered.

Savage shook his head. "You go with Nate. It's important he makes it back in one piece."

There was a pause as they considered the validity of his statement.

"Okay." Nate handed Savage his hunting rifle. "You'd better take this just in case whatever did this comes back."

"Thanks." Savage slung it over his shoulder. The weight of it was comforting.

"Hang tight. We'll tell them to be as quick as they can, but the nearest base is in Durango."

It could be hours.

Savage gritted his teeth. "Do me a favor after you get a hold of the search team, call the station and update Barbara on the situation."

With a nod, the two men set off, striding knee-deep through the snow. Standing at the barn door, Savage watched them go, then turned back to the frigid darkness inside the barn.

Hell, it was cold. He'd never experienced temperatures like this, and he was from Denver. Rubbing his gloved hands together, he tried to generate some body heat. His frigid breath steamed in front of him before dissipating like smoke. The glacial air clung to his face, prickling his skin.

Savage returned to the body. The beam from his flashlight was the only light source, and it sliced through the heavy darkness like a laser. He drew in a breath, steeling himself, then bent down to take a closer look.

Young, in her early twenties, and pretty – or she would have been at one time, before this. Dark lashes framing those petrified eyes. Was she wearing mascara? Up close, he realized that her face was actually an eerie shade of pale blue, blending with the frost that clung delicately to her hair and sprinkled the ground around her. Ice crystals had formed on her eyelashes and the edges of her nostrils, and her clothes were stiff and unbending, preserving the position in which she'd died.

Her hands, rigid and curled into stiff claws, were surprisingly unmarked. Ruby red nails, vivid against her ashen skin. No scars, no scratches or lacerations. It didn't look like she'd tried to fend off the frenzied animal that had claimed her life.

Frowning, he shone his flashlight on the floor, looking for blood spatter, but there was very little. Maybe it had frozen beneath her body. He thought about moving her but decided against it. He didn't want to destroy what little evidence was there. Hopefully the CSI team could tell them what kind of animal had mauled her.

Not even a portable AFIS machine would help, since there was no internet connection out here. The fingerprint analysis would have to wait until they got her back to the morgue. If she was on the police database, they'd be able to get an ID. But a girl like this, with her quality clothes and manicured nails, probably wouldn't have a police record.

Slowly and deliberately, he moved his flashlight down her body. Slim, dressed in jeans and a cream winter jumper. No scarf. No coat. What the hell was she doing here without protection from the snowstorm? It had been on the news for weeks, the series of cold fronts moving south, freezing everything in their path. Hardly sudden.

He was about to turn away when a metallic glint caught his eye. Bending down, he stared at the area beside her body. A silver chain lay on the ground. He almost hadn't seen it, half hidden as it was beneath the straw.

Hers? Or did it belong to the Thompsons, lost here in warmer months and forgotten about?

Reaching down, he picked up the chain with his gloved hand and studied it. It had snapped, the chain-link severed but not at the clasp.

He supposed it could have been ripped off during the attack. There was something else too. A pendant. Round, flat, silver-rimmed with a glass center.

Hang on... He squinted. There was something inside the glass. Shining the flashlight onto the pendant, he made out a delicate paper snowflake, intricate and detailed.

Carefully, he got a forensic glove out of his pocket and slipped the chain and pendant into it. That would have to do until he could get an evidence bag to put them in. Then he placed the glove in his inside jacket pocket. It would be safe there, the chain of evidence uninterrupted. It might help identify her.

Two hours later, and the plummeting night temperature was becoming a problem. Savage's feet had gone numb, and he could no longer feel his pinkie fingers. Pacing up and down the barn didn't help much, but at least it kept his circulation going. If he'd known he would be spending his evening outdoors, he'd have brought additional protection and supplies.

Becca would be wondering where he was. Hopefully, she'd have called the office by now and spoken with Barb. Cringing, he stomped his feet, dislodging more snow. He should have called her before he'd set off, but he'd been focused on the call-out and hadn't expected it to take so long.

The dark was getting to him too. He'd turned his flashlight off to conserve the battery, but the wind whistled around the structure, emitting a low screech that worked on his nerves. Where the hell was the rescue team?

The snowcat wasn't fast, but it was effective in this weather. It was the only way the search and rescue crew would get here with their equipment and a stretcher to remove the body.

Nearly three hours later, and on the point of turning blue, Savage was relieved to hear the distinct rumble of the snowcat's turbo diesel engine.

"Thank God for that," he muttered, as they pulled up outside the barn. For the last half hour, he'd been doing star jumps and running on the spot to stave off hypothermia.

As it turned out, he'd been right. Visibility was so bad, the team hadn't got helicopter clearance, and so they'd driven from the base to the ranch in the machine.

"She's in here," he called to the crew, who rushed in, grateful for the temporary respite from the snow. To his surprise, Grizzly was with them. The mountain man looked to be in good shape, despite having made the trip three times. A veteran of this unforgiving wilderness, he'd guided the paramedics back to the barn.

"Thanks for coming back," Savage told him.

He grunted. "Want to see the girl to safety."

As if she were still alive.

Savage nodded. He too hadn't wanted to leave her out here alone in the cold and the dark. After the crew had strapped her onto the gurney, the Search and Rescue team leader, a broad-shouldered man who'd introduced himself as Clinton, said, "We're ready to go."

Savage nodded. "Okay, then. Let's head back."

The journey back in the snowcat took a brief fifteen minutes, compared to the hour-long walk to get there. It had stopped snowing, too, which helped with visibility.

"A brief respite," Clinton said grimly. "There's more on the way."

The ranch house loomed out of the snow like a welcome mirage, becoming clearer the nearer they got. Savage sighed in relief when the door opened and Nate let them in. The victim was taken to a waiting ambulance.

"I called your deputies," Nate told him, as he walked inside and saw Sinclair and Thorpe waiting in the living room. Deputy Sinclair had grown up in La Plata County, so she knew the general area pretty well, while Thorpe was a Tennessee local, and had only been in Hawk's Landing for a few years.

"We came as soon as we could." Thorpe handed Savage a dry, fur-lined winter jacket that he hadn't seen before. It must be one of his own. With a grateful grunt, Savage shrugged off his sheriff's one, now wet and stiff with cold, and pulled on his deputy's. Slowly, the feeling began to return to his fingers.

"You got the AFIS machine?" he asked, when his teeth had stopped chattering.

"Yeah, it's in the car." Thorpe raised his eyebrows. "Want me to get it?"

He gave a stiff nod. "Let's see if she's in the system before they take her away."

"I'll be right back." Thorpe disappeared, then gave a shout a few minutes later. "Hey, out here."

Savage and Sinclair went to see what was happening. "I got a match," he called from the back of the ambulance.

"Yeah? Who is she?"

"Her name is Anita Cullen. She was arrested five years ago for shoplifting. Minor offense. Got a suspended sentence."

Not such a long shot after all.

"Did you say Cullen?" Nate frowned.

"Yeah, you know her?"

"I know her grandparents," he said with a shake of his head. "They run the general store in Hawk's Landing. Good folk. Been here for generations. They'll be devastated to hear about their granddaughter's death."

"What about her parents?" Savage asked.

"They live in that big house up in the foothills."

He knew it. It spread out on the lower slopes of the mountain, accessible only by a winding forest service road that led up from the town. "Well, that's our next stop."

It was nearly two in the morning, but it felt later. Much later. This had been one hell of a night – and it was about to get longer.

THREE

"YOU'RE SURE this isn't hers?" Savage showed a photograph of the snowflake pendant to Anita Cullen's shellshocked parents. After the initial blow, they'd collapsed on the four-seater couch in their spacious living room and were holding each other like they were afraid to let go. Afraid of what else might befall them.

"I'm sure," Anita's father croaked, his voice heavy with grief. "We've never seen it before."

"Did she suffer?" Mrs. Cullen glanced up fearfully. She wore silk pajamas and her fine, blonde hair tinged with gray hung loosely around her face. Her feet were bare, despite the cold.

"No," lied Savage. "The attack was sudden. It would have been over quickly." That much was true, at least, but the fear and pain up to that point must have been substantial. He blinked away the image of her terrified eyes staring up at him.

Her mother closed her eyes. "Thank God."

"Is there anyone we can call for you?" Sinclair asked. "A relative, a friend?"

"My parents live close by," Mr. Cullen said. "We'll call them in the morning." The grandparents who owned the general store.

Mrs. Cullen nodded, stifling a sob.

"We'll have to tell Logan," Mr. Cullen added.

"Oh, God." Mrs. Cullen grasped his hand.

"Logan?"

"Logan Maddox, her boyfriend." Mr. Cullen grimaced, or perhaps he was just trying to keep it together. "They were dating."

Maybe it was Logan who'd given her the necklace.

"We can do it, if you like?" offered Sinclair.

Her father dropped his head. "That would be a relief, thank you. It's going to be hard enough telling Mom and Pop—" His face crumpled, and he didn't finish.

"That's okay." Sinclair replied somberly. "Leave it with us."

"I don't understand what she was doing out there," her mother whispered. "I mean, she knows better than to go skiing in this weather."

"Skiing?" Savage arched an eyebrow.

"She was an avid cross-country skier," her father said. "We assumed that's what she was doing when... when she was attacked."

"We didn't find any skis or snow boots at the barn," Savage said, frowning. "It looks like she was on foot."

"No way." Her mother shook her head. "That's impossible."

"Anita grew up in these parts," her father explained. "My wife is right, she wouldn't be out there on the Thompsons' ranch on foot, and especially not in this weather. She knows better than that."

"How did she get there, then?" Savage glanced at Sinclair. The barn was at least a mile from the ranch. Still on the Thompsons' property, but not easy to reach in the snow. It had taken them over an hour to walk there. Plus, Anita had been wearing tennis shoes, jeans and a cashmere sweater. No coat or ski jacket. She definitely had not been dressed for the outdoors.

Sinclair gave a puzzled shrug. "Where would she have set out from?"

"West Mountain Resort. That's where Logan works. He's a ski

instructor there. It's where they met." Something in Mr. Cullen's voice made Savage think he wasn't a fan of his daughter's boyfriend.

He saw Sinclair make a note on her phone. The resort wasn't far from here. The south and west-facing slopes of the mountain were perfect for skiing, and several resorts had sprung up over the last ten years, or so he'd been told. He wasn't a skier. Preferred hiking the trails in the summer, although he didn't get to do that very often these days.

"How long have they been dating?" He watched Mr. Cullen's face.

"Couple of months."

"What's he like?"

"He's okay. Handsome fellow. Strikes me as something of a ladies' man."

"Anita was crazy about him," her mother said. "He treated her well."

Her father gave a soft snort.

"Okay, we'll pay him a visit first thing in the morning," Savage said. The early hours were not the time to go knocking on doors at the ski resort. Neither Mr. nor Mrs. Cullen reacted. Logan Maddox wasn't important enough to pierce their grief. Ashen faces, lines deeply engraved into their foreheads, the all-too-familiar haunted expressions. He'd seen it all before, and it never got easier.

"I'm so sorry for your loss," Sinclair said as they got up to leave. "Please let us know if there's anything we can do."

"Thank you." Mr. Cullen managed, his voice trembling. His wife had retreated into herself. She twiddled the wedding ring on her finger. Round and round, unaware of what she was doing. Savage's heart went out to them. Nothing they could do would bring back their daughter.

They left the sprawling property and walked back to their cars. Neither spoke. In the valley below, the streetlights of the town twinkled brightly, oblivious to the pain of the residents on the hill. Both Savage's Suburban and Sinclair's cruiser were parked outside, already glittering with frost.

"I don't remember it ever being this cold," Sinclair muttered, stomping her feet to get rid of the snow. "I hope you've got heating in your new place."

"Yeah, got it installed last month."

"That's good. See you tomorrow," she said, then glanced at her watch. "Make that in a couple of hours."

It was nearly five o'clock. "Get some sleep. We have to talk to Logan Maddox before he heads out onto the slopes."

"I know."

Savage cast one last lingering glance back at the house. "What the hell was she doing out there?"

"It's a mystery," Sinclair replied, rubbing her eyes.

"I don't like mysteries."

She gave a tired smile. "I know, that's what makes you a good sheriff."

He grunted and watched her drive off. The sky lightened to the east. The pre-dawn glow bled into the inky black, diffusing it. He felt wired, the events of the night leaving him strung-out. Sleep wouldn't come, not while everything was so fresh in his head. He also didn't want to wake Becca, who needed her sleep. He'd send her a text message once he got to the office. Climbing back into his SUV, Savage drove straight to the Sheriff's department.

THE SLOPES OPENED AT NINE, which gave Savage and Sinclair half an hour to find and question Logan Maddox. Parking outside the clubhouse at the West Mountain Ski Resort, they ignored the startled looks from the guests who'd noticed the unmistakable colors and insignia of the county sheriff's department on the side of their vehicle.

Stifling a yawn, Savage followed Sinclair into the clubhouse. A large sprawling building, it housed the administrative offices, the resort hotel, and a pub-style bar with a separate entrance called the Snow Plough.

Inside was warm and inviting and filled with the tempting aroma of bacon and coffee. Breakfast was in full swing. Savage's stomach rumbled. Going directly to the office after the Cullens' meant he hadn't had breakfast.

Sinclair glanced over at him. "Coffee?"

"Yeah, but first, let me call Maddox."

"I'll do it. You grab us a table."

He wasn't going to argue with that. Savage went into the restaurant and looked around. Situated off the main lobby, it was contemporary and elegant with expansive windows that overlooked the majestic snow-drenched mountains. They stretched upwards, their white peaks piercing the soft underbelly of the cloudy sky. Savage had never been here before, and he had to admit, the view was spectacular.

As soon as he sat down, a smiling waitress came over. Ordering two coffees, he sat back to admire the view. On closer inspection, he could make out the rocky outcrops peering through the snow, the edges hard and jagged. Between them sluiced curved valleys, steep and dangerous – reserved for only the most advanced skiers.

Sinclair returned. "He's on his way."

"Great."

Half a cup later, Logan Maddox strode in. He walked with a confident swagger and smiled indiscriminately at everyone he passed, particularly the women.

"Reminds me of a high school jock," murmured Sinclair, as he made his way over to their table.

Savage sized him up. Mid-30s, athletic build with sun-kissed hair that framed a face used to smiling. As Mr. Cullen had said, he was a handsome man. Roughly six feet tall with a long-legged stride and broad shoulders, Maddox wore a pale blue ski jacket, the zipper open, and reflective sunglasses on his head.

"You must be Sheriff Savage." He extended a hand.

Savage shook it, then introduced Sinclair. "This is Deputy Sinclair."

Maddox's smile widened, and his gaze lingered on her face. "Good to meet you."

Savage felt her tense. He gestured to the vacant chair. "Please take a seat, Mr. Maddox."

The ski instructor eased into the chair, stretching his long legs out in front of him. They bumped into Sinclair's, but he didn't apologize. Instead, he flashed her a grin and shifted them ever so slightly to the side.

"What is this about?" He seemed genuinely curious.

"I'm sorry, Logan, but we have some bad news," Sinclair began. On the way there, Savage had asked her to break the news about Anita. It wasn't just for the experience. He just had a feeling a guy like Logan would respond better to a woman, and he was right.

The spark faded, replaced by a look of concern. "What about?"

"It's your girlfriend, Anita Cullen." Sinclair hesitated.

A flirty smile. "Anita isn't my girlfriend."

"Oh?" Sinclair glanced at Savage, thrown. "That's not what we heard."

"We aren't in a relationship, we just... see each other every now and then. Our relationship is more physical, if you know what I mean." He winked at her. "Anyway, what's up with Anita? Has something happened to her?"

Sinclair frowned at his blatant attempt at flirting while she tried to regain her train of thought. Savage gave her a moment. Eventually, she said, "Anita Cullen was found dead last night."

There was a stunned silence as her words sank in. Logan stared at Sinclair, then looked at Savage for confirmation. "For real?"

He nodded. "For real."

Logan sucked in a breath. "Holy crap. How? I mean... what happened?"

"It looks like she was attacked by a wild animal," Sinclair explained. "Her parents asked us to inform you."

"Oh, yeah. Sure. Of course." The frown deepened and he shook his head. "That's crazy. I only saw her yesterday."

"When?" Savage asked.

"Lunchtime. We ate here at the resort. I can't believe she's... dead." He ran a hand through his hair, dislodging his sunglasses. They fell to the floor, and he bent to retrieve them. Despite their relationship being mostly physical, he did appear to be shocked by the news.

"Where did it happen?" he asked, setting them on the table.

"We're still piecing it all together," Sinclair replied.

"You don't know, or you're not telling me?" He looked confused.

"Ever been to the Thompson's ranch?"

"Sure. That's her granddaddy's land."

"What?" Savage leaned in.

"Yeah, didn't you know? Her grandaddy owns most of this side of the mountain. Leases it to the ranchers. I think he used to own this site too, but Austin Lambert – that's my boss – bought it from them to build the resort."

Savage glanced at Sinclair, who also looked surprised. Neither of them had known that. Nate hadn't said anything about it.

"You said she was attacked?" Logan turned to Sinclair.

"Yes, from what we can tell," she said, careful not to give out too much information. "We'll know more after the autopsy."

He exhaled loudly. "I still can't believe it."

"Mr. Maddox, did you give her a necklace?" asked Savage. "We found one next to her body."

The ski instructor looked surprised at the question. "No, we weren't really at the gift-giving stage yet."

Sinclair's eyes hardened. "Was she wearing a necklace when you last saw her?"

"I don't think so." He looked at each of them in turn. "Why? Is it important?"

Savage shrugged. "Probably not."

Savage finished his coffee then pushed himself up from the table. "Mr. Maddox, would you mind showing us where Anita kept her skis?"

"Sure, they're at the back of the ski shop. There's a shed where we store our stuff. Come with me."

They followed him out of the warm clubhouse into the crisp, invigorating air at the base of the slopes where the chairlift station was situated. The lift itself was stationary, but the operator was in his little hut, getting ready to kickstart the day. Soon it would be ferrying adventurers toward the frosted peaks.

They walked past a kaleidoscope of skiers, swathed in jackets of every hue, waiting in a line to board the ski lift. Most chatted in a low hum while waiting for the slopes to open, skis already secured to booted feet, scraping gently against the snow.

"Best runs in the county," Logan boasted, as they approached a wooden shop with a big banner that read, *Ski School & Private Lessons or Ski Rentals* on the side.

Logan didn't seem that upset about Anita, now that he'd gotten over the initial shock. A woman in her forties waved as they walked past, and he threw her a cheeky wink. The guy was obviously an incorrigible womanizer. He wondered if Anita knew what he was really like.

They slipped through a nondescript door at the rear of the building and found themselves in a well-used workshop. The air was thick with the earthy scent of wood and the slightly acrid tang of varnish and fiberglass, a testament to the countless repairs and tune-ups that had taken place within these walls.

Skis in various stages of repair and maintenance lay scattered across worn wooden benches, and the overhead shelves were a jumble of wax, screws, and an assortment of tools. How the people who worked here knew where anything was, Savage had no idea.

"Organized chaos." Logan chuckled, reading his mind.

Toward the back, a robust rack groaned under the weight of numerous colorful skis. Some, scarred by previous descents, were well-used, while others appeared pristine and filled with untouched potential.

"These are hers." Logan took out a pair of streamlined cross-country skis with bindings attached. Black, with a red and gold stripe across the nose, they looked sleek and expensive.

"You sure?" Savage took them from him and inspected them. They were dry, didn't look used.

"Of course I'm sure."

Savage ignored his irritated look. "Did she have another pair?"

"I have no idea. All I know is these are the ones she kept here."

"Okay." He nodded at Sinclair for them to go. There was nothing else they could do here. "Thanks for your time."

"Deputy," Logan called to Sinclair as they walked away. They both turned around. "You know where to find me if you want to ask me any more questions." Savage was annoyed at the suggestive remark, so he could only imagine how Sinclair felt.

"I don't think that'll be necessary," she said coldly.

Savage watched smugly as Logan's smile faded.

"Come on," he said to Sinclair. "Let's get out of here."

"What a prick," Sinclair muttered, as they made their way back to the SUV.

They were on their way back to the station when Barb came over the radio. "Sheriff, I've got Ray on the line for you." Ray was a medical examiner who, along with his wife, Pearl, a forensic expert, had moved to Hawk's Landing to get away from the big city. Savage had used their expertise on a number of cases over the last year. They made a trustworthy and reliable team.

"Patch him through. Thanks, Barb."

"Dalton, it's Ray. I've got those autopsy results you wanted."

Savage slowed to navigate a particularly icy stretch of road. The tire chains crunched as they struggled for grip. "Yeah? What have you got?"

"You do bring me the most unusual cases."

He frowned. "What do you mean?" A mauling wasn't that unusual.

"I mean, your victim was dead long before she was attacked by whatever took a bite out of her."

Savage froze, his hand gripping the steering wheel.

"You there?" Ray asked.

"Yeah, I'm still here." His voice was a rasp. "Are you saying what I think you're saying?"

"That she was murdered?"

"Yes."

"No, for once that is not what I'm saying."

Savage shot Sinclair a puzzled look. "I'm confused, Ray. What *are* you saying?"

"I'm saying your victim died of hypothermia at least a couple of hours before she was mauled."

"I guess that explains why there was no blood inside the barn?"

"I'll send over the paperwork once I've got it typed up."

Savage ended the call. His gaze pierced the smudged windshield to the pale sky stretched across the snow-capped trees. Somewhere out there, Anita Cullen had frozen to death and then her body had been moved, leaving him with more questions than answers.

And buried beneath it all lay the truth.

FOUR

"HYPOTHERMIA?" Sinclair stared at him.

"That's what he said."

"She froze to death?" Thorpe swiveled around in his chair.

"Yep. For whatever reason, she was stranded out in the snowstorm and took cover in the barn. It was so cold, and as we know, she wasn't dressed for it, so she developed hypothermia and died. A couple of hours later, the mountain lion found her."

Barbara closed her eyes. "How awful."

"Why didn't she call for help?" asked Littleton, who was working on some reports in the corner.

"There's no cellphone coverage in the vicinity," Savage confirmed. "I tried to call the search and rescue team when we found her body. That's why Nate and Grizzly had to hike back to the ranch."

"At least that will bring her parents some comfort," Sinclair muttered. Savage nodded. It would help knowing she succumbed to hypothermia and fell asleep, rather than was mauled to death by a lion. Not that there was any good way to go.

Sinclair stood up. "I'll let them know."

"So that's it, then?" Thorpe asked. "Natural causes."

Savage nodded. “Yeah, the autopsy is pretty definitive. Tragic, but nothing suspicious.”

“Except how she got there in the first place.” Thorpe glanced at Savage over his glasses.

He shrugged. “That’s not enough to build a case on.”

Although, he had to admit, Thorpe wasn’t wrong. When Savage had been on paternity leave, he’d made Thorpe Acting Sheriff, a role the deputy had performed admirably. Savage had been worried that he wouldn’t like going back to a deputy when he returned to work, but to his surprise, his colleague had stepped down willingly. “I’m more of a data geek,” he'd explained, with a rueful grin. “I only agreed because I knew it was temporary.”

Thorpe shrugged. “So, case closed?”

Savage gave a reluctant nod. “Yeah. Case closed.”

IT WAS mid-afternoon when Savage heard a commotion coming from the lobby at the Sheriff’s station. He opened his office door and poked his head out.

“What’s going on?”

Sinclair shrugged, but they were all staring at the lobby where the usually passive Barb was having a fiery confrontation with a mystery woman. From where Savage was standing, he could only see the back of her very blonde head.

There was a steely edge to Barb’s voice. “If you’ll wait here, Ms. Dahl, I will go and get the Sheriff.”

“It’s *Special Agent Dahl*,” came the insistent reply. “I’m with the FBI. Here’s my ID.” There was a strange twang to her accent, but he couldn’t place it. American, but mixed with something else. Something foreign.

There was shuffling as Barb checked out her credentials. “One minute, please. I’ll tell him you’re here.”

His desk phone rang, but he was already at the security door to the lobby. “It’s all right, Barbara. You can let her through.”

Barbara gave a stiff nod and opened the security doors using the button underneath her desk. They hissed apart, and the blonde woman whooshed through, her heels clacking on the wooden floor. She was petite, about five-four, with sharp features, rimmed glasses, and a slim frame drowning in an enormous black coat at least two sizes too big.

"I'm Sheriff Savage." He held out a hand, but she either ignored it or didn't see it. A pent-up, nervous energy radiated off her like electricity. He could feel it, and he was sure the others could too. "How can I help?"

"Special Agent Avril Dahl. FBI." She pushed her glasses up her nose, just like Thorpe did when he got excited. "I believe you found a woman, Anita Cullen, frozen to death."

It was more of a statement than a question.

"How did you—?"

"I have an alert set up in the system," she said, waving a dismissive hand in the air. "Could you tell me what happened?"

Savage frowned. "I'm sorry, but why is the FBI interested in our victim?"

"I don't know if I am yet."

"I?"

"We. The FBI." She let out an exasperated breath. "Please, how did you find her?"

He frowned, puzzled by her urgency. "On a local ranch. She froze to death."

"Hypothermia?"

"Yes. I really don't see—"

She took a deep breath, her eyes lighting up. "She was just lying there, frozen? No strangulation marks? No stab wounds? Not a suicide?"

"That's right. Agent Dahl—?"

"Sheriff, I have reason to believe Anita Cullen was murdered."

There was a shocked pause. Everybody stared at her, including Barbara who'd followed her into the squadroom.

Savage cleared his throat. "I'm sorry, Agent Dahl, but Anita Cullen died of hypothermia. I have an autopsy report that proves it."

"It's incorrect."

He was beginning to get ticked off. Who did she think she was coming into his station and telling him that the verdict was incorrect? "I trust my ME implicitly, Agent Dahl. I assure you, there is no mistake."

She shuffled from foot to foot, as if trying to decide what to say next. He noticed she had tiny ankles and very shiny shoes. A strand of hair fell into her face, and she blew it away, a short angry burst of air. Her hair was pulled up in a messy bun, except half of it had fallen down thanks to the gusty wind.

"What makes you think it's incorrect?" he asked, breaking the silence.

She fixed her clear, blue gaze on him. "Because I've seen it before."

He shook his head. "I'm not following. Seen what before?"

"This exact circumstance. The start of winter, the snowstorm, a woman supposedly frozen to death in an isolated spot. The body posed."

Savage studied her. She didn't look nuts. Intense and impassioned, but not crazy.

"Her body wasn't posed," he said, finally, even though he didn't like discussing Anita's death with an outsider. "She was mauled by a mountain lion. At first, we thought that's what killed her, until the autopsy proved otherwise."

Dahl froze. "How do you know the body wasn't posed if she was mauled by a wild animal? It could have disturbed the original crime scene."

It was an interesting question and one they hadn't thought to ask. There'd been no need.

"There was no crime scene," he said quietly. "She froze to death."

There was a loaded pause as Dahl inspected him over her glasses. He noticed she had very big, pale-blue eyes. Nobody else uttered a word. The FBI agent looked away first.

“Sheriff, can we talk in private?”

Savage gave a stiff nod. “Come into my office.”

He had no idea what the FBI agent was doing here in Hawk's Landing, or whether she really did have information about Anita Cullen’s death, but he was professional enough to find out before he showed her the door.

“Do you mind if I see your credentials? He closed the office door. Call him petty, but he wasn’t about to discuss the case with a woman who’d just walked in off the street claiming to be an FBI agent until he knew for sure she was who she claimed to be. ID badges could be faked, and she sounded foreign, which was unusual for an FBI agent.

Dahl reached into her coat pocket and pulled out a leather holder which she opened and slid across the desk toward him. It was an FBI identification card.

Federal Bureau of Investigation
Special Agent Avril Dahl

HE TURNED it over in his hand, inspected the back. On it was stamped the insignia of the FBI. It seemed official. He’d get Barbara to do some further checks, but the woman seemed legit.

“Are you American?” he asked.

She gave a curt nod. “My mother was American, although she never lived here. I have both US and Swedish passports. Would you like to see those too?”

He nodded. She produced the documents which he studied for a long moment. Everything seemed to be in order. Savage gestured for her to sit down. “Special Agent Dahl, you must admit, this is all pretty strange – you barging in here out of the blue, claiming to have knowledge of Anita Cullen’s death.”

"You don't have to call me Special Agent," she snapped. "Agent Dahl is fine."

He nodded.

She sank into the chair opposite him and balanced her briefcase on her lap. He watched as she opened it and pulled out a file. Thick, worn, curling at the edges. She dropped it onto the desk with an abrupt thud.

"What's this?"

"This is just a small part of a fifteen-year hunt for a serial killer known as Frostmördaren – The Frost Killer," she said, her gaze still on the folder. "He began his killing spree in Stockholm in the winter of 2006."

"Okay, so what does this Frost Killer have to do with us?"

"His MO is always the same. He strikes one town every year, killing four women in rapid succession. It starts in December and sometimes lasts until February. He chooses his locations carefully – small towns, out of the way, often cut off because of the snow." She pushed her glasses up her nose. "I've tracked him across two continents, five countries, and seven states in the last decade, and that's only since I've been on the case."

Savage stared at her. Had he heard that right? "You're saying Anita Cullen was killed by a serial killer?"

"That's exactly what I'm saying."

Maybe she *was* nuts. There was a fanatical gleam in her eyes that worried him. "But there is no evidence she was murdered. The autopsy—"

"You won't pick up how he killed her on a tox screen because you don't know what to look for. He renders his victims unconscious long enough for them to freeze to death. That's his MO. He positions them on their backs in the snow, hands over their chests, eyes closed as if in prayer."

Savage thought of Anita, the way they'd found her. She'd been on her back but sprawled on top of the straw as if thrown or dragged. That *could* have been the mountain lion's doing. Her eyes were shut, her left arm draped across her body, the right outstretched to the side. It was possible it had fallen there during the attack.

Still...

"I don't know." He raked a hand through his hair. "It seems premature to be attributing this death to your... Frost Killer. I mean, why would he come here? Why now?"

"There is one way to know for sure whether this was him." Dahl glanced up from the folder.

Savage raised an eyebrow. "What's that?"

She leaned across the desk, the intensity of her gaze pulling him in. He found he was doing the same. "Did you find a pendant on the body? A snowflake encased in glass."

He gasped. "How—?"

She gave a triumphant nod. "I thought so. That's his calling card." Her eyes blazed like blue fire as she said, "It's the same killer."

FIVE

SAVAGE FACED HIS TEAM, his face sombre. After hearing Agent Dahl's revelation, he'd stopped her from telling him anything more, and they'd moved to the squad room so the others could hear.

"Agent Dahl has something she'd like to share with us," he announced, while she took off her coat and draped it over Sinclair's desk. Underneath, she wore a grey skirt-suit with a white shirt. It also looked slightly too big, and he wondered if she'd lost weight recently.

He nodded, giving her the go-ahead. "Why don't you start from the beginning?"

A hush fell over the office.

Barbara, who wasn't about to miss out on this, perched against Thorpe's desk. All eyes were on the petite FBI agent.

Dahl's expression was intense. Savage was beginning to doubt she had any other setting. He could tell this serial killer, this Frost Killer, was personal to her, or had become so over the years. A decade was a long time to be hunting someone.

"It starts the same way every year," she began, her voice soft and low. They had to strain to hear her. "The first snowfall of winter is usually when the first body is found. Always posed in the snow, always female, always blonde."

Sinclair raised a hand. "Well, there's your first discrepancy. She wasn't posed, and her body was found in a barn, not outside in the snow."

Savage held up a hand and Sinclair stopped talking. He gestured for Dahl to continue. "Your victim was found by a wild animal. A mountain lion, I think?"

Savage nodded in confirmation.

"It could be that she was dragged into the barn by this animal."

"It is possible," he admitted. "The ME said she'd been dead for at least two hours before she was mauled. The barn was cold, but I'm not sure if it was cold enough for someone to freeze to death. Not in the space of several hours."

Dahl gave a nod of agreement. "The Frost Killer drugs his victims, rendering them unconscious. He then positions them in the snow, so they freeze to death like they're asleep." She spoke like she knew the killer personally. He wondered how many 'sleeping' bodies she'd seen over the years.

"We didn't find any drugs in her system," Thorpe pointed out.

"Chloroform doesn't stay in the system for long. A small amount will leave the victim unconscious for several hours, depending on how much is administered. It depresses the central nervous system, producing a deep coma."

"Wouldn't the autopsy pick that up?" Sinclair frowned.

"Only if it's conducted a short time after death. Otherwise, it's rarely detected." Dahl glanced around the room, becoming more confident and self-assured. In this field, she was the expert. "Sometimes a minute amount is found in blood and tissue samples using gas chromatographic or mass spectrometric analysis." She turned to Savage. "But I'm guessing you don't have that type of equipment here in—" She looked blank.

"Hawk's Landing," Barb supplied, shooting Savage a worried glance.

"You guessed right," Savage said.

Not even Durango had that type of equipment. When something complicated was required, they sent the samples to Colorado Springs, the nearest big city forensic lab.

"Then how do we know for sure it's the same killer?" Sinclair narrowed her eyes. "So far, all you've got to link Anita to this psycho is the time of year."

That had been Savage's initial thought too. "Tell them about the pendant."

Dahl gave a little nod. "The killer leaves a snowflake pendant on his victims' bodies. It's slightly different every year, but the concept is always the same. A paper snowflake encased in glass."

Sinclair fell silent, while Barb, Thorpe and Littleton stared at her, mouths gaping. Savage, who'd anticipated their reaction, got to his feet. "In light of this, we have to consider the possibility that we're dealing with the same killer."

The silence lengthened. The telephone rang, but nobody answered it.

"Barbara?" Savage said, pointedly. She started, then hurried back to her desk to pick it up.

"How many women has he killed?" Sinclair whispered.

Dahl didn't have to think about it. "Fifty-three, including Anita Cullen."

"Fifty-three." Sinclair's eyes widened. Even Savage was stunned. That was way more than any active serial killer he'd ever heard of.

"Why haven't we heard of this guy?" Thorpe questioned. "Normally, a killer as prolific as this would have been in all the newspapers at some time or another."

"We tried to keep it out of the press," she replied. "Didn't want to send the killer underground. Unfortunately, there were instances when the case appeared in local newspapers, but I don't think it ever made the National Press."

"How long has he been doing this?" Littleton asked.

"He's been active for fifteen years," Dahl replied.

"You said you've been hunting him for ten," Savage remembered.

"That's right." She turned to him. "When I joined the FBI, he'd already been killing for five years. It wasn't a new investigation."

That made more sense.

"But four victims per year, for fifteen years is sixty victims." Thorpe did the math.

"He hasn't been operational for the last two years," she said tersely, breaking eye contact. "I thought I'd missed him, or he'd moved to another country, or dropped off the radar. Until this." She spread her arms. "Here."

Two years unaccounted for.

"Why do you think he came here?" Savage asked her. Hawk's Landing was a small mountain town, hardly worth mentioning. It barely made it onto the map.

"I don't know." She bit down on her lower lip in frustration. "There doesn't seem to be any pattern to where he kills. It's like he closes his eyes and picks a place on a map. The last six years prior to the two when I couldn't find him were in the United States."

"What about before that?" Sinclair asked.

"Sweden... Norway... Finland.... Denmark." She shook her head. "He moves around."

"Confusing for the police," Savage said. "Cross-border crimes make it harder to track him."

"After the first murder in Sweden—" Her accent thickened with emotion as she broke off her sentence. "He disappeared and the police gave up. It was three years later, when he killed four women in Copenhagen, that they put two and two together and realized he'd been doing it every winter since Sweden. By that stage, though, they couldn't attribute the other deaths to him. Too much time had passed."

"What about DNA?" asked Savage.

"The bodies had been cremated or buried, the evidence lost. The only thing they had to link him to the crimes were the pendants."

"That's a long time to be killing," Sinclair murmured.

"Four women every year," Thorpe whispered, shaking his head. Littleton seemed stunned into silence.

"Age group?" asked Savage.

"Twenties and thirties. His first victim was thirty-six years old. The second twenty-two."

Sinclair exhaled loudly. "He's not particular, then."

"Not when it comes to age."

The team went quiet, staring at her and each other in bewilderment. It was a lot to take in. Savage cleared his throat. It was up to him to make some sense of this, to decide how they were going to handle the shocking new information.

"Okay, listen up," he said.

Eager eyes turned to him. "First, we need to ask Ray to look for chloroform in her blood and tissue. If we can confirm that, we'll know Agent Dahl is right."

"I thought you said you didn't have the technology," Dahl said, frowning.

"We don't, but we have a very enterprising medical examiner, and he might be able to come up with a workaround, even if it takes a day or two."

She frowned but nodded.

"In the meantime, let's track Anita Cullen's last moves on the day she died. If we're working on the assumption she was taken, let's find out how and from where."

"We know she was at the West Mountain Ski Resort at lunch time," Sinclair pointed out. "Logan Maddox confirmed that."

He nodded. "That's a good place to start."

Dahl turned to Savage. "Can you take me to this West Mountain Resort?"

"I'll take you," Sinclair offered.

Savage shot his deputy a grateful smile. He wanted to get on the phone to Ray. Dahl would want to question Logan Maddox, and they'd already done that. He wondered how the insouciant ski instructor would fare when pitted against the intense FBI agent. The thought almost made him smile.

"THE FROST KILLER," Becca whispered, when Savage told her what had transpired that day. They were sitting together in the living room, enjoying a rare moment of peace after having put Connor down for the night. Having not slept the night before, Savage was battling to keep his eyes open. "That's quite a moniker."

"Yeah, I know. I hate it when the media comes up with nicknames for serial killers. It just serves to boost their ego and give them the notoriety they crave, when really, they're the scum of the earth and should be left to rot in obscurity."

"Wow. You are tired."

He scoffed at how well she knew him. "This guy has been killing for fifteen years, except for the last two." He went on to describe the killer's MO, and how many women he'd murdered.

"What happened to make him stop?" she asked.

"Agent Dahl doesn't know."

Becca took a deep breath. A trained psychologist, she ran an in-patient clinic for challenged youth over in Pagosa Springs, but, while she was still on maternity leave, she had started seeing clients privately again. "Well, the man is obviously seriously disturbed, mentally unstable, or psychopathic. Probably a mixture of all three."

"Great," he muttered.

"There are several reasons why people turn into killers," she said. "And I don't mean a one-off, I mean a repeated pattern of murders."

"A serial killer."

"If you like." She cringed at the use of the word. "The first is the type who suffers from hallucinations, schizophrenia, paranoia. A demented individual who hears voices telling him or her to kill. Psychologists have termed them visionary killers, but in real life, this is a very disturbed person with severe untreated mental health problems."

Savage tried to keep an open mind, although from what he'd heard, the Frost Killer didn't appear to be delusional. He was too careful, too methodical.

"They have no pattern in terms of victimology, and there's a different MO every time. They're messy, frenzied, unpredictable."

Savage shook his head. "This guy isn't messy or frenzied. He plans everything."

"Which leads me to the second type of killer," Becca said.

He sat back and listened.

"The kind that targets a specific type of person. Prostitutes, vagrants, homosexuals, the elderly." She looked pointedly at him. "Blondes of a certain age."

Savage nodded.

"He believes them to be evil, unclean, or sinful and is convinced the world would be a better place without them."

"Hmm." Savage stopped nodding.

"The type is significant," she went on. "It links back to a previous experience."

"Like a childhood trauma?"

She nodded. "Could be. For example, they may have negative associations with that particular type of person, suffered abuse or neglect at their hands. They may have lost them under dramatic circumstances."

Savage thought about this. "I don't have access to all of Agent Dahl's files."

Becca tilted her head. "You'll have to go back to the beginning, try to find the trigger."

"Trigger?"

"Starting point. What set him off."

Savage scratched his two-day old stubble. "What about winter? Why do you think he kills then?"

"For the same reason he targets a specific type of person. It's significant for him."

Savage rubbed his eyes, suddenly feeling overwhelmed. He knew it was just because he was tired. "Okay, I get it. Anything else I should consider?"

"It's important to bear in mind that killers don't have to fall into one specific category," Becca told him. "These are general categorizations, but in reality, it's often more complex, and the groups overlap."

"What are the other categories?"

"Well, the most common killer is the one who murders for power and control. They like to dominate their victims. Often, they'll rape or torture their victim before killing them. They like to see them suffer, to feel powerful and in control. They take their time."

"Plan their kills?" he asked.

She nodded. "To the finest detail. Sometimes they stalk their victims before they kill them, even been known to break into potential victims' houses and look around."

Savage exhaled.

Becca put her hand on his arm. "After they've committed the offense, this type of killer usually takes a memento, something to remember their victim by."

"I know they sometimes take a memento, but what about leaving a memento behind, like a calling card?"

She nodded. "Yes."

He told her about the snowflake pendant.

"I'd guess that someone close to him wore one. His mother, maybe, or a sister or girlfriend. He's trying to recreate a moment, or a place in time."

"We should concentrate on the pendant, then," Savage muttered. "Find out where he got it from."

"That would be a good place to start."

"I'm sure Agent Dahl has delved into this. She's been on the case for ten years. If she hasn't found anything, then maybe there wasn't anything to find."

"Or she'd missed it somehow. There's always a reason," Becca said quietly.

"Why four victims?" he mused.

"Everything is significant," Becca replied. "He has his process, and for some reason, four kills is what satiates him."

Savage pulled a face. "He's a monster."

Becca gave a grim nod. "Yes, and by the sounds of things, he's now in Hawk's Landing, and if what this FBI agent says is true, he's only just getting started."

SIX

SAVAGE BRACED himself against the cold as he strode across the road to the sheriff's office early the next morning. The temperature had plummeted overnight, and, as if that wasn't enough, the frigid wind had strengthened, freezing everything in its path and turning roads, sidewalks and vehicles into slick, gleaming hazards. They'd have their work cut out for them today.

He was running late because it had taken several attempts to start the Suburban, usually a reliable vehicle, and he'd had to drive at a snail's pace down his treacherous driveway to reach Durango Road to avoid going into a skid.

He'd been looking forward to the warmth of the office, but instead of heat, it was tension that hit him as he walked through the door. Barbara shot him an exasperated look. "She's here," she mouthed, as he swiped his fob to release the door lock and gain entry.

"Mornin'."

Savage walked through the silent squadroom to his office. Agent Dahl sat at Sinclair's desk, her coat thrown over the back of the chair, typing furiously on her laptop. A sulky Sinclair was now at Littleton's desk since he hadn't come in yet. She just shook her head when he raised an eyebrow.

Dahl stopped pounding the keypad and glanced up. "Sheriff, do you have a moment?"

"Sure." He took off his jacket and hung it on the hook behind his door. "Come on through." She snapped her laptop shut, then clip-clopped after him in her heels.

"Actually, I wanted to ask you something," he said, before she'd even had a chance to open her mouth.

Startled, she froze. "Oh?"

"I'd like to take a look at the original files. I'm particularly interested in the old cases, especially the first murder in Stockholm back in 2006."

Her glasses slid down her nose and she didn't bother pushing them back up. "Why?"

He forced a smile. "Isn't it obvious? You muscle in on our investigation claiming that this victim was killed by a serial killer who began his killing spree in Sweden fifteen years ago. Something must have triggered it, and I'd like to read what conclusions the Swedish police came to."

"I can tell you everything you need to know about that."

"Thank you, that would be useful, but I'd like to read the original police reports too. The first twenty murders occurred before you started working for the FBI."

She didn't respond.

"You do have them here, don't you?" He didn't think she'd travel halfway across the world without all the important files.

"Yes." Her tone was clipped.

"Okay, so if you don't mind giving them to my assistant, Barbara. She'll make copies of them."

Dahl hesitated.

"Is there a problem?" he enquired.

She cleared her throat. "No problem. I'll give them to her right away."

"Thank you. Now, what is it you wanted to talk to me about?"

"Er." She seemed to have drawn a blank. His question had thrown her. She hadn't wanted him looking at her files. It was a territorial thing, he got it, but the flow of information had to go both ways. "Oh, yes. The victim. What do you know about the victim? Her family, where she lives, what she does for a living and so on."

"We're in the process of collating that information," he said. "Once my deputies have finished, we'll have a briefing so everyone's on the same page. Does that work for you?" His tone implied that if it didn't, that was tough luck. They were working together on this, or not at all.

She gave a stiff nod. "You will let me know when you hear back from your medical examiner?"

"Of course."

Reluctantly, she left his office, and he closed the door behind her. Barbara came in a short while later with a cup of coffee and a pile of photocopies.

"Here's the first batch." She placed them on his desk. "There are more coming."

He smiled his thanks and picked up the coffee. It smelled good, and he still hadn't thawed out from the short drive to the station in his frigid vehicle. By the time the heat had kicked on, he was pulling into the parking lot across the road.

The phone rang as he was about to take his first sip. Holding the cup in one hand, he answered the phone with the other. "Yup?"

Barbara screened all his calls, so if she put it through to his desk, it must be important. "Ray on Line One for you, Sheriff."

That was fast. Surely, he couldn't have found anything already.

"Ray, what have you got for me?"

"Your Agent Dahl was right," he said, his voice upbeat. "Chloroform was used to subdue her."

"How do you know that?" Savage set his cup back down on the desk. "Don't tell me you managed to get hold of a chromatograph?"

"Don't be crazy. We'd have to send the sample to Colorado Springs for that."

He scratched his head. "Then how?"

"Well, Pearl had the bright idea to test the skin around the victim's mouth for traces of chloroform, and there it was. Whoever did this to her held a cloth laced with the stuff over her mouth. She would have been out in seconds."

"Well, I'll be—" he muttered.

"Yeah, I'm sorry we missed it the first time. It's not something we routinely test for."

"Understandable."

Savage rubbed his forehead. Up to now, he hadn't fully committed to the idea of Dahl's Frost Killer operating in La Plata County, even with the snowflake pendant. Without evidence that Anita Cullen had actually been murdered, it had all been a little too circumstantial. Now there was no doubt. The chloroform confirmed it.

After he'd thanked Ray and replaced the receiver, he stared at the wall for a long moment before pushing back in his chair and getting up. Time to tell Dahl, although he knew it would only confirm what she already knew.

As expected, her reaction was muted. "Do you believe me now, Sheriff?"

"Never doubted you." He turned to the rest of his team. "What have we got on Anita Cullen?"

Thorpe spun around in his chair. "I can give you an overview."

"Go for it."

"She was twenty-four years old and worked at her family's general store. For the last four years, she's been studying economics and politics at the University of Virginia. She graduated in July."

"Five months ago," murmured Sinclair. "She had the rest of her life ahead of her."

It was terribly sad, but then murder always was.

"Like Nate Thompson told us, her family has owned the general supply store for generations. They're wealthy if that makes a difference. They own substantial property in the area, mostly on this side of the West Mountain. The ski resort was also on their land, as is the Thompsons' farm."

Sinclair gave a low whistle.

"Their wealth is irrelevant," Dahl said abruptly. "The other victims fell into a wide range of income groups."

Savage hadn't had time to read the photocopied files of the earlier crimes yet, so he had to go on her pre-existing knowledge of the investigation.

"The victimology is simple. Female, blonde, in their twenties and thirties. That's it. That's all we've got." Dahl tossed her own blonde hair out of her face.

"You never found a link between any of the victims?" Savage asked.

"Don't think I haven't tried," she snapped. "I've driven myself crazy trying to find a connection between them, to understand how he's targeting them, but it appears to be completely random." It struck Savage that she was exactly the killer's type. The right age group, blonde and female.

"Were they all single?" Sinclair asked.

She shook her head. "No, again there's no apparent pattern. Most were single, but that's because of their age. Seventeen of the victims were married, nine had children."

Savage had to admit she had memorized the details of the case, but then that would be expected after a decade. It was incredible how she'd kept going for so long. Eventually, this kind of case would consume you. Eat away at your core until there was nothing left. He'd had cases like this before, but thankfully, he had always managed to solve the ones that got to him the most. He thought of his last trip to Denver, the one that had almost ended in disaster. The one that had taken him almost ten years to solve. Perhaps Dahl and he weren't so different after all.

"Well, he must be targeting them somehow," he said, refocusing. "Did you speak to Logan Maddox yesterday?"

Sinclair suppressed a grin. "Agent Dahl spoke to him. He was very helpful."

"We ascertained that Anita Cullen left the resort at 3:15pm," Dahl said. "She drove to her grandparents' store, parked the car in the lot behind the main street, but never made it inside."

"I've arranged for her car to be taken to the lab for analysis," Sinclair added. "It doesn't look like it's been tampered with, and we couldn't see any signs of a scuffle."

"So that's where she was taken." He raised an eyebrow. "In the center of town in broad daylight."

"It looks that way," Dahl confirmed. "Of course, she may have gone somewhere else before she was snatched, but we don't know that for sure. Your deputy, Littleton, is going door-to-door to see if anyone saw her." Littleton, the youngest member of the team, was still a little green, but he'd come a long way in the last year.

"I'm looking at the CCTV camera on the main street and trying to pinpoint where she was when her cellphone signal was lost," Thorpe said.

"We didn't find any personal belongings on her," Savage reminded them. "No purse, no phone. She wasn't even wearing a jacket."

"The killer must have them," Sinclair said ominously. She turned to Thorpe. "He'll have gotten rid of the phone by now."

"What did Logan Maddox do after Anita left him at the resort?" Savage asked.

"He took some of the more advanced skiers up to the black run at Purgatory," Dahl said, consulting her notebook.

"Any chance he could have gotten from there to the Thompson's ranch?"

"It's not him," she said, dismissively. "He'd have been fifteen at the time of the original murders, and he's never been outside of the United States."

Sinclair rolled her eyes.

Dahl was right, of course. Logan Maddox did not fit the Frost Killer's profile.

"Okay, but how does Anita's disappearance relate to previous victims?" Savage asked.

"Some were taken in daylight," Dahl confirmed. "Others were kidnapped outside their apartments or walking home after dark. Again, no pattern."

"So, he watches them," Savage concluded, thinking of Becca's categorization. "He stalks them, waiting to catch them unawares. This is not an opportunistic killer. He knows their routines and surprises them when there are no witnesses."

"We came close once," Dahl said quietly. Everybody turned to look at her. "In Chicago, back in 2014. A woman was attacked, but she managed to get away."

"Did she give a description?" Savage asked.

"Dark hair, dark eyes, a structured jawline. Good looking." She snorted. "That's probably how he fooled so many women."

"Any DNA?"

She shook her head. "No, he was wearing gloves, but there was a witness. A nearby skateboarder thought he'd gotten out of a blue Ford Fiesta. We followed up on it, but the kid didn't get a plate. I checked all the car-hire companies in the area and found several rented blue Ford Fiestas. It's one of the most common makes in America. We ran all the renters' drivers' licenses, but they checked out." She shrugged, but Savage could sense her frustration.

It was hard to believe nobody had seen anything in all the years the killer had been active. "Out of fifty-two murders, not including Anita Cullen's, you've only had one failed attempt and one eyewitness?"

Her face flushed. "What can I say? He's careful. We had a few possible sightings over the years, but nothing conclusive. You must understand that he only kills during one phase of the year, and always in different geographical locations. Nobody knows where he'll strike next. We followed up on them at the time, but they led nowhere." She sighed. "When he's done, he disappears again until the following winter. Drops off the grid. Vanishes into thin air."

"These sightings, are they in the case notes?" asked Savage.

She nodded. "Most of them, yes. I have more files at my office in

D.C., but they're mostly supporting documentation. It's all on the FBI network, anyway. I can access it at any time."

He couldn't, though. He didn't have clearance. If there was anything extra, he'd just have to ask her to get it for him.

"Okay, that's it for now." He nodded at his deputies. "You guys keep working on Anita's background. Cross reference anything unusual with the other victims. See if you can find a link."

"Other victims?" Thorpe asked.

"There's a stack of case files on my desk, compliments of Agent Dahl." He smiled politely at her, but she didn't smile back. "It might be a good idea to scan them to our drive, so we've all got a copy."

"I can do that," Barb said.

"What are you going to do?" Sinclair asked him.

"I'm going to talk to Anita's grandparents. They seem to be the head of the family and may know something about Anita's whereabouts the day she went missing."

Dahl jumped out of her seat. "I'll come with you."

He'd had a feeling she was going to say that. Shooting Sinclair an apologetic look, he left the office, Agent Dahl close on his heels.

SEVEN

THE GENERAL STORE was a large wooden building in the center of town. It took up two plots and sold everything from building supplies to cosmetics. Behind it was the public parking lot where Savage parked his Suburban. The snow had piled up along the sides, turning it into a shallow pool of brown slush.

"This is where we found her car." Agent Dahl walked over to a cordoned off area in the parking lot. A strand of yellow police tape had come loose and flapped in the wind.

Savage studied the area, but like his deputy and the FBI agent, he didn't see any signs of a struggle. There were no scuff marks or blood in the snow. The wind sliced straight through him, and he pulled his jacket tighter. "Pearl, our forensic technician, hasn't found anything significant in her vehicle."

Dahl glanced up at the two streetlights angled above the parking lot. He knew what she was thinking. "There's no CCTV here." Her shoulders drooped. "If there was, we'd know what happened to her. Where's the nearest one?"

"There's a camera at each end of Main Street." He shrugged.

"That's all we have here in Hawk's Landing. It's not really big enough to warrant more."

"Pity." Her mouth tightened into a sulky pout.

He let it slide, but only because he knew how desperate she was to find a lead. She wasn't alone in that. Unfortunately, the town budget didn't stretch to additional surveillance cameras.

"Let's go inside." He strode across the murky puddle that was the parking lot to the general store.

Savage suspected the building hadn't changed much over the years. The wooden façade had faded and was now weathered and chipped, looking like something out of the late eighteen hundreds. A classic, hand-painted sign swayed in the wind, the words 'Cullens' General Store' barely visible, but it was known to all who resided in the town. Hell, it was one of the first stores he'd come to when he arrived in Hawk's Landing.

A bell above the door chimed as he pushed it open, alerting the shopkeeper they were there. Old Mr. Cullen, a stoic, weathered man, glanced up from behind the counter where he was unpacking boxes of stock.

Agent Dahl stopped and looked around, admiring the antiquated, rustic charm. Her gaze wandered to the walls covered with black and white photographs, old newspaper clippings, and mining paraphernalia. They told the story of the town's vibrant past. He'd done the same thing himself, the first time he'd walked in. It was an interesting read.

"Good to see you, Bob." Savage held out his hand. "I'm sorry for your loss." He knew Bob Cullen well, since Savage had had to refurnish his entire house – twice – in the last few years. Once when he'd moved here from Denver, and the other a couple of months back when his old house had burned to the ground.

"I WONDERED when you'd be around, Sheriff." Bob shook his hand over the counter. Above his head, aged shelves were filled with a peculiar mix of modern necessities and vintage items that seemed to have been there for an eternity. Savage couldn't even identify some of the items.

"Need to ask you a couple of questions about Anita," he said.

Bob glanced at Dahl, who was inhaling deeply. The scent of aged wood, tinged with the faint aroma of tobacco and old paper, permeated the store. It was a pleasant and oddly comforting smell, like when you went to visit your grandparents' house as a kid.

"This is Agent Dahl," Savage said, introducing the FBI agent, who blinked several times and came over to the counter.

She nodded at him. "You have a lovely store."

"Thank you. We like it."

Savage raised an eyebrow, surprised. Dahl didn't look at him, she was still admiring the old wooden beams and assortment of items. He turned back to Bob. The old man had aged. His hair was completely white now, and there were deep lines etched into his weathered forehead. His eyes had sunken into his head, giving him a skeletal appearance, and his skin was tinged with gray. He didn't look well.

"Do you know what happened?" Savage asked.

"My son told us she was attacked out on the Thompsons' ranch." His face twisted with emotion. "Margery is devastated. She can't leave the house." Margery was Bob's wife, a normally energetic seventy-year-old.

"That's right," Savage said, carefully. "We're trying to figure out how Anita got to the barn on the ranch."

Bob stared at Savage. "Phillis told me you'd asked about that. I thought she skied there. You know she loved to ski cross-country."

"I know, but we didn't find any skis at the barn. She wasn't wearing a ski jacket, or any jacket for that matter. We think someone took her there."

"Took her? How?" His eyes creased as he narrowed them.

"I don't know. They could have driven to the trailhead up at Boulder's Point and walked the rest of the way. Maybe they used a trail groomer or snowmobile." Although there weren't any tracks. A groomer would have left deep ruts, clearly noticeable to anyone on foot. A snowmobile not so much, and any subsequent snowfall could have covered them up.

"Why would someone take her out there?" Bob frowned. "What aren't you telling me, Dalton?"

Agent Dahl glanced at him.

The old guy was savvy, he'd give him that much.

"It's a loose end that doesn't make sense," Savage said, honestly. Even before Dahl had arrived with her serial killer connection, he'd been wondering about that.

The old guy scratched his chin. "All I know is she was on her way to see me, or so she said. She parked her car behind the store, I found it there myself and called your lot, who came to pick it up."

"Didn't you think it was odd when she didn't turn up?" Dahl asked.

"Not really." Bob sighed. "I wish I had, but she's twenty-four years old and dating that ski instructor up at the resort. I figured she'd gone for coffee with him or gone shopping with a friend, or something. It's not like she kept regular hours at the store."

"She didn't work shifts?" Savage asked.

"No, in fact we told her she didn't have to help out, but she insisted. That's the kind of girl she was. We didn't pay her for it either, not officially, although I gave her some spending money at the end of each week to keep her going."

"Was she planning on sticking around?" Savage asked. "I know she recently graduated from VU."

Bob clenched his jaw, the muscles working overtime to control his grief. "Anita was trying to figure out what she wanted to do with her life. She had offers, good offers, but she said she wanted to spend some time at home before making up her mind." His voice broke. "God knows, I wish she had gone somewhere. Anywhere, but here."

Then she'd still be alive.

The unspoken words echoed around the store.

"What did you think of her boyfriend?" Savage asked.

Bob shrugged. "Didn't really know him, although Anita was crazy about him."

"She tell you that?" Savage asked.

"Yeah, she confided in me. We were close." His eyes clouded. "I'll miss our chats."

"It must be very hard," Savage said quietly.

Bob nodded somberly. "What is it you really want to know, Sheriff?"

Savage gave a wry smile.

"Did my granddaughter really get mauled by a mountain lion?" His gaze flickered from Savage to Dahl. "I'm sure the FBI don't go around investigating random wild animal attacks."

Savage bowed his head. "There are some unexplained details," he admitted. "We don't know yet if they mean anything, but—"

"But they mean something to you, eh?" He nodded at Dahl.

She nodded. "Yes, sir. They do."

"Bob, did Anita have a routine?" Savage interjected, before Dahl said something she shouldn't. "I know you said she didn't need to work, but did she keep regular hours at the store?"

"You're thinking someone was watching her? Waiting for her to show up?"

Dahl nodded again.

He sighed. "I guess so. She'd come in most afternoons. She had a deep sense of duty, just like I did at her age. You know the Cullens have been in Hawk's Landing since it was a mining town?"

"I didn't, no."

"Yeah, my great-grandparents came over from Wales. They were pioneers, known for their sturdy work ethic and deep respect for the land. They were experts in processing ore and developing smelting techniques. After the mining dried up, they started the blacksmith forge, then this general store as well as a packaging company. In the process, they acquired a fair bit of land. We've sold some of it over the years, to that young man who owns the ski resort and a few others. Now my son looks after our investments, and the properties."

"That's an impressive legacy." Savage didn't know much about the history of Hawk's Landing, having only arrived a few years back. He was practically a newcomer, compared to these folk.

Bob's chin rose a notch. "My forefathers were hard workers. I like to think we've done them proud."

"Indeed you have." Savage saw the old man nod appreciatively.

"If you need any help in figuring out what happened to my Anita, you just have to ask." He met Savage's gaze head on. "If someone did take her up there and left her to get attacked by a wild animal, I'd like to know who."

Savage nodded. "I promise I'll keep you posted."

IT WAS Becca's idea to invite Avril Dahl over for dinner. Savage had just gotten off the phone with yet another snowmobile rental company who said they hadn't rented any out to visitors in the last few days.

"It's the right thing to do," Becca insisted, as she chopped vegetables in the kitchen. "She's new in town and doesn't know anybody. Besides, I'm sure she'd appreciate a home-cooked meal."

Savage gave in, but he wasn't thrilled about it. Hopefully, the weather would put her off.

Unfortunately, it didn't.

An Uber dropped Dahl off outside the farmhouse, after clawing its way up the snow-covered driveway a couple of hours later. She wore the same thick, black coat over several layers of clothing, which she peeled off once she got inside. He was surprised to find her in jeans and a cobalt blue sweater that made her eyes appear even more intense. She looked different. More human, less agent.

The farmhouse was cozy and warm, thanks to the new central heating system, and there was a fire going in the grate.

"Come on in," Becca said, after Savage had hung the multitude of clothing on the peg by the door. "It's good to meet you, Agent Dahl."

"Please, call me Avril." Dahl smiled at Becca, her glacial eyes softening slightly. Savage relaxed a little bit. Maybe this wasn't going to be as excruciating as he'd first thought.

"Can I get you a drink, Avril?" he asked. "We have wine, or I can get you a beer, if you'd prefer?"

"Wine is fine."

He nodded and poured her a glass of the Merlot Becca was drinking. Connor was fast asleep in his room, but that could change at any moment. The baby monitor was on in the kitchen, but so far, all seemed quiet.

He noticed Dahl looking around. "We've only just moved in." He gestured to the exposed wooden beams that needed sanding and revarnishing, and the wooden floorboards covered with rugs to disguise the scratches. "There's still a lot we need to do to the place."

"It was a rather impromptu move," Becca explained, leading them through a peeling door frame into the living room. They still hadn't figured out what had happened to the actual door. Somewhere along the line it had been removed, and probably discarded or used for firewood. "Our previous house burned down."

Dahl gasped. "How terrible. Was it an accident?"

"Not exactly." Becca met Savage's gaze.

"It was arson," he explained. "But we caught the man who did it."

Dahl tactfully didn't ask any more questions, but something in her expression told Savage she suspected there was more to the story.

"Where in Sweden are you from, Avril?" Becca asked, as they sat down.

"Täby. It's a small town near Stockholm," she replied, "but I haven't been back in years. Last time I was in Sweden was six years ago."

"Wow." Becca raised her eyebrows. "Where is home, then?"

"Washington D.C." Dahl stared into the burgundy depths of her glass. "That's where I'm currently stationed, although I move around a lot."

"I've never heard of the Frost Killer," Becca admitted. "We're kind of obsessed with prolific serial killers in this country, especially one who has murdered so many women. The media sucks it up."

Dahl shot Savage a hard look, presumably for telling Becca about an active investigation.

"Becca is a clinical psychiatrist," he explained. "She's worked with me before and helps out on most of our cases."

A nod.

"We didn't broadcast it," Dahl said, "although some press attention was unavoidable. There was a podcaster in New York who got hold of the story, but luckily, they weren't very popular, and the story dried up when the killer disappeared. That was nearly three years ago."

Dahl moved to push her nonexistent glasses up the bridge of her nose, and that's when Savage realized what was different about her. She wasn't wearing her frames tonight. It softened her appearance, but also made her eyes appear wider and more vivid than usual.

"At first it was because the authorities didn't think the cases were linked," she continued, "but after the snowflake pendant was found, it became clear it was the same killer moving around year after year."

"Why do you think he only kills during the winter?" Becca asked.

Dahl was silent for a moment. "I think he likes the snow. It preserves the bodies."

Becca gave a slow nod. "Something from his past, maybe? Someone he knew froze to death, or perhaps they died, and he wanted to preserve the body?"

Dahl glanced at her in surprise. "I couldn't find any incidents like that in Sweden in the years preceding the killings."

Savage had known she'd look into it. "Maybe you didn't go back far enough."

"It's possible. I went back ten years, but you never know." She shrugged. "It could have been earlier, or it could have been in a different country. I only have access to certain files, and some juvenile records are protected."

"They wouldn't give you access?" Savage was surprised. This was an important case. They should have waived protocol to catch a serial offender like the Frost Killer.

"No." She didn't meet his gaze. That meant she'd gotten the information another way, but still hadn't found anything.

He nodded. "I'd like to take a look at your notes on that."

"I will email them over to you, but there is nothing worthwhile."

"Tell us about the first murder," said Becca, her gaze flickering to Dahl's face.

Savage thought he saw a faint flush of color on the FBI agent's cheek, but she nodded and put her wine glass down on the table.

"Okay, but I must warn you. This one is personal for me."

"I'm sorry." Becca didn't look that surprised. "Did you know the victim?"

"Yes. She was my mother."

EIGHT

SAVAGE STARED at the FBI agent. That explained a lot. Her drive. Her intensity. The duration of the investigation. Avril Dahl had dedicated her life to tracking down the man who'd killed her mother.

It was also heartbreaking.

Becca reached out and touched her hand. "I'm sorry, Avril. We didn't know."

She retracted her hand and placed it in her lap. "That's okay. It was bound to come out eventually. Her name was Olivia. Olivia Dahl."

"Was there a reason why you didn't tell me before?" Savage asked.

"It's been my experience that when police forces discover my family connection to the investigation, they think I'm crazy." She made a circular motion next to her head with her finger. "They think I'm obsessed with the case."

They weren't wrong there.

"It's understandable," Becca said softly. "You want answers, and you feel only you can get them."

Avril gazed at her. "No one else has been able to come close. I nearly caught him in Chicago, but he got away again."

Savage frowned. "That was when the skateboarder saw him?"

"Yes, a young woman, Kerry Musgrave, was approached by a man while she was out jogging. He asked her for directions, before trying to grab her. Luckily, she was a black belt at karate and was able to get away."

"That is lucky," Becca murmured.

"The woman smelled alcohol on him," Avril continued, "but I think that was the chloroform."

Savage narrowed his eyes. "What about the skateboarder? Did he actually see the attack?"

"Yeah. He came running over, but by that point, Kerry had fought him off, and he'd run back to his car."

"A Ford Fiesta?"

"That's right, but it was probably a rental car or a stolen vehicle. He wouldn't have used his own."

Savage nodded in agreement. "You said this was back in 2014?"

"Yes, but the first murder occurred in 2006. I was fourteen at the time."

"Do you mind telling us about it?" Becca whispered.

Dahl gave a reluctant nod.

"I remember because it was my birthday. We'd had a party at our house, and a few of my close friends and their parents were there."

Savage and Becca both leaned forward as Avril told her story.

"It was a fun afternoon. Everybody left around five o'clock, after which my mother took the dog for a walk in a park nearby. It was her routine. She did it every evening. Sometimes I went with her, but I was tired after the party, so I didn't go."

She glanced down at her hands. Savage knew what she was thinking. If only she'd gone with her mother, maybe it wouldn't have happened.

"It wasn't your fault," Becca murmured.

"I know." Avril took a steadying breath. He wondered how long it had taken for her to come to terms with that. "When she didn't come home, my father went looking for her. He discovered Roffe – that's our dog – running around in the park, but my mother was nowhere to be found."

"That must have been very hard for you and your father," Becca said.

"It was." A shaky whisper. Still so raw after all these years. "That night, a search party went out. They looked all night but couldn't find any sign of her. The police thought she'd run away, as they found no trace of a struggle, no blood, no nothing."

That was often the first consideration, after which the spouse became the primary person of interest. He nodded at her to continue.

"Then they took my father into custody. They questioned him for hours, but he'd been home all evening."

"You were his alibi?" Savage asked.

She gave a concise nod. "I was in my bedroom while he was downstairs tidying up. I saw him take out the trash from my window."

"What happened next?"

"It was the following evening when they finally found her."

"Where?"

"In a forest west of the town. She was lying in the snow, hands folded over her chest, eyes shut, just like she was sleeping. She'd frozen to death."

Becca inhaled. "Except she hadn't?"

"No, but at the time, there was no reason to believe she hadn't. She was the first victim, you see. There was nothing to compare it to. The verdict was suicide."

Savage could see how they thought she'd laid down and succumbed to the cold.

"But you weren't convinced?"

"Of course not. My parents were happy. It was my birthday. She wouldn't have done that to me. Anyway, she'd never have killed herself, she wasn't that type of person."

"And then there was the pendant," Becca whispered.

"Yes. It was around her neck. My father insisted he hadn't given it to her, and neither of us had seen her wear it before, but the police—" She cut off with a sad little shrug.

"They didn't believe you?" Savage finished.

"They thought it was a gift from a secret lover." She scoffed, her cheeks coloring. "They even had the audacity to suggest she'd been having an affair, which had ended badly. That's why she'd killed herself."

The police had obviously looked at all feasible options. Something must have convinced them her mother had been seeing someone else. It was quite a conclusion to jump to without evidence. Looking at Avril's face, he decided not to go there. Not now. Maybe he'd find more answers in the files.

"How did your father take it?"

"Not well, as you can imagine. I tried to convince him it was all nonsense, that Mom wouldn't do that, but he felt betrayed. He actually believed her capable of that. That's when . . . Well, that's when our relationship fell apart."

"I'm so sorry," whispered Becca.

"So, the case went unsolved. That winter, three other women went missing. Two turned up dead, the third was never found."

"The police didn't link them?"

"No, the two murdered women were in neighboring Norway, so their deaths weren't linked. The missing woman was also Swedish, but because they didn't have a body, there was nothing they could do."

"Didn't the Norwegian police connect those murders with your mother's?" Savage asked.

She shook her head. "The death in Bergen was ruled an accident, while the other was on the opposite side of the country. Two different police forces, and they didn't communicate with each other back then like they do now. Today, the systems are interlinked. We share information in a central database in Europe, but back then, it was still in development. The similarities were missed. The pendant wasn't entered as evidence."

"So, he got away with it," Becca summed up.

Avril gave a sad nod. "My mother's murder was never solved."

AT THE STATION the next day, Savage thought about what Avril had told them. Avril's mother had been abducted during her evening walk. If they were sticking to the stalker theory, that meant the killer had been watching her house and was familiar with her movements.

It had been his first kill, that they knew of. Was it possible it had been an opportunistic crime? Avril's mother had simply been in the wrong place at the wrong time. Except, the murderer had enjoyed it so much, he'd gone on a killing spree that had spanned fifteen years.

Nah. He discounted that theory almost immediately. Everything's significant, Becca had said, and he trusted her professional judgement. Avril's mother had been chosen for a reason.

"Avril," he called, opening his office door.

Sinclair glanced up, surprised at the use of Dahl's first name. He'd already briefed his team on the FBI agent's connection to the first victim before she'd come in that morning, but none of them had realized they were on a first name basis. "Did your mother notice anything unusual in the weeks leading up to her death?"

The FBI agent frowned. "I'm not sure I understand?"

"Well, we know the killer watches his victims, gets to know their routines. That's why he doesn't get caught because he's thought about how he's going to take them. He strikes when nobody else is around. When the victim's vulnerable. I was thinking—"

"Did my mother know she was being watched?"

He nodded.

Her eyes glazed as she thought back to the past. "I don't think so. I don't recall her mentioning anything like that, but if she had, it would have been to my father, not to me."

"Did your father ever mention anything?"

"I didn't get a chance to have that conversation with him. He passed away a few years back." Her shoulders tensed. "Heart attack."

"I'm sorry."

That was disappointing. It would help if her father had sensed something was up, even if his wife hadn't thought it important enough to mention. Maybe that's why he'd so readily believed she'd been having an affair. Something had made him suspicious. Except now, they'd never know.

"Yeah. I regret not going back now, but like I said, we weren't close." Avril would have been in the States when her father died, and obviously hadn't gone home for the funeral.

"When he was alive, did he—?"

"Nope." She shook her head. "I don't remember him mentioning anything like that. I questioned him several times when I was first assigned the case, but he never once mentioned a stalker or my mother saying she felt uneasy."

"Okay." It was possible, however, that someone had been following Olivia Dahl. That someone had known she'd take the dog for a walk that evening. Had been lying in wait. Ready to pounce.

The question then became: Why her? Why Olivia Dahl? What had brought her to the killer's attention? Was it an unfortunate coincidence? A random sighting? Or was it something more calculated? A work colleague? An unwelcome infatuation? Or even a secret lover?

Savage returned to his office. The next step was to familiarize himself with the history of the investigation, and there was a stack of files he had to get through. With the snow still pelting down and the wind howling through town, he took advantage of the lull in emergency callouts and settled down to read.

NINE

IT WAS PRETTY MUCH like Avril had said. Olivia Dahl had gone out after dinner to walk the dog and never returned. When the police analyzed her call logs, they found multiple phone calls to a mystery man called Michael. The calls had taken place over the span of the last month, at infrequent intervals.

Michael, it turned out, had a burner phone, so they couldn't trace the number. This is what led the police to assume she'd been having an affair. That, and the unidentified necklace.

Of course, Michael could also have been her killer. Savage wondered if they'd thought of that, or had they been so quick to fit the evidence to their narrative that they'd ignored it? He bet Avril hadn't.

Sure enough, slotted into the file, he found a hand-written page containing her own notes.

Michael Forsberg. Colleague. 40 years old. Married. Four children.

Michael Olsson. Family doctor. 45 years old. Married. Two children.

Michael Brolin. Reporter. 34 years old. Single. Gay?

It appeared Avril had been investigating all the Michaels in her mother's life. All three of them. There were photographs too, and by the looks of things, they'd been taken without the subject's permission. Leaving the office. Going into a bar. Getting into a vehicle. None of the subjects looked at the camera. The photographs were dated and named. Avril was nothing if not thorough. Presumably, she'd ruled them out as suspects.

Michael Forsberg was on holiday with his family when my mother was murdered.

Michael Olsson was at a conference in Denmark.

Michael Brolin was in Bosnia.

They all had alibis.

So, who was the mysterious Michael on her mother's phone?

Grimacing in frustration, Savage closed that file and opened the next one and read the name at the top.

Lene Hansen.

Lene disappeared almost two weeks to the day after Olivia Dahl. A twenty-six-year-old from Bergen on the Norwegian coast, she worked for a ferry operator and was engaged to be married when she disappeared. Her body was found two days later in the foothills of Fløyen Mountain, which overlooked the city. There was a photograph of the crime scene.

Serene. Posed. Peaceful. Those were the words that first sprung to mind as he studied the pale, slender form of Lene Hansen. She looked like an angel, her blonde hair spread out in the snow, hands folded across her chest.

He squinted at the necklace around her neck. A snowflake, perfectly formed and carved from paper, encased in glass. It was slightly different from the one found on Anita Cullen, but then the killer probably made them himself. It made sense that they'd change over time as he evolved, as he got better at it.

Savage sat back in his chair, studying the necklace. That was the key, he was sure of it. The killer's chilling calling card. If they could find out who supplied the glass cases, or how they were made, it might lead them to him.

"Any luck on the pendant?" he asked Thorpe, poking his head around his office door.

"Not yet," the Deputy replied. "We've sent a photograph to every jeweler in town, and Littleton is following up, but so far, nothing."

"My theory is that he makes them," Avril said.

Savage could imagine the killer meticulously carving the intricate shape of the snowflake with a scalpel. Taking his time, getting it perfect. "But how does he encase it in glass and make it into a pendant? He'd need help for that, wouldn't he?"

"You can buy glass slides." Avril rubbed her eyes. He guessed this wasn't the first time she'd had this conversation. "Then you slot in the snowflake and place a silver rim around the edge. I found them online once, but the supplier hadn't had any recent orders and didn't ship to Scandinavia."

Sinclair looked up. "There could be any number of websites out there that provides the same thing."

Avril gave a tired nod. "There are. These craft stores pop up all the time. If he's getting them online, it's going to be hard to trace."

"I'll keep looking," Thorpe muttered. "We might get lucky."

Savage nodded and went back to his office to continue reading through the case files.

Helene Basken was a young woman from Oslo with a history of minor infringements and misdemeanors. She'd dabbled with drugs, had been caught using several times, and been arrested for shoplifting. Growing up in Norway's child welfare system, she'd never had a stable home life and, therefore, lacked not only love and affection, but also discipline.

Yet, at the time of her murder, she had a decent job working as a receptionist at an upmarket hotel in the city center. One night, after work, she'd left the hotel and vanished. Her roommate had told police she hadn't come home after her shift.

Helene's body had been found a week later near a hiking trail on the Bygdøy Peninsula, west of central Oslo. The official verdict was that she'd passed out and died of exposure, although they hadn't found any drugs or alcohol in her system to back that up. It was her background that had condemned her, and consequently, her death was never registered as suspicious. No one considered the pendant around her neck to be significant, nor did they consider she might be a victim of the Frost Killer until Avril had connected the dots half a decade later.

Savage exhaled.

Four.

Avril had said there were typically four women murdered each winter. A nice, even number. It would appeal to a man with an obsessive personality. A man who would painstakingly craft a snowflake out of a piece of paper. A man that took the trouble to pose his victims so that they were perfectly preserved in the snow.

There were no official reports of a fourth woman's body being found that season, though as Avril had pointed out in her notes, Anna Hollman, a Swedish university student, had gone missing just before Christmas. She'd left her residence hall at the University of Stockholm where she was studying medicine but never made it to her boyfriend's place in Helsinki, Finland.

According to the ferry operator, she'd boarded the ship in Stockholm, but hadn't gotten off the other side. Avril had written that the killer could have followed Anna on board and taken her off the other side. One of the wheelchairs onboard the ferry had gone missing after that particular voyage. Had the killer used that to wheel his unconscious or drugged prey off the ship?

Friends at the university had reported that Anna had been under a lot of strain after an uncharacteristic fall in grades, which led the authorities to reach a verdict of suicide, even though her body was never found.

Savage wondered what had caused Anna's grades to drop. Fear? A stalker, maybe? Someone harassing her? Following her?

Avril had been right to question it. Many women went missing in Scandinavia every year, and they couldn't hunt them all down, but Anna Hollman's case was interesting, and Savage could see why Avril had added it to the investigation. Unfortunately, she'd gotten no support from the Finnish or Swedish police who'd just wanted to close the case. There was even a note from an Inspector Eriksen saying the wheelchair theft was inconclusive and the depressed young woman had most likely thrown herself overboard.

Another brick wall.

Had Anna been the fourth victim? If so, where was her body? Forever locked in an icy coffin somewhere in Finland, covered by snow?

Savage sighed and stretched his neck. He was frustrated after reading the report, so he could only imagine how Avril must feel after ten years of this.

They *had* to catch this guy.

Savage stared down at the open folder until the words on the page swam in front of his eyes. If the bastard was operating in Hawk's Landing, it was going to be his last rodeo.

Four women dead every year.

“Not in my county,” he muttered, closing the file.

TEN

THE KILLER WATCHED as the object of his attention left her house and climbed into her fancy SUV. It was enormous, even by American standards, and completely dwarfed her petite frame. Dark black, tinted windows, hybrid technology. It didn't make a sound as it eased away from the curb.

The killer waited a moment before he followed. It wasn't essential to keep eyes on her since he already knew where she was going. Same place she went every morning.

Renegade Creek.

There was a hiking trail that ran alongside the river. Not right next to it, but farther back, hidden by the trees. The track was isolated, quiet, and relatively straight, which made it perfect for running. Perfect for killing, too.

The track was overgrown with trees — dark firs and pines bending over the path as if they were protecting it, touching at the top. The arching green canopy prevented the ground from being covered in snow, another reason why it was favored by runners.

He followed her to the gravel parking lot near the trailhead, keeping well back in the early morning traffic. People drove slowly on account of the weather. There were a few other vehicles scattered about, but not many. It was too cold for leisurely hikers or joggers. Only the dedicated were out today.

She parked the SUV and climbed out. He watched as she looked around her, then slipped the car key behind the front left tire. Stupid bitch. She thought nobody was watching, but he was always watching.

After a quick stretch, she took off at her usual brisk pace. Long, loping strides in an easy, practiced rhythm. He shook his head. That girl ran like the wolves were snapping at her heels. Little did she know they were. A wolf in sheep's clothing. He chuckled at his own little joke.

What was she running from? Some deep-seated desire to get away from herself, or maybe it was to prove herself? With her family's wealth came a whole host of problems. Expectation. Responsibility. Always being in the public eye.

Wasn't that what she wanted?

Why else study politics? Why else become engaged to a local politician?

"Don't you worry. You will be famous, sweetheart," he whispered into the icy morning air. "Soon, everybody will know your name."

KEVIN LITTLETON, the youngest of Sheriff Savage's deputies, walked into the Bouncing Bean coffee shop and looked around. It was busy, but then it was the lunchtime rush. Maybe he should have waited until after lunch to question the girl behind the bar.

The rich coffee aroma smelled good, and his mouth watered as he joined the line. Maybe he'd get one to go. The door-to-door visits had taken all morning, and he could do with a break. So far, his search for a witness had turned up zilch.

How was it that nobody had seen Anita Cullen park her car and walk down the main street toward her granddaddy's store? This wasn't a big city. A girl like Anita stood out here. Striking, blonde, and well-dressed. She was the type of person strangers gawked at and locals smiled at. Almost everybody in Hawk's Landing knew who she was. Hell, even he knew who she was, and he'd only been here a couple of years.

The line moved quickly, and in no time at all, he was at the counter. Littleton gave what he hoped was a friendly smile and produced his ID card. "Hey there. I'd like a double-shot macchiato to go, but I'd also like to ask you if you saw this woman come into the shop the day before yesterday." He held up Anita's photograph. It had been lifted from her social media profile and portrayed Anita with the sun shining on her face, her hair glowing like a halo, laughing at the camera.

The barista's eyes glazed over. "What?"

It was like she didn't know what to do first.

"Have you seen this woman?" He held the photograph closer to her face. Someone behind him stomped their foot. He ignored them. This was police business.

"Uh, yeah. That's Anita Cullen. She's always in here."

Littleton's heart skipped a beat. "She is?" He cleared his throat. "I mean, that's great. Do you remember seeing her two days ago?"

The barista thought for a moment. "You mean Tuesday?"

"Yeah. Tuesday afternoon." That ski instructor boyfriend of hers had said he'd last seen her around three fifteen.

The barista screwed up her forehead. "Yeah. Yeah, I think I did. She ordered two extra-hot cappuccinos."

Littleton inhaled sharply. He was having trouble believing what he'd heard. "You're sure? It was definitely Tuesday afternoon?"

"I can check the order log, but I'm pretty sure it was Tuesday. Must have been around three thirty. Didn't see her yesterday, though."

Littleton's heart was beating so fast, he couldn't think straight. "Okay. If you could check, that would be great. Um, do you remember if she met anyone here?"

The barista frowned. "I don't think so, but I can't be sure. I was busy, you know? Tuesdays I'm here on my own. I don't have time to watch the customers to see who they're meeting."

Damn. His heart sank. "Okay. Do you have any surveillance cameras in the store?" He knew that was the first thing the sheriff would ask, so he'd better have the answer.

"Only the camera aimed at the till." She nodded at the small roving eye on the shelf behind her head, not very well disguised between a bottle of vanilla syrup and one that was a spicy cinnamon flavor.

"Can I see it?"

She glanced behind him at the rapidly lengthening line. "What, now? It's lunch time. I'm kinda busy."

"Yes, of course. No, sorry. It doesn't have to be now." He was babbling, but it was because he was so excited. The footage might give them a lead. "Could you do it as soon as possible, then give me a call at the station? Here's my card." He slid it across the counter.

"Are you going to be much longer?" the man behind him asked.

"No, sir. Almost done," he replied, without turning around.

"It's urgent," he told the barista.

She nodded. "Sure, I'll do it as soon as it calms down."

"That's fine." He made to move out of the way, then remembered he was about to order a drink. "Oh, and that double-shot macchiato?"

"Coming right up."

The man behind him groaned, but he stood his ground, hoping against hope that the video would show them who Anita Cullen had been with. Two coffees, the barista had said. That meant she was meeting someone. Could her killer be somebody she knew? Her boyfriend? Had Logan Maddox been lying about when he'd last seen her?

Littleton shook his head. He mustn't jump to conclusions.

Just get the evidence, he told himself, moving to the side while the girl made his coffee. The man behind him grunted and stepped forward.

"There you go. Have a good one." The barista put it down on the counter.

"Thanks. Don't forget the footage," he reminded her.

But she was taking the next guy's order and didn't respond.

ELEVEN

THE TEAM POURED over the surveillance footage. The barista had dutifully sent the digital CCTV file to Littleton's email address.

"It's her," Avril breathed.

Savage could feel the excitement radiating off her. "She's ordering two takeout coffees, all right. I wonder who the second is for?"

"The barista didn't remember her meeting anyone in the shop," Littleton said, "but she couldn't be sure."

"It could be her grandpa." Sinclair straightened up. "She was on her way to the general store. It would make sense for her to get coffee on the way."

"Why don't you head down there and ask old Mr. Cullen if that's something she'd do?" he said. "Maybe it was their routine."

"Sure." Sinclair moved away from Littleton's desk to grab her jacket. The store was close enough to walk to.

"Pity we can't see where she goes," Thorpe muttered. The footage was a confirmation that Anita had indeed been in the Bouncing Bean coffee shop a little after three thirty the afternoon she was killed, but it didn't help to identify who took her. Unfortunately, after she collected the coffees, she disappeared off-screen, out of range of the camera.

They couldn't even tell whether she'd sat down in the cafe or gone out the door.

"At least we know she wasn't taken from the parking lot," Littleton murmured.

Savage patted him on the shoulder. "It does help us with her last movements. Good work, Deputy." The back of Littleton's neck turned pink.

"If she wasn't taken from the parking lot, then she must have been abducted between the coffee shop and the general store." Avril tapped the side of her glasses. "Assuming that's where she was headed."

"Let's wait for her grandfather to confirm that, first." Savage didn't want to jump to any conclusions. Even if it was Anita's practice to pick up coffees before work, it didn't mean she was doing it on that particular day. She may have been meeting someone they didn't know about. A friend, perhaps.

"Have we talked to her friends?" he asked Thorpe, who nodded.

"Yes. Anita's only been back in town for five months, but her old school friend, Maisie Fowley, said she hadn't seen her for a few weeks. Maisie works in Pagosa Springs, so they usually only get together on the weekends, but with the weather being so bad, they hadn't gone out in a while."

He nodded. That made sense. Even though most folks were used to harsh winters here in La Plata County, this one was particularly severe.

"Anyone else she'd buy coffee for?"

"Maisie said there was a guy she went cross-country skiing with," Thorpe added. "Ed Winslow. But I checked, and he's gone to Denver to see his family for Christmas, so he's not around. I checked her phone records, to be sure, but the last call she made before her phone went offline was earlier that morning, on her way to the resort. She'd called Logan Maddox to tell him she was on her way."

"That's it?" asked Savage. "No other calls or texts?"

"Nope. Then her phone goes offline later that afternoon. Last known lookup was the cell tower near the resort." He shrugged.

"Okay." Savage backed away from the computer. "Our goal is to find out who she was meeting. Littleton, see if you can identify any of the other people in this video. Maybe the girl at the Bouncing Bean knows them. One of them might remember something."

Littleton nodded and shut down his computer. Thorpe went back to his desk. Avril hovered. "How far is the Bouncing Bean from here?"

"Not far. Take the first left and you'll get to the main street. The Bouncing Bean is halfway down on the right."

"I think I'll take a walk," she said.

He nodded. If he didn't know this town so well, he'd have done the same. She was retracing Anita Cullen's steps to see where she might have been abducted. The problem was, the Bouncing Bean was situated on the busiest street in Hawk's Landing. At mid-afternoon on a Tuesday, there weren't many places she could have been taken without somebody seeing.

"Maybe we should put an appeal out for information?" Littleton asked, pulling on his jacket.

"If we do, everyone will know it wasn't an accidental death," Thorpe pointed out.

He was right. They didn't want the press sniffing around. Any hint of a serial killer, and they'd descend on this town like an army. He'd seen it happen before.

Barb hurried into the squadroom, wringing her hands.

"What's up?" asked Savage. "You okay?"

"That was Jed Russell on the phone." Her voice was a hoarse whisper. "Apparently, he's found a body near the creek that borders the Hatch farm."

"IT'S HIM," Avril whispered, as they sped out to the farm. "It's the second kill. I know it." The FBI agent sat in the backseat of Savage's Suburban, biting her nails. Her face was pale in his rearview mirror.

"Let's not jump to conclusions." He tried to be rational. "There could be any number of reasons why there's a body out there."

"Jed said there was no blood, and she was female," Sinclair said grimly.

He had to admit, it did sound like the killer's MO.

Savage drove as fast as he dared on the icy roads. They got to the farm, only to have Jasmine Hatch rush out to meet them. Savage had first met Jasmine several years back when she'd come into the station to report her daughter missing. They'd been friends ever since.

"Oh, Dalton, it's just awful. Jed said she's just lying there in the snow." Her unusual teal eyes overflowed with sadness, and her long, silver hair whipped about her face in the frigid wind. He knew she was thinking of her daughter, whose body had been discovered in a lake several miles away.

Dalton hugged her. "Don't worry, we're heading up there now. Does the service road go all the way to the river?"

"Yeah, but you'll have to cross on foot. Jed says she's on the other side."

"Gotcha." That would make things more difficult, but not impossible. The creek wasn't wide, but it was rocky, and the currents – particularly this time of year – were deceptive. "Medics have been called, but they'll be lagging behind. Send them up to the river when they get here."

She nodded and hurried back into the house.

Savage climbed back into the SUV and reversed onto the service road. The Suburban bounced along the uneven surface, its tire chains rattling and spitting up ice and snow. At least Jed had gone before them so there were deep ridges in the snow from his tire tracks. It would make it easier for the emergency vehicles, too.

He spotted Jed's truck parked near the creek and pulled up next to it. With this much snow melting into it at the source, the shallow channel swirled and twisted with eddies. Come Spring, it would be lethal. Steam hissed off the surface, but underneath, it looked cold and gray, and he didn't relish wading across it.

Jed beckoned from across the river. He stood on the opposite bank, waving.

"I can't see the body." Avril craned her neck.

"Jed said it was in the woods, about fifty yards from the creek."

"You got waders?" Sinclair gazed at the rapidly running water.

"In the back."

"What about me?" Avril asked.

"I've only got two sets. You'll have to wait here, unless you want to cross in those?" He glanced at her smart trousers.

She scowled, but there was nothing she could say. Crossing in her clothes wasn't an option.

Sinclair went in first, gasping as the water rose to her mid-thighs. "Jeeze, it's freezing!"

"Look out for that fast-flowing gully on the inside of the meander," Jed called, standing on the bank. "Nearly grabbed my legs out from under me."

Savage went in after Sinclair, gritting his teeth against the cold. How Jed managed it in his jeans, he had no idea. Then again, the old guy was a retired Screaming Eagle from the 101st Airborne Division. They were made differently.

They trod carefully, making sure they were on stable footing before taking the next step. The current tugged at their legs, sucking them downstream.

"You okay?" Savage called to Sinclair, whose face was pinched with concentration.

"Yep. Nearly there."

Finally, they emerged onto the opposite bank. Jed shook both their hands, his expression grim. "Glad you could come. She's over here."

He led them into the forest. It was dark, but sheltered, and it was a relief to get out of the biting wind. A dirt track ran through it, parallel to the river. Savage couldn't see any sign of a body.

"Where is she, Jed?"

"Over here." He moved deeper into the woods. Even surrounded by foliage, they could still hear the creek behind them as it sputtered and hissed its way toward the lake. A few seconds later, the trees parted, and they were in some sort of clearing. Mounds of fresh snow covered the ground, deep and undisturbed. In the center lay a protrusion in the shape of a body.

She would have been easy to miss, being off the track and given the amount of snow that had fallen on top of her. At least two inches covered her body in a thick, icy shroud. The shape was distinctly feminine, however, and both Savage and Sinclair stared at the frozen figure with morbid fascination.

"How'd you find her?" Savage asked.

"A couple of local boys spotted her," he explained. "They were up here taking photographs. You can see their prints around the edges of the clearing."

Savage looked at two sets of deep prints and nodded. Made sense.

"They knew we were the closest residents," Jed continued, "so they crossed the river and followed the service road down to our place to use the phone." At Sinclair's questioning look, he said, "There's no cell reception up here. I said I'd call you."

"Where are they now?" Savage asked.

"They've gone home, but I have their contact details." He patted his pocket. "They're good kids. I've known them for years. They're always out here in the summer. Not so often in winter, though."

"Okay, thanks." He'd ask Littleton to pay them a visit and get their statements.

"No footprints in the clearing itself," Sinclair pointed out, looking around. The clearing was filled with fresh powder. Not a dent disturbed it.

"He knew to cover his tracks," Savage said, "or it snowed so much that they've been buried. We'll get Pearl to come up here and take a look." That would have to wait till he got back to the Suburban and could use the radio.

"It sure looks like him," Sinclair murmured.

"Looks like who?" Jed frowned.

"No one." Savage shot her a warning look. "Thanks, Jed. We've got it from here."

"You sure? You don't want my help moving the body? The easiest way to get her out is across the river, otherwise it's a good four-mile hike back to the trailhead." He looked back down the dirt track.

Looked like he was going to have to give Clinton from Search and Rescue another call. They'd have to carry her over the fast-flowing water to get her to the ambulance.

"All right, let's cordon off the area and head back to the truck. I need to use the radio."

Sinclair nodded and took the police tape out of her backpack. She set about cordoning off the clearing, wrapping the yellow tape around the trees on the perimeter. While she was doing that, Savage took a few steps closer to the body. He risked contaminating the crime scene, but he needed to know. Was this the Frost Killer?

Wearing gloves, he bent down and dusted some of the snow off her chest. She was icy cold, her body frozen stiff.

"What are you looking for?" Jed called.

"Just taking a closer look."

There was a silver chain around her neck. Holding his breath, he wiped away more of the snow. A pendant lay against her sternum.

It was a snowflake.

TWELVE

"THE MEDIA ARE GOING to be all over this one." Sinclair raised her eyebrows at Savage. "Do you know who the vic is?"

"Enlighten me."

"Stephanie Harcourt. She was engaged to Commissioner Albright's son, and as we know, the Commissioner is not a man to take his daughter-in-law's death lying down."

Shit.

The District Commissioner was known for his quick thinking and sharp tongue. Elected by the community for his second term, the general feeling was that while he might not be the most likable politician in the county, he got the job done. People felt like he had their backs, particularly on issues like affordable housing, improving the county's infrastructure, and protecting residents from the perils of climate change – drought and wildfires in the dry season being of primary concern.

Apart from one or two official meetings, Savage didn't have much to do with him. It looked like that was about to change.

"We'd better notify the family," he said. "Before they read about their daughter's death in the papers."

"Nobody knows yet," Littleton pointed out.

"You mean apart from Jed and Jasmine Hatch, their grandchildren, the Search and Rescue team, and those two photographers?"

The junior deputy colored.

Savage picked up the keys to his Suburban. "Things have a habit of getting out, no matter how hard you try to keep them under wraps. Sinclair, let's go see the victim's parents, and then we'll pay Commissioner Albright a visit."

"I'm coming too," Avril said, getting up.

Damn. He'd almost forgotten she was along for the ride. The Swedish Agent had the uncanny ability to sit quietly, her slender frame almost blending into the furniture, but when she wanted something, she was a simmering pinball of tension that whizzed around the room, disrupting everything.

"You sure you want to come to the next of kin notification?"

"Ja," she replied. "They might tell us something about the victim. Something that could help the case."

He sighed. She wasn't wrong there.

"All right. Let's go."

STEPHANIE HARCOURT'S parents lived in a large, two-story house in an upmarket part of Durango. It wasn't a match for the Cullen's sweeping mountainside property, but it wasn't bad. Savage pressed the gleaming gold buzzer, and they waited to be let in.

"I wonder if he's home," he muttered.

"Thorpe said he works from home. Property developer," Sinclair replied. "He should be here."

The door swung open. "I told you not to go ahead without me." A middle-aged man in smart trousers and a shirt, who Savage assumed to be Mr. Harcourt, stood there, phone pressed to his ear. Savage wasn't sure if he was talking to them or the caller. Regardless, the personal call would have to wait.

He cleared his throat. "I'm sorry to disturb you, Mr. Harcourt, but

I'm Sheriff Savage and this is Deputy Sinclair and Agent Dahl. We need to talk to you about your daughter, Stephanie?"

The man frowned. "Sorry, Bill. I'll call you back." Turning to the detectives, he said, "What's she done now?"

"What makes you think she's done something?" Savage asked.

"You wouldn't be here, otherwise." Mr. Harcourt held the door open so they could file in.

"Is your wife home?" Savage asked, looking around the entrance hall.

"Emily passed away ten months ago." His expression remained neutral, although his eyelids flickered as he said the words.

"I'm sorry to hear that."

Mr. Harcourt studied them. He hadn't invited them into the living room and didn't look like he was going to, so they stood awkwardly in the entrance hall. "What's going on?"

Savage noticed a side cabinet covered with family photographs, mostly Mr. and Mrs. Harcourt in happier times, and several of his daughter, Stephanie.

"I'm afraid we have some bad news," Savage began, gritting his teeth. Damn, he hated doing this. The man had recently lost his wife, and now they had to inform him that his daughter had died, too. Life could be a bitch sometimes. "Maybe we should sit down."

"Tell me." His tone was clipped.

Savage cleared his throat. "I'm sorry to have to tell you that Stephanie was found dead this morning."

There was a long pause as Harcourt registered what Savage had said. He stumbled backwards against the wall and put his hand against it to stabilize himself.

Sinclair made to take his arm, but he waved her away. "Where?" he rasped. "Where was she found?"

"Out on the hiking trail near Renegade Creek."

Harcourt closed his eyes. "She ran there every morning. Never missed it, no matter what." When he opened them again, they glistened with tears.

"We've very sorry for your loss," Savage said quietly. Sinclair gulped beside him, while Avril just stared at him with wide, vacant eyes.

Mr. Harcourt struggled to keep it together. Savage suspected he didn't show his emotions often. Probably thought it was weak.

"How did she die?" He blinked several times and took a ragged breath.

Avril opened her mouth to speak, but Savage cut her off. "We don't know yet. We're waiting for the medical examiner's report."

It was the truth, as far as they knew it. Nothing else had been confirmed. Besides, telling him she could be the second victim of a crazed serial killer who freezes his victims to death sounded a bit far-fetched, even if it was the bizarre reality.

"How could you not know?" He rubbed his forehead, agitated. "I mean, you saw her body, didn't you?"

Savage nodded. "We did, yes."

"Was she attacked while she was running? Were there any marks on her? Did she have any injuries?"

"Not that we could see, sir."

Harcourt clawed at his thinning hair. "I don't understand. She wouldn't have just dropped dead. She was a healthy young woman."

"We'll let you know as soon as we find out." Savage tried to placate the man. He didn't blame him for all the questions. If it was his daughter, he'd want answers too.

All he got in reply was a stiff nod.

Avril stepped forward. "Mr. Harcourt, do you mind if we ask you some questions about your daughter?"

The bereaved father gave her a look that said: Really? You want to do this now?

"Um, maybe we should come back, Avril." Sinclair put a cautionary hand on Avril's arm. Harcourt was in no state to answer questions. The poor man was still leaning against the wall for support, his face gray and pinched.

Avril seemed surprised, then looked at Savage and pushed her glasses up her nose. "Oh, yes. Of course. I'm sorry."

"Would you like us to call anyone for you, Mr. Harcourt?" Sinclair said.

He shook his head. "No. I—I'll be okay."

He didn't look it.

Savage led them out, leaving Harcourt alone with his grief, his phone still clutched in his hand.

"Sorry," Avril muttered from the back seat as they drove to Clifford Albright's house. It was after four o'clock, and the sun had set unnoticed behind the mountains. Darkness seeped over the valley, dropping the temperatures again.

"Sometimes, I—I get so consumed with the case that I forget. . ."

Savage nodded. In the short time he'd known her, he'd realized the FBI agent didn't do the empathy thing too well. Her natural intensity meant she forgot people had feelings.

"It's okay. Usually, I would ask a couple of questions too, but in that case, I think we needed to give him some time to grieve."

Sinclair, sitting up front with Savage, nodded. "Yeah, poor guy was barely holding it together."

They drove out of town to the Albright's family estate. The radio crackled just as they pulled up to the steel electric gate at the foot of the driveway.

"Yeah, Barb. We're here."

"It's Thorpe," came his deputy's voice.

"What d'ya got?" Although Savage thought he knew. While Pearl had gone up to the hiking trail to analyze the crime scene, Ray had met the Search and Rescue team at the hospital and was going to test the victim for chloroform. Given that it was such a low-tech test, it wouldn't have taken long, and the results would have been almost instantaneous.

"Ray found chloroform around her mouth," Thorpe confirmed. "Looks like it's our guy."

THIRTEEN

THE ALBRIGHT ESTATE was a sweeping ranch-style property situated on the lower slopes of the San Juan Mountain. In the daytime, the view would have been spectacular. The air smelled fresh and clean, with a hint of fern or pine, he wasn't sure which. Looking up, rough, jagged peaks plastered in snow and ice pierced the indigo sky.

The road to the estate had recently been cleared, otherwise it would have been impassable, even in the SUV. Snow drifts covered the slopes on either side, the dark shadows of the evergreens poking through. The hillside, adorned with wildflowers in the summer, was now one continuous expanse of snow.

"It's beautiful," breathed Sinclair, staring out of the window.

"Looks like Sweden," was Avril's curt reply. Savage couldn't work out if that was a good or bad thing.

They paused at a gatehouse manned by armed security personnel and had to show ID before being allowed to proceed.

"Bit much for a local politician, isn't it?" Sinclair muttered, as they drove up the winding driveway to the house.

"I heard the Commissioner is an avid art collector," Savage murmured, as they parked and got out of the SUV. "Maybe that's why."

The air was biting cold, now that the sun had gone, and his eyes watered as he walked toward the front door. Savage pressed the buzzer, and they waited to be let in. Eventually, a smart, middle-aged woman with readers perched on her head opened the door. She squinted at them. “Can I help you?”

“We’re looking for Clifford Albright.”

“My son is in the study with his father. I’ll get him for you. You can wait in the living room.”

With a sweep of her hand, she led them to a spacious room filled with expensive leather furniture, elaborate lighting, and an ornate coffee table on which sat an enormous centerpiece of white and pale-yellow flowers. It both warmed and chilled the room at the same time.

Savage’s gaze landed on a gilt-framed painting hanging over the fireplace. It was of a group of men mounted on white steeds. They appeared to be on a hunt, judging by the rifles across their chests. One horse reared up, its rider hanging on triumphantly. The artwork seemed to glow from within, illuminating the characters’ faces, while the edges faded into a dark, forest green.

Savage could just make out the artist’s name from where he was standing. *Alfred Jacob Miller*. He didn’t know whether it was a copy or an original, but judging by the security at the gate, he was guessing real, and probably one of several treasures on display in this house.

“Can I help you, Sheriff?” Commissioner Albright strode into the room. He wore a checked shirt, jeans, and cowboy boots, and looked decidedly normal, not suited and booted like his onscreen persona.

“Actually, we’re here to talk to your son,” he replied.

Clifford stepped into the room. “Is something wrong?” He was as self-assured as his father and had the same heavy jawline and dense black hair.

“I’m afraid so.” Savage dove straight in. “Stephanie Harcourt was found dead this morning.”

“Oh, God!” Clifford stared at them, dumbfounded. “Stephanie’s dead?”

Savage gave a stiff nod. "Her body was found out by Renegade Creek a few hours ago."

"She jogs along there." Clifford collapsed onto one of the sofas, his eyes glazing over. His mother put a shaky hand on his shoulder.

"What happened?" Commissioner Albright turned to Savage. "Was it an accident?"

There was no point in avoiding the truth. The Commissioner could easily read the police report. "I don't think so, sir."

Mrs. Albright gasped. "You mean she was murdered?"

"We're still putting the case facts together, but it's the direction our investigation is leaning."

There was a stunned silence.

Clifford's face crumpled. "Was she—? Did anyone—touch her?" He couldn't bring himself to say the words.

"It doesn't look like it," Savage confirmed.

Clifford exhaled shakily. "Thank God."

"Then why kill her?" Albright frowned. "This doesn't have anything to do with Clifford, does it? Someone trying to get to him? To us?"

Savage noted the narcissistic tendency to think it was all about him or his family.

"We're not sure at this stage," he said. "We think it might be someone targeting women in the area."

"Oh, Lord." Mrs. Albright walked around the back of the sofa and sat down next to her son. "A serial killer?"

How people loved to bandy that term around.

Albright glanced at Savage. "Is this true? There've been others?"

"Yes," Avril cut in. "Stephanie Harcourt is the second woman to be targeted this week."

Savage cringed. The blunt delivery was not how he wanted to break it to Albright.

"I'm sorry." The Commissioner peered behind Savage at Avril as if noticing her for the first time. "Who are you?"

"FBI Special Agent Dahl," she said, stiffly. "I'm working with the Hawk's Landing Sheriff's Department on this investigation."

"FBI?" Albright glanced from Avril to Savage and back again. "Sheriff, can I have a word in private?"

"Yes, sir." He relished the opportunity to get away from Avril. It would give him a chance to smooth things over.

Albright led him down a short, carpeted corridor to his private office. Once inside, he gestured for Savage to take a seat while he went over to a cabinet and poured himself a tumbler of whiskey. "Want one?"

"No, thank you. I'm on duty."

Albright knocked it back, took a deep breath, and turned to Savage. "Okay, Dalton, what the hell is going on, and why is the damn FBI involved?"

Savage sat down and waited while Albright eased himself into the leather-bound chair behind his desk. Once he had the Commissioner's full attention, he said, "On Tuesday, a woman called Anita Cullen was found dead in a barn on the Thompson's ranch. She froze to death."

"I heard about the Cullen girl. Terrible tragedy." He scratched his head. "Wasn't that an accident?"

"No. She'd been knocked out using chloroform and left in the barn to freeze to death."

"Jesus," he whispered.

"The next day, Agent Dahl arrived and informed us that the modus operandi of Anita's death was exactly the same as that of a serial killer the FBI have been hunting for the last ten years."

"Ten years?"

Savage nodded.

Albright stared at him, shaking his head.

Savage went on, "Once his victims are unconscious, he leaves them to freeze, posing their bodies in the snow." He purposely left out the bit about the snowflake pendant.

Albright's voice was low. "What kind of sicko does that?"

Savage didn't answer.

The Frost Killer.

"Why has it taken them so long to catch the bastard?"

Savage grimaced. "It's complicated. He operates across country and state borders, which makes him difficult to track, and he only kills during the winter months, then he disappears again until the following year. And he never kills in the same place twice."

Albright blew out a slow breath.

"This is his latest spate of murders," Savage said. "First Anita, now Stephanie."

There was a pause as what Savage said sunk in. To give Albright credit, he managed to stay composed. "Was Stephanie left to freeze in the snow too?"

Savage nodded, then showed Albright a photograph on his phone. It was one he'd taken from the crime scene, before they'd moved her body. An angel, frozen forever in her icy grave. Her hands resting on her chest, her face dusted with snow. "This is how we found her."

Albright stared at it for a long time, then glanced away.

"We have to stop him, Dalton. We have to make him pay for what he's done." His beefy hands clenched into fists.

"We're giving it our full attention, sir."

"Anything you need." Albright got to his feet. "You give me a call. I want this monster caught before he kills any more women. You hear me?"

Savage couldn't agree more.

"Yes, sir."

FOURTEEN

THE NEXT MORNING, there was a small gathering of reporters outside the Sheriff's office dressed in thick coats and woolen hats. They cradled coffees from The Bouncing Bean and stomped their feet to ward off the cold.

"Here we go," muttered Savage, as he walked toward them.

"I knew Stephanie Harcourt's death would cause problems," Sinclair said, trailing behind him. "Anything with a hint of celebrity, and they're all over it."

"She was famous?" Avril looked surprised.

Savage shrugged. "Local politicians and old money are as close as we get to celeb status around here."

"How did Stephanie Harcourt die, Sheriff?" called one reporter, shoving a microphone in his face.

"Was it an accident?" asked another.

"Could you give us the cause of death?" shouted a third.

"No comment at this time." Savage forced his way past them into the office, Sinclair and Avril right behind him.

Barbara rolled her eyes as they burst through the door. "They've been out there for the last hour," she moaned. "Someone must have leaked it."

"Bad news travels fast." Savage marched across the squadroom to his office.

"You gonna give a statement?" Barb called after him.

"I'll have to, otherwise it'll make us look like we aren't doing anything, or we don't have anything to go on. Either way, it's not good for the department."

"I hated this part about being Sheriff," Thorpe murmured, looking out the window at the reporters.

"Give me an hour," Savage said, disappearing into his office. Before he gave a statement to the press, he had to be sure they hadn't missed anything.

First, he called Ray, who answered on the first ring. "Nothing else wrong with her," he told Savage. "It's a real shame, healthy girl like that cut down in her prime."

It always was.

"Pearl with you?" he asked.

"Yeah, hang on. I'll put her on."

Pearl came on the line. "Hey, Dalton. I nearly froze my ass off at your crime scene yesterday."

"Find anything?"

"Nothing useful. She was laid out in the middle of that clearing and made to look like she was praying. I didn't find any signs of a struggle, no DNA beneath her nails, no bruising or scratches anywhere on her body. The killer didn't leave any trace of himself behind. Not even a footprint. The snowfall did a good job of covering up any clues."

"She was unconscious when she died?"

"That's my conclusion." There was a brief pause. "I don't think she suffered, if that's any consolation."

He supposed it was a small mercy.

"Okay, thanks Pearl."

Savage sighed. It was time to face the media.

. . .

"GOOD MORNING," he began, standing on the steps, waiting for the group to quieten down. Hawk's Landing only had one small press that put out a monthly local newspaper, while Durango had a daily as well as a couple of smaller monthlies. A regional press had also sent a reporter, probably because Stephanie's soon-to-be father-in-law was the County Commissioner.

"Thank you for coming. Yesterday, the Hawk's Landing Sheriff's Department recovered the body of Stephanie Harcourt, from the Renegade Creek hiking trail. According to the medical examiner, the cause of death was cardiac failure as a result of exposure to cold."

There was a dull silence, then someone muttered, "She froze to death?"

"That is correct. The Sheriff's Department will continue to investigate the circumstances around Stephanie Harcourt's death in order to obtain a clearer picture of what happened to her."

Savage turned and walked back up the steps, just as the reporters registered what he'd said.

"How did she freeze to death?"

"How long was she out there for?"

"Did she get lost?"

"Was she under the influence of alcohol or drugs?"

He ignored them all and walked back inside.

"I'm not sure if I made that better or worse," he said.

Barb chuckled. "They're never going to be satisfied, no matter what you say."

Unfortunately, he feared that was true.

"You didn't mention that her death was suspicious," Sinclair said.

"I didn't want to start a mass panic. Can you imagine if we told them a serial killer was on the loose, targeting young, blonde women?"

"Maybe we should warn them," Sinclair said. "That way they can take precautions."

"I'd rather not right now. It might also send the killer to ground. It would be better if he thought we're still under the impression these two deaths were unfortunate accidents."

Sinclair gnawed on her lower lip, uncertain.

Avril gave a little nod. "I agree. We can't let him know we're onto him."

"We're not," Sinclair pointed out. "We don't have a freakin' clue who 'he' is."

"Not yet," said Thorpe, and there was an optimistic glint in his eye that bolstered Savage.

Littleton chose that moment to come rushing in, out of breath. "What the hell's going on?"

"Press got wind of it," Sinclair said. "Stephanie Harcourt's death has caused quite a stir."

Littleton glanced back at the door. "Nearly clawed me to shreds out there."

"Any luck with those two photographers?" Savage asked, making his youngest deputy refocus.

"No. They were both shocked by the discovery, but they didn't pass anyone else on the trail. They said the place was deserted."

"Typical." Savage huffed. "What were they doing in the clearing?"

"Looking for the perfect shot," Littleton said. "They knew about the clearing from before. It's like a secret spot for photographers."

It was beautiful. He pictured the pristine snow, the frosted trees reaching for the sky in a circle around the body, steel-gray clouds diffusing the light.

"Whatever happens, we can't mention the pendant," Savage warned them. "I don't want that in the papers. Nobody must know about it."

"It was in the original news reports," Avril remarked. "We can't hide it."

"No one's made that connection yet," Savage stressed. "The natural assumption is going to be that Stephanie Harcourt went for a run, got lost, and died from exposure. Let's keep it that way."

"I was looking into Stephanie's background." Thorpe tapped a report on his desk. "They've been around for generations, too."

"Just like the Cullens," muttered Savage.

Thorpe went on. "By all accounts, Stephanie was a little wild. In the articles that mention her engagement to Clifford Albright, it says how she'd calmed down a lot since she'd met him."

Savage pursed his lips thoughtfully. "Her mother's death may have affected her badly."

Sinclair nodded. "It would have done, I'm sure. Losing a parent can cause one to go off the rails for a while."

He glanced at her, wondering if she was talking from experience. He hadn't ever asked Sinclair about her parents.

"None of that matters." Avril gave a sulky pout. "The Frost Killer doesn't discriminate based on wealth, status or historical significance. He strikes at random, which is why it's so hard to catch him."

Savage sighed. As onerous as it was having Avril contradicting their every move, she did have a point. The Frost Killer was an out-of-towner. A stranger to Hawk's Landing. Why would he care whether his victims were wealthy landowners? Whether they were politically connected?

Historically, there had been no pattern to his kills. Nothing that linked the victims.

Four women.

That's what Avril had said, and all the case reports he'd read supported that. Every year, the Frost Killer murdered four more women. No more. No less. That meant two more women in Hawk's Landing or Durango were at risk. His county.

He sat down at his desk and wrote down what they knew so far. Female, twenties or thirties, blonde hair, fit and active, unmarried, wealthy or prestigious, but as Avril pointed out, that last one was probably just a coincidence.

Anita was a cross-country skier, Stephanie a runner. Did that mean anything? He frowned and rubbed his temples with his forefingers. Maybe. Maybe not.

Frustrated, he called Barb in. She had lived in Hawk's Landing most of her life and knew everyone worth knowing in the town. "Barb, who are some of the other prominent families in the county?"

"Oh, gosh. I only know those families that live around here," she said.

"Okay, give me those."

"Well, apart from the Harcourts and the Cullens, there's old Matt Madden out near Bayfield. He's fallen on hard times, but when he gets drunk, he tells anyone who'll listen how his family was one of the first to work the mines."

She thought for a moment. "I suppose the Calhouns would be considered prominent. They've been in Hawk's Landing since the beginning too, but they weren't miners, I don't think, although I could be wrong."

Savage made a note. "Anyone else?"

Barb clicked her fingers. "You know, there's a local historian called Rex Haverly who works at the library. You should go talk to him. He'd know more than me."

"Thanks, Barb."

Savage wasn't a big fan of internet searches. Too much unverified information out there that could be misleading. He preferred to do his own research. But without anything concrete to go on, he logged on and ran each of the names Barb had given him through Google.

The Cullens had set up a foundation that had funded the local high school, Black Rock High. It wasn't a big school, but it drew kids from the surrounding farmland and ranches, as well as Hawk's Landing.

Interestingly, they were now funding environmental projects, particularly water related. A lot of Clifford Albright's charity work was environmental. Was that a link? Or was he grasping at straws?

Likewise, there was no mention of a Matthew Madden, despite the family name going back to the town's roots.

The Calhouns were originally from Scotland. They weren't miners, but they had provided a lot of the town's essential services. The local inn, the doctor's office, and eventually, a hospital. Currently, however, he could only find reference to one descendant living in Hawk's Landing. A daughter, Grace. She was twenty-four years old and worked at Black Rock High School as a teacher.

The webpage showed a picture of her taken a couple of years back, standing by a horse and holding a rosette. She had a wide smile and pale blonde hair.

FIFTEEN

"IDIOTS."

The killer turned away from the Sheriff's office in disgust. How could they think this was an accident?

Two girls, both frozen in the snow, both wearing his signature pendant.

What the hell did he have to do to get noticed? Write his moniker in blood in the snow?

He sighed, frustrated. Then again, what could you expect from a small-town Sheriff in a backwards place like this?

There'd been nothing in the newspapers about his first victim, Anita Cullen. Zilch. It was as if she never existed. Didn't anybody care? They must have found her body by now. It'd been a week since he'd preserved her. Out on the range, the majestic La Plata Mountains guarding her body, the snowflakes gently caressing her perfect skin.

He was tempted to go back there and check, but that would be foolish. He wouldn't make the same mistake other killers made – returning to the crime scene. They were weak because they couldn't stay away. They wanted to relive the experience. Needed to see the impact of their crime.

He wasn't like that. He wasn't weak.

Of course, he could have just asked the Sheriff. With his camera over his shoulder, nobody would have guessed he wasn't a reporter. Another blood-thirsty journalist out for a story. They were almost as bad as he was. Preying on human emotion. Scaremongering.

But he couldn't take the chance. Drawing attention to himself would be foolish. There was a CCTV camera above the entrance to the sheriff's office, but he'd made sure to wear a cap and keep his face behind his bulky camera. That way nobody would be able to identify him, even if they did check the footage.

He wasn't stupid.

The killer walked back to his truck, boots crunching on the icy tarmac. He glanced up at the sleet-gray sky. A damp cold hung in the air like a moist cloth. It was going to snow again. He could smell it. His pulse quickened.

Good.

He was almost ready.

Two down, two to go. He must follow the pattern. It had to be that way.

Overcome with anticipation, he deviated from his normal route home and drove toward the reservation. He wanted a glimpse of his next target.

The casino was out of his way, but not by much. The road had been cleared since the last snowfall, making the trek easy. Parking in the lot outside, he hurried to the entrance, turning up his collar against the cold. He sniffed the air. Another couple of hours, then it would come down.

An overwhelming pinging, beeping and jingling from the slot machines greeted him as he entered the building. The heating was turned up, and he relaxed, enjoying the warmth. There was something nurturing about the soft lighting, the plush carpeting, and the rich colors, like they were luring you into a false sense of security, so you'd spend all your money on the one-arm bandits or the craps tables.

As the killer walked toward the blackjack table where she worked, he listened to the clatter of roulette balls, the rustling of cards and the clink of chips being stacked. Sounds he'd grown familiar with over the last few weeks. This angel might come close on the heels of the last, but he'd been watching them all for a long time. He knew who, he knew how, and in what order. His planning had been meticulous. Nothing was left to chance.

Her routine seldom varied. She worked five eight-hour shifts per week. One week, the shifts were during the day, and the following week, at night. From Monday to Friday, she stayed at the hotel in a room on the fourth floor. He'd seen other staff members up there and figured the more permanent workers had some sort of temporary accommodation deal in their contract.

On the weekends, she went home to her apartment in Durango. It wasn't a great apartment, just a dingy one-bedroom on the first floor of a cold, brick building. She could do better, but perhaps she didn't want to spend her money. Five nights out of seven, she lived at the hotel.

This honey was a naughty girl. Not content with the money she made dealing, or the generous tips she received, she also entertained men back in her room for substantially more.

He'd engaged her services once – hadn't been able to resist. To feel the warmth of her body before he snuffed it out had been too great a temptation. Besides, she was asking for it, right? Any girl who put out like that knew the risks.

He sidled past the table, behind her. Nobody noticed him, they were too occupied with their hands. Unaware of his movements, she dealt cards, collected chips and offered practiced, sympathetic smiles. The consummate professional.

He wondered if her employers knew about her lucrative side hustle. Probably not. Or maybe they did and turned a blind eye. After all, it was a service she was offering. Some men liked to celebrate their winnings by buying a nice piece of ass. He'd just wanted to feel her, inhale her, taste her, before she was gone.

No, not gone.

Preserved.

It was almost time for her break. Admiring her slim neck, her long, blonde hair clipped up in a neat coiffe, and her blood-red nails as she dealt the cards, he felt himself grow hard.

"Soon," he murmured to her back. "Soon it will be your turn."

SIXTEEN

SAVAGE PULLED up in front of Black Rock High School. It was a modern, H-shaped building with plenty of outdoor space. As he walked into the building, he noticed a few curious young faces peering at him through the windows. The black Suburban with LA PLATA COUNTY SHERIFF written in gold along the side drew attention.

"Excuse me, could you show me where the office is?" he asked a lone student, hurrying to class.

"Down the hall on the left," the boy said without making eye contact, then scuttled off, backpack slung over his shoulder.

Savage followed his directions. After knocking, he pushed open the door and found himself in a waiting room, with a row of blue plastic chairs positioned against the wall. It smelled of ink and sweaty kids. Through a plexiglass window was a young woman with flaming red hair typing furiously on a clunky, out-of-date computer.

Behind her, a printer whirred as it spat out pages, and a phone rang incessantly. Sighing, she stopped typing, held one finger up at him, then answered the phone. "Black Rock High School, how can I help you?"

Savage waited while she directed the call. When she looked up at him expectantly, he tipped his head in greeting. "Morning. I'm Sheriff Savage from Hawk's Landing. I'd like to talk to Grace Calhoun, please. Could you tell me where she is?"

The woman's brow wrinkled. "Is Grace in some kind of trouble, Sheriff?" While her expression was one of concern, he noticed a curious sparkle in her gaze. She looked like the type to gossip.

"No, not at all, Miss—" He glanced at the laminated card around her neck. "Pettigrew." He didn't elaborate. It was none of her business.

"She's in class now." Pettigrew checked her computer. "But she'll be done in... seven minutes. If you'd like to wait outside Classroom 35, you should catch her coming out."

"Great. Where is that?"

"Oh, how silly of me. You don't know your way around, do you? I'll show you." She made to get up.

"No, that's okay. I won't pull you away from your desk." He wasn't going to give her a chance to overhear what he had to say.

A flash of disappointment. "Oh, okay. Well, it's straight ahead as you come out of this office, then take a right at the end of the corridor. Classroom 35 is halfway down on the right."

"Thank you."

He set off, walking through the deserted halls, glancing at rows of sometimes bored, sometimes concentrating faces through the glass panels in the classroom doors. His school in Denver was nothing like this one. Urban, tight on space, and mostly concrete, he'd gotten the bare bones of an education. Thankfully, he'd liked to read and was bright enough to get into the Police Academy. That's all he'd ever wanted to do, anyway.

Five minutes later, the doors flung open, and a tide of students surged into the corridors. He flattened himself against the wall outside the classroom, waiting for the chaos to subside. Eventually, a slender, blonde woman wearing jeans, a cream blouse, and a maroon cardigan emerged.

"Miss Calhoun?"

Her gaze flitted over his uniform, lingering on the star pinned to his jacket. “Yes?” Her tongue darted out as she wet her lips. “Is something wrong? Has something happened?”

“No, nothing like that,” he reassured her. Most people feared the worst when they saw him. It was one of the downsides of the job.

“Oh, thank goodness.” She let out a shaky breath.

“Is there somewhere we can talk?”

“Sure, why don’t you come into the classroom. I’ve got a break now, and this room isn’t occupied until the next period.”

He followed her in. She stood in front of her desk, so he did the same, feeling awkward. How was he going to warn her without sounding melodramatic or divulging the whole story?

“What is it, Sheriff?” Her eyes were a cobalt blue, like the sky on a hot summer’s day. There was a warmth about her, an empathy that he liked. She smiled, hesitantly. “Have I done something wrong?”

“No, not at all. This is a precautionary visit.” He hesitated while she stared at him, waiting for him to spit it out. “We’ve had a few instances of attacks on young, blonde women,” he began, opting for a half-truth rather than the full story. “So, we’re asking everyone who fits that profile to be ultra-vigilant and not to take any unnecessary risks until we’ve apprehended the suspect.”

She gave a little gasp, and her hand fluttered to her chest. “How awful! What kind of attacks?”

“Assaults, mostly.” He wasn’t going to go there. She didn’t need to know the Frost Killer’s lethal MO.

Grace Calhoun studied him, her blue eyes filled with concern. “Well, how worried should I be?”

“We have intelligence that suggests the perpetrator is operating in this area, so it’s best to be on high alert.”

“Wow, okay. That sounds scary.”

“Stay vigilant. Don’t go anywhere alone for the next couple of weeks. Not until we’ve caught this guy. Stay in well-lit places, lock your door when you get home, take all the usual precautions.”

She exhaled, and smoothed a hand over hair that was pulled back in a neat bun. It didn't really need smoothing. "I will. Thank you for coming here to warn me in person."

"ALL PART OF THE JOB, Miss Calhoun."

SINCLAIR CAME INTO HIS OFFICE, closing the door behind her. "Where have you been?"

"I went to see Grace Calhoun."

Her eyes widened. "What? You didn't tell her about the killer, did you?"

"Of course not. I did warn her to be careful, though. I said there'd been a spate of attacks on young, blonde women in the area."

Sinclair sat opposite him. "Good move."

He nodded. "I think she bought it."

"You know, you can't warn every blonde woman in the county, not without going public with this."

He sniffed. "I know that, but I can't help feeling she's one of the most likely candidates. Her family's heritage is tied to the town, and from what I can see, they have quite a legacy."

"Why is she working in a school?" Sinclair asked. "With that kind of old money—"

"We don't know that they have money," Savage interrupted.

Sinclair shrugged. "What about her parents?"

"I didn't ask."

She gave a contemplative nod. "What about the Maddens?"

He sighed. "There's a Matthew Madden living in Bayfield, who Barb thinks is connected to the original family, but I couldn't see if there were any women who fit the profile." He grimaced. "The Google search didn't turn up anything."

"I'll look into it," she said.

"Great. I want to talk to that historian, Rex Haverly. He might be able to shed some light on the history of the town and the founding families."

"Agent Dahl doesn't think the family thing has any bearing on the case."

"She's probably right, but what else do we have to go on?" He got up.

"I'll keep working on this," Sinclair said. "You can take Agent Dahl with you to the library."

Sinclair wasn't a fan, that much was obvious.

He masked a grin. "Fine, we'll have a briefing when I get back."

"HE DOESN'T TARGET his victims based on wealth or status," Avril insisted as they walked the short distance to the library. Barb had called ahead, and despite it being a Saturday, Rex Haverly was working in the archives.

"I went back over my case notes last night, and there is nothing like that. Some are rich, some poor, some in between. I can't see how this is relevant."

"You don't have to come with me." Savage thrust his hands into his pockets and kept walking.

She bit her lip. "I know, but I'd like to find out about the history of this place, even if it is a waste of time." He raised his eyebrows. For some reason, he couldn't picture the intense FBI agent having any interests outside of this case. He realized that was narrow-minded, but so far, she'd had tunnel vision when it came to The Frost Killer.

"It might seem like a waste of time to you, but I would be remiss if I didn't follow up on the only link we've got between the two victims."

"It's just that I've been down this road before—"

"I know, but it's my first time, so humor me, okay?"

He received the faintest of smiles. "Okay." Avril stopped and stared up at the Victorian-era building with its faded stone exterior and intricate carvings. It stood several stories high and was one of the oldest and most beautiful buildings in Hawk's Landing. "Wow, is this the library?"

"Yes, impressive, isn't it?" He felt a surge of pride, even though he wasn't from here.

They opened a gate and walked through a small, landscaped garden, which Savage knew was maintained by a team of volunteers. "Usually, this is filled with native Colorado plants," he explained, stomping over the flattened snow to the front door. Avril glanced up at a bronze statue of a miner with a pickaxe over his shoulder, a silent nod to the town's origins.

Inside the library, the high ceilings gave it an open, spacious feel. Savage had only been here once before, but he remembered the welcoming, cozy atmosphere. The floorboards, darkened over time, creaked as they walked over to the reception desk. Natural light flooded through the tall windows with wavy vintage glass and cast gentle shadows over the wooden bookshelves lining the walls.

"Can I help you?" the bespectacled librarian asked. He had small eyes and an overbite, reminding Savage of a rabbit.

"We'd like to speak with Rex Haverly."

The librarian glanced at the sheriff's badge and nodded. "One moment, please. He's in the archives. I'll call him."

They waited at the main reading area and browsed the books that lined the shelves. There was everything from modern bestsellers to historical non-fiction detailing the history of mining in Colorado and beyond.

Avril moved toward an enormous fireplace with logs glowing in the hearth. There was a semicircle of comfy chairs positioned around it, presumably for book clubs and gatherings, and she sat down gingerly, extending her hands toward the warmth.

It was a girlish gesture, and in that moment, Savage felt sorry for her. How many towns had she been to in the middle of winter, hunting the man who'd killed her mother? Eight? Nine? No wonder she acted like she was on autopilot. Like she'd seen it all before.

She had. And every time was a disappointment.

How much of herself had she given to this case? It must have broken her several times over, but here she was, a decade later, still chasing him down.

"We're going to do our best to catch him," he told her, coming to stand beside her. She started, then gave him a whisper of a smile.

"I know."

SEVENTEEN

A THROAT CLEARED BEHIND THEM, and Avril jumped clean out of her chair. The pair of them turned to take in the newcomer.

"I'm Rex Haverly. I believe you wanted to speak to me?"

"Yes, thank you for meeting with us." Savage studied the diminutive man in a waistcoat, with a bushy mustache and John Lennon round glasses. He looked like he could have stepped straight out of the nineteenth century. "We'd like to ask you about the history of Hawk's Landing, in particular the old families who came here to work the mines."

His mustache fluttered as his face broke into a wide smile. "Ah, my area of expertise! You've come to the right place, officers." He shuffled over to one of the armchairs and sat down. Savage and Avril did the same.

"Where would you like me to begin?"

"How about with the mining boom?" Savage suggested. While he'd heard stories of the gold rush and the town's origins, he'd never taken the time to read up on it.

"Ah, yes. The Dawn of Prosperity." His eyes gleamed. The historian was in his element. Savage leaned back to listen.

"It all began in 1858 as news of gold discoveries spread across the land. Pioneers flocked to Colorado, and among them were the original settlers of Hawk's Landing. Drawn by tales of abundant gold, these settlers founded the town, hoping to stake their claim to prosperity. The Maddens, Irish immigrants fleeing the Great Famine, were among the first to strike gold. Their fortune attracted more settlers, and the town quickly grew."

Haverly had a rich, theatrical tone to his voice, and although Savage wasn't that interested in history, he found himself enthralled by the story. Even Avril leaned forward in her chair. The Maddens must be the great-grandparents of Matthew Madden, the loner Barb had mentioned.

"By the 1870s, Hawk's Landing had transitioned from gold to silver. The town's mines, particularly those controlled by the Harcourts, an English family with a keen eye for geology, became a hub of silver extraction. The town's prosperity was reflected in its bustling streets and ornate houses, just like this one." He waved a hand in the air.

Stephanie Harcourt's ancestors.

"The library is that old?" Avril asked.

"Yes. In fact, it once was the residence of the Harcourts, before they moved on and donated it to the town."

Now that was interesting.

Haverly continued. "It was during this era that the Strombergs introduced their signature silverwork. You may have seen various items dotted around the library and in the museum." When they both shook their heads, he pursed his lips, his mustache quivering again. "You should take a look sometime. It's wonderful craftsmanship."

"We will," Savage assured him.

"Anyway, they transformed raw silver into exquisite artifacts. Hawk's Landing wasn't just mining silver. It was crafting history."

Rex Havelry could be on stage, he was that accomplished a storyteller. Savage thought about what the historian was saying. "So, we've got the Maddens, the Harcourts and the Strombergs as three of the founding families?"

"That's correct." He gazed down at them through his owl-like glasses. "But there's more."

"Oh?"

"Yes, lots more."

Not too much, Savage hoped. His brain was almost at its saturation point.

"The prosperity, sadly, was not to last," Haverly continued. "The Panic of 1893, triggered by the repeal of the Sherman Silver Purchase Act, was a gut-punch to the town. Silver prices plummeted, mines closed down, and many miners found themselves unemployed. The town's population dwindled, and the once-bustling streets grew quieter."

Avril's eyes were huge, like a little girl being read a fairy tale. Savage, on the other hand, grew tired of the theatrics.

"What happened to the families?" he asked.

"The economic challenges intensified tensions within the town. The Cullens, originally from Wales and known for their ore processing techniques, attempted to diversify their operations. Meanwhile, the Calhouns, who provided essential services, felt the pinch as residents left or were unable to afford their services. The Strombergs tried moving from silver craft to agricultural equipment, but it wasn't the same."

Savage now understood why Anita Cullen's family owned plenty of land, and why Grace Calhoun worked as a teacher at the local school.

"This is not a unique story," Haverly concluded, placing his hands in his lap. "It's indicative of Colorado's mining history, a microcosm, if you like, of the hopes, challenges, and enduring spirit of our founders."

Savage felt like he ought to applaud.

Avril shook herself out of her trance. "That was *very* interesting, Mr. Haverly. Thank you for sharing it with us."

"I'm glad you enjoyed it." He broke into a wide grin. "We have many books on the subject. If you like, I can point them out to you."

She shook her head, a small frown gracing her face. "I'd love to, but we're actually investigating a crime."

"Oh, you are?" Haverly glanced from Avril to Savage.

He cleared his throat. "There's a possibility it might have something to do with the history of the town, which is why we wanted to speak with you."

"I see." Haverly frowned. "I hope I was helpful."

"You were. Very helpful." Savage shook the man's hand. "Thanks again."

"Harcourt is the name of the second victim," Avril said, once they were back in the Suburban. "Stephanie Harcourt."

"Correct." Savage tried to recall the names the historian had mentioned. "The Cullens, the Harcourts, the Maddens and the Calhouns were all descendants of the founding families."

"Don't forget the Strombergs," Avril added. For someone who didn't think it was relevant, she had paid close attention.

"You like history?" he asked.

She seemed surprised by his question. "Yes. If I hadn't joined the FBI, I would have been a historian or something similar."

That explained her enraptured look back at the library.

"Maybe you still can, one day," he said. "You know, when all this is over."

A wistful look passed over her face.

"Maybe."

"I JUST DON'T KNOW if we're on the right track," Savage said to Becca later that evening. She breastfed Connor while he stirred a stew on the stove. The rich, meaty aroma made his stomach growl.

"Two victims aren't enough to classify him as a serial offender," she pointed out.

"I know, but considering how long he's been active..."

She grimaced. "That does put a different spin on it. And there's no other connection between the victims other than their physical appearance and status?"

"Nothing we can find, and even the status part is thin. It could be a coincidence that both Anita Cullen and Stephanie Harcourt are from well-to-do families. As you said, two victims aren't enough for a pattern."

She rubbed Connor gently on the back. "What does Avril think?"

"She thinks we're wrong to be looking into their backgrounds. According to her research, his previous victims have been random targets. They look similar, but their backgrounds are vastly different."

"Maybe she's right."

"You think I should give up on this theory?"

"I didn't say that."

"Huh?" He turned to her, confused.

"There is always a pattern," she said, shifting Connor so she was more comfortable. "With repeat offenders like this, particularly someone who's been active for over ten years, nothing is random. He might not even know it himself, but he will be following a pattern. You already know he has a type. That's a pattern."

Savage nodded. "It's not enough." Sinclair's words sprung to mind. "I can't protect every blonde woman in Hawk's Landing."

"*How* he's targeting them will also fall into a pattern. If he's not from the area, he'll be hunting for his victims, which means he'll have a routine. Where does he hunt? Does he cruise the streets, the strip malls, the ski resorts? He's limited by the snow as to where he can go."

"What if he's done prior research? He could know who his victims are before he even gets to town."

"Again, that will fall into a pattern. Where is he looking for them? Online chat rooms, social media, town records?"

Savage frowned. "Rex Haverly, the historian we spoke to, works in the archives."

"Is he a local?"

"I think so. Barb knows him."

"Unless he's been traveling around the world for the last decade, he's unlikely to be your killer, but he might know how someone can access the archives online or through a catalog."

Savage stroked his jaw. It was rough and scratchy. "What you're saying is our killer might not have targeted Anita and Stephanie because they're from notable families, he might just have found them that way."

"Your killer could be a bit of a history buff."

He stifled a yawn. "We'll just have to look harder for a pattern."

Becca looked up and smiled. "If anyone can do it, you can."

BEING on an active case meant you didn't get the weekend off. Savage woke early, leaving Becca asleep with only a kiss on the cheek as a goodbye. He checked on Connor, who was curled up on his side, sucking his thumb. He watched him for a moment, feeling the love swelling in his heart, then dragging himself away, headed to the station. His talk with Becca the previous night had given him a weird sort of perspective. She was the voice of reason, the one who helped him understand the criminal minds he hunted.

Savage faced his team, all of whom were in except Barb. Even Avril was there, but that was to be expected. He doubted she slept much. "I think the Frost Killer may select his victims in advance."

They all stared at him, Avril more intently than the others. "What makes you say that?"

"We know he's not from here because he moves around every year, seeking fresh hunting grounds. As we know, winter is not the best time to go hunting. There are fewer people outdoors, roads can be closed, getting around is difficult – so it stands to reason he's preselected his targets before he gets to town."

"You know, you could be right," Littleton said. They all turned to him. "I've been looking into the pendants, and nobody makes anything like that around here. I couldn't even find anything similar online. I think the killer makes them himself and brings them with him."

Avril nodded. "It fits with what we already know."

Savage continued. "Our killer's a planner. It stands to reason that everything he does is thought out well in advance."

Avril perched her glasses on her head. "How does he choose who to kill?"

Savage pursed his lips. "That's what we have to find out."

Sinclair gave a jerky nod. "If he's preselected his victims, all he has to do is watch them for a few days, then choose the best time to ambush them."

"Exactly. Now I know there isn't much of a link between Anita and Stephanie, but their family history could be how he's choosing them."

Avril nibbled at her thumbnail. He knew she thought the selection was random, but perhaps she needed to start looking further afield.

"Thorpe, I want you to get ahold of the historian, Rex Haverly. The library is closed today, but you might be able to catch him on his cellphone. Find out if there's any way to access the archives online. And first thing tomorrow, head to the library and ask if anyone has taken out a book on the history of the town. Haverly said they had several."

Thorpe nodded and reached for the phone.

The rest of them divided up the families between them and got to work. A couple of hours later, they had a list of seven existing descendants of the founding families who were still living in the area.

"Matthew Madden lives on a smallholding outside of town," said Littleton. "According to Barb, he's something of a loner. I checked his birth certificate, and he is a descendant of the original Maddens, but is the only surviving relative. He had a twin brother who died when they were kids. Drowned out by Horseshoe Lake. I found a news article in the Durango Herald."

Savage frowned. "Any offspring?"

"One daughter, Naomi. She's twenty-six. I'm still trying to find an address for her."

"Littleton, you head out there and talk to her father. Find out where Naomi is now." The young deputy nodded, pleased to be doing something.

"Then there's Grace Calhoun, who you visited yesterday," Sinclair said.

Avril looked up sharply. "You went to see her? Why didn't you tell me?"

"I just told her to be careful," he explained. "She fits the profile."

"Did you tell her about—"

"Hell no," Savage interjected. "I made out like it was some local thug assaulting blondes."

She frowned but didn't ask any more questions.

"What about you? Find anything new?" Savage asked the FBI agent.

She consulted her notes. "I've been looking into the Strombergs. There are two descendants who fit our criteria. Ava and Hugo. Ava lives here, in Hawk's Landing, but there is no address for Hugo. They'd both be in their thirties now."

"What about their parents?" Savage asked.

"Deceased. It looks like they got divorced pretty early on, too."

Savage raised an eyebrow. "Let's go talk to Ava."

Avril tapped her notebook. "She works at a place called Gold Rush Beauty."

Sinclair straightened up. "I know it! That's where I get my eyebrows done." She flushed, then frowned. "Actually, I think I know the girl you mean, but they call her Evie at the salon. She's also blonde."

EIGHTEEN

GOLD RUSH BEAUTY was situated on the main street, where most of the businesses were located. Today, however, the road was quiet with most of the stores either shut or not doing much business. Only Church Street, which ran off it, was filled with vehicles.

The repurposed building, adorned with aged timber panels, substantial front-facing windows, and a shingle-clad roof, bore the distinct marks of a bygone era. Savage had walked past it many times, but never appreciated the historical significance before.

A hand-painted sign hanging above the door displayed the salon's name. It was tinged with gold leaf, a nod to the town's prestigious past.

"Isn't it cute?" Sinclair grinned as she pushed open the door.

Inside smelled of acetate and hairspray. Savage fought back a sneeze. A male hair stylist rolling an elderly woman's hair onto fat curlers glanced up. "Be with you in a minute, Deputy."

"No rush, Hamish." Sinclair waved for him to finish.

"How old is this place?" Savage studied the framed black and white photographs on the wall. Some appeared to be quite old, dating back to the late eighteen hundreds. The town looked completely different then. Dusty roads, clapboard buildings, men and women in old-fashioned dress. He stared at the same gold-leafed sign outside the salon. It seemed unchanged. It was as if the store had been plucked out of the photograph and dumped in modern-day Hawk's Landing.

"Fairly old," she said. "Obviously it's had different owners over the years, but it's been here for as long as I can remember." Sinclair craned her neck. "I don't see Evie."

Savage glanced up as a girl holding a dish of blue paste appeared from a back room. "Maybe it's her day off."

Hamish put in the last curler, wheeled the lady under what Savage assumed was a standing hair dryer with a large, metal dome that looked like some kind of alien experiment, and rushed over. "I'm afraid we've got nothing today, sweetie. We're short-staffed."

"Oh? Evie not here?"

"No, she didn't turn up for her shift." He ran a harassed hand through his hair. "She knows she's got to work Sundays. It's our busiest day. I've had to call Bianca in. Poor thing's only just got back from her honeymoon."

"Is it like Evie to miss a shift?" Savage asked, frowning.

"No, sir. She's usually right on time."

"Did you try calling her?"

"Yes, her phone's off or something." He shrugged. "I don't have time to chase her. As you can see, we're frantic. Mrs. Rigby's waiting for a facial, and I've got another customer who needs acrylic infills." He rolled his eyes. "It's crazy."

It did sound chaotic.

"Do you have Evie's address?" Sinclair asked.

He rubbed his forehead. "I think so. Give me a second." He shuffled around the counter and opened a large notebook. "I know we should be on a system," he said, "but I kinda like it this way." A system would certainly be more efficient, Savage thought, as Hamish turned the pages, looking for Evie's details.

"Ah, here you go." The salon manager wrote the address down on a scrap of paper and handed it to Sinclair. "I know the weather's diabolical, but unless she's sick or snowed in, it's no excuse to skip work. If you see her, tell her to come in as soon as possible." He waved his hands in the air. "We're pretty desperate."

"Will do. Thanks Hamish."

He nodded and went back to his customers.

"I'm getting a bad feeling about this," Savage murmured, as they walked back to the Suburban.

Sinclair turned her collar up against the cold. "Yeah, me too."

Savage drove as fast as he dared across town to Evie Stromberg's house.

"This is it." Sinclair pointed to a small, wood house set back from the road. The paint peeled in places, and the gate hung off its hinges, but it seemed decent enough.

As they walked up the path to the front door, it started snowing again. Sinclair glanced up. "I think we're going to have another snowstorm tonight."

"That's what the weather report says."

Savage rapped on the door. They waited, but there was no answer.

Sinclair leaned forward. "Is that music?"

Savage listened. "Yeah, I think so. There's definitely someone home." He rapped harder.

Eventually, they heard floorboards creaking and the door opened. A young woman stood there, barefoot despite the cold, her dark hair streaked with blue, and a ring through her nose. "Yeah?"

Savage held up his badge. "I'm Sheriff Savage. This is Deputy Sinclair. What's your name?"

"Emily."

"Emily, is Evie home?"

Suspicious eyes glared at them. "What do you want with Evie?"

"That's not what I asked." A snowflake fell down the back of his collar and icy water trickled along his back. The music was louder now that the door was open. It appeared to be some sort of heavy metal.

The girl looked sulky. "She's not here."

"Do you know where she is?"

"Her boyfriend's probably. She stays there most nights."

Savage glanced at Sinclair.

"Where does her boyfriend live?" Sinclair asked.

"Durango. I don't know where exactly."

"Does he have a name?" Sinclair raised an eyebrow.

"Yeah, Richie. Richie Vines."

"Richie Vines? That's his real name?" Sinclair looked doubtful.

She shrugged. "That's what he goes by."

"Any idea where we can find Richie Vines?" Savage asked.

"He works at the Bar-T on 8th Street. That's where she met him."

"Thank you." Sinclair turned away. The girl was about to close the door when Savage put his hand against it.

"Hey, when did you last see Evie?"

She thought for a moment. "Not for two days, but I know she came back after work yesterday, because she made something to eat and messed up the kitchen."

"You weren't here?"

"Nah, I work at the Comfort Inn out on the interstate. I don't get back till late."

"Okay, thanks for your help."

Back in the SUV, Sinclair dusted the snow from her hair. "Do you think he'll be there now? It's three twenty. Might be too early for his shift."

"Call them," Savage suggested, as he pulled out into the trickle of traffic. Not many vehicles were on the road now that it had started snowing. Already, it was coming down heavier than before. He put the wipers on.

Sinclair put the phone on speaker. "Good afternoon. Could you tell me if Richie Vines is working today?"

"Yeah, sure. Richie's shift starts at five."

"Okay, great. Thank you." She hesitated. "Do you have an address for him?"

A pause.

"Who is this?"

"It's Deputy Sinclair from Hawk's Landing Sheriff's Department."

"I'm afraid I'm going to have to see some ID before I give out employee details."

She glanced at Savage.

"We may as well drive out there and wait," He glanced up at the sky. It looked like a sheet of gray metal, thick and unyielding. "This is only going to get worse."

She nodded. "Okay, no problem. We'll be there soon."

THE WINDSHIELD WIPERS screeched as Savage tried to shake off the relentless snowflakes. Sighing with relief, he pulled over in front of a neon sign that said, Bar-T.

"We might not find it on the way out," Sinclair warned, blinking at the other cars in the street, which were completely buried by large mounds of snow.

In response, Savage pressed the button on his fob and the Suburban, with a cheeky flash of its headlights, locked with a beep.

The Bar-T was an authentic western-style bar, complete with double doors on the inside, and a jukebox playing country and western music in the corner. It was quiet, since it had just opened, and apart from a lonely bartender wiping down the tables, it was empty.

The man glanced up as they entered. "Hey, what can I get you folks?"

"Sheriff Savage and Deputy Sinclair," Savage said. "We called earlier wanting to speak to Richie Vines?"

"Oh yeah. Richie's not in yet."

Savage gestured to an empty table. "Do you mind if we wait? Weather's terrible."

"Sure, have a seat. Can I get you a drink?"

"Do you do coffee?"

He grinned. "Only 'cause you're law enforcement."

"Great."

"Richie worked here long?" Sinclair asked when the bartender came back with their coffees.

"A couple of years." He set them on the table and straightened up. "He's a good guy. We have a high turnover of staff, like most bars, but he's stuck around longer than most."

"You the manager?" Savage asked.

"Sure am. Fred Greaney." He gave a quick nod. "Give me a shout if you need anything else."

"Thanks, Fred."

Sinclair took off her gloves and wrapped her hands around the coffee mug. "What if Richie Vine doesn't know where Evie is?"

"If nobody's seen her, then we'll have to assume she's missing," Savage said grimly. "It might be nothing. She might be at his place right now and just hadn't gone back on account of the snow."

Sinclair gave a hesitant nod. "Maybe."

A few minutes before five o'clock, a stocky guy in ripped jeans and a black shirt under a weathered leather jacket walked in. His swagger spoke of confidence, and he had a spring in his step, along with a backpack slung over his shoulder.

"Richie Vines?" Savage said, as he passed their table.

The guy turned, surprised. "Yeah, who wants to know?"

Savage would have thought that was obvious. "Sheriff Savage and Deputy Sinclair from Hawk's Landing Sheriff's Department. Mind if we have a word?"

"I'm about to go on shift."

"It's okay, Rich," the manager called from behind the bar, raising a hand.

Savage gestured to the empty chair. "Take a seat."

Richie hesitated, then sat down. "What's this about?"

"We're looking for your girlfriend, Evie Stromberg. Do you know where she is?"

He shot them a quizzical look. "She's working at the salon in Hawk's Landing."

Sinclair narrowed her gaze. "Did she stay at your place last night?"

"Yeah, she usually stays over. What's this about?"

"Did she leave this morning to go to work?"

"Yeah."

"What car?"

"Huh?"

"What car does she drive?"

He gave them a weird look. "She drives a shitty Corolla. It's falling apart, but she can't afford a new car." He stared at them, his dark eyes filled with worry. "Why? Has she been in some sort of accident?"

"She didn't make it into work, Richie," Sinclair said. "We've just been there. She missed her shift."

"What?" He scraped a hand through his hair. "I don't understand. She's gotta be there."

"Do you know where else she might have gone?" Savage asked, his voice low. "Would she have gone home to change first, do you think?"

"Yeah. Yeah, she would have done that." He was frazzled, they could tell. "Have you tried her house?"

"Her roommate hasn't seen her in two days."

"Shit." He scraped his chair back but didn't get up. "Do you think something's happened to her? Like an accident or something?"

"It's possible," Savage said. "We'll put out a BOLO on her vehicle. That way if she's stuck on one of the roads, we'll find her."

Richie gnawed at his lip.

"You know her license plate?"

He frowned. "Um... not really, no. Colorado plates."

"Okay, don't worry. We'll look it up."

"You'll tell me when you find her?"

Savage studied the wrinkled forehead, the worried eyes. He seemed genuinely concerned.

"If you give us your number, we'll give you a call when we find her." Sinclair took out her phone.

He rattled off his number, which Sinclair recorded with a blur of her fingers over the screen of her phone.

"Thanks for your time, Richie." Savage stood up. "One last thing.

Do you think she'd go back to your place, if she couldn't get home for some reason?"

"She might, but she wasn't there when I left."

"Does she have a key to your apartment?"

"No, but she knows where I hide the spare." When they didn't move, his eyes widened. "Oh, shit. You wanna go check?"

Savage nodded.

"Sure, go for it. I can't leave the bar, though. I'm on duty till midnight."

"That's okay. We'll swing by your place, if that's okay. The address?"

He gave it to them, and Sinclair wrote it down.

"Where do you hide the spare key?" Savage asked.

He hesitated. "On top of the doorframe. You'll have to buzz someone else to get access to the building."

"Right, thanks for your help."

"Do you really think she's there?" Sinclair asked, once they'd left the bar.

"I don't know, but we should check it out before we head back to Hawk's Landing. Richie Vines may not have been telling the truth. She may not want to be found."

Sinclair came to a stop next to the SUV. "You don't take anyone at face value, do you?"

He gave a rueful grin. "In this business, it's best not to."

Savage swept most of the snow off the hood and windshield, then climbed in. The doors were already frosting closed.

"You okay to drive in this?" Sinclair peered through the front window. Visibility was less than a hundred yards.

"Let's see how far we get. The Suburban can handle most things, if we drive slowly."

"All right, you're the boss. Let's go see if Evie Madden is hiding out at her boyfriend's pad, and all this is just a big fat false alarm."

Savage nodded. They could only hope.

NINETEEN

RICHIE VINES' apartment was in a redeveloped block that appeared to have once been a warehouse. Made of brick and weathered steel, it had a certain old-style charm to it that Savage found appealing. The front entrance was a large, wooden door with an awning above it, in keeping with the nineteenth-century style.

They waited until one of the residents came out, then slipped in before the door shut.

"He's on the ground floor," Sinclair said, as they walked down an exposed brick corridor with steel beams above their head and fluorescent lighting.

She stopped outside apartment 4. "This is it."

Savage ran his fingers along the top of the door frame. "Got it," he said, taking the key down.

"Should we buzz first?" Sinclair asked.

"Nope, we have permission to enter." He inserted the key into the lock and opened the door. Standing still, they listened for sounds from inside, but the apartment was silent. All they could hear was the wind whistling through the crevices, and a slight hum from a generator somewhere in the building.

Sinclair ventured farther in. "There's nobody here."

"Let's do a quick check to be sure."

It wasn't a big apartment.

"The bed hasn't been made," Sinclair called from the bedroom. Savage followed her in. The sheets were rumpled, and the pillows had two dents in them.

"At least we know she slept here," Savage nodded to a beaded necklace on the bedside table. Evie must have forgotten to take it with her that morning.

Sinclair went to check the bathroom, while he opened the wardrobe.

"Two toothbrushes, and there are some feminine products in the cabinet," she said, coming back.

"Her roommate did say she stayed here regularly. There are also a couple of skirts and blouses in the closet."

They went back to the living room.

"Now what?" asked Sinclair.

Savage grimaced. "I think we have a missing person on our hands."

"EVIE STROMBERG IS OFFICIALLY MISSING," announced Savage, when they got back to the station. Despite the bad weather and the fact that it was after six o'clock in the evening, everyone was still at work. "She left her boyfriend's to go to work and never arrived. She's not at her place, and there's no sign of her vehicle."

"It's *him,*" whispered Avril, turning ashen.

"Let's not jump to conclusions," Savage said, although he had to admit, it wasn't looking good.

"She could still be alive." Thorpe frowned as he looked at Savage. "If he does have her, she could be out there somewhere, unconscious, but alive."

Savage forced himself to focus on what they could control. "Check her cellphone. Get her last known location. Also, put out an urgent BOLO on her vehicle."

Thorpe and Littleton spun back to their computers and got to work.

"We might have to go public with this one." Sinclair eyed Savage. "If she's out there—"

"I know." He raked a hand through his hair. "After Stephanie's death, the press is likely to start connecting the dots."

"It can't be helped," Sinclair insisted. "There's a young woman's life at stake."

"You're right. Let's put out a Critical Missing Adult Alert on Evie Stromberg. Have we got a photograph of her?"

Sinclair reached for the phone. "I'll ask her boyfriend."

"You never know, someone might have seen her," Thorpe said.

Savage gave a gruff nod. "There's always a chance."

Things happened quickly after that. Richie Vines sent through a smiling photograph of Evie, which Savage found hard to look at. Her blue eyes sparkled with life. He couldn't imagine them empty and stark, glazed by death. He held too many of those images in his head already, and he knew he'd never get rid of them.

"Let's stay positive," Barb said, coming in with yet more coffee. "It might be a false alarm."

A few somber nods. Nobody really believed that.

Not now.

Outside, the wind howled like an injured prairie dog, and the windows rattled. The snow was so heavy, they couldn't see across the street.

A hushed silence fell over the office, apart from the few urgent phone calls and follow-ups on the missing person alert. Savage knew they were all thinking the same thing: if Evie Stromberg was outside in this weather, she wouldn't last long.

Retiring to his office, he called Sheriff Shelby from the Durango Sheriff's Department. Shelby had joined forces with his team on more than one occasion. He was a good man, trustworthy and reliable. He also had a soft spot for Barb, which helped.

"I hear you've got a missing person," Shelby said, as soon as he answered. “My boys are keeping a lookout.” He was obviously still working too. Durango was larger than Hawk's Landing, and had a bigger force, which meant they could cover more ground. Savage filled him in on the situation, including the FBI’s involvement.

“You’re shitting me,” Shelby exclaimed when Savage confided that this was potentially the third victim of the same killer.

“Wish I was,” he grumbled.

“Damn. Okay, I’ll inform my men this is urgent. So far, we’ve come up with nothing. Nobody has seen her vehicle or received any calls about a body.”

Savage sucked in a breath. Hearing the words made it all the more real. He didn’t want to think about that. Not yet. Not while there was still a chance. “Thanks, Shelby.”

“You got it. Be in touch.”

Next, Savage called Darryl Clearwater, head of the Tribal Police. Even though they didn't want anything to do with his or the Durango Sheriff’s Department, Savage believed the various law enforcement agencies operating in the county should have some degree of cooperation. They all wanted the same thing, after all, although sometimes it didn’t seem that way.

He answered cautiously, “This is Clearwater.”

Already suspicious.

“Captain, this is Dalton Savage. Got a minute?”

“I saw your missing person alert. No, we haven't seen her. I’d have called if we had.”

The reality was the killer could have taken her onto the reservation. The area was large and relatively isolated in parts, even if the community was a small one. Savage’s team had no jurisdiction there, which made it an attractive killing spot for a savvy murderer.

“I know that. Reason for my call is to let you know this is the third woman to have disappeared in the last week or so. The first two showed up dead.”

There was a heavy pause.

Savage continued, taking advantage of the stunned silence. “We found their bodies laid out in the snow. He left them to freeze to death."

"He?"

"The killer. He drugs his victims, then leaves them outside to die."

A low whistle. "You're sure it's the same guy?"

"Positive. MO's identical. Here's the thing. Evie Stromberg could still be alive. She went missing this morning."

Another briefer pause.

"I'll send out a patrol, but just to be clear, we're looking for a white woman, lying out in the snow?"

"That's right. She's blonde, five foot five, or thereabouts, and will look like she's asleep. You'll know it when you see it."

He purposely didn't mention the pendant. That was something he wanted to keep back, in case it got to the media. Nobody must link this killer to the Frost Killer who'd been terrorizing women for the last decade. He suppressed a shiver. Not only would there be widespread panic, but they'd risk losing the murdering scumbag for another year.

"Okay, Sheriff. We'll let you know if we find anything."

"I'd appreciate that." He hung up.

Savage drummed his fingers on his desk. He should be out there searching for her or doing something other than sitting in his office. To distract himself, he called Becca. She was holed up at home with Connor, staying out of the storm.

"Don't worry, we're fine." He could hear the weariness in her voice. She'd been alone with Connor all day and needed a break.

"I'll make it up to you," he promised her. "There's a young woman missing. She could still be alive."

"I heard the broadcast on the radio. Do you really think she's out in this weather?"

"I hope not, but she didn't make it into work today."

"Does she fit the profile?"

He tensed. "Yeah, she does."

Becca hesitated. "Be careful, Dalton. Don't take any unnecessary risks."

"I won't."

"I love you." Her voice was strained.

"I love you too."

The wind rattled the windows, and glancing outside, all he could see was swirling snowflakes. If Evie Stromberg was still alive, she wouldn't last much longer.

He pulled open his office door. "Anything?"

"It's only been twenty minutes since we put out the alert," Sinclair said.

"I'm going to look for her," Savage growled. He couldn't stay here anymore. Not when he could be out there doing something.

"You don't know where to look," Barb complained. "She could be anywhere in the county."

"I have to do something."

"Dalton, look at the weather," Barb pleaded. "There are patrols out looking for her. If they find anything, you need to be ready to go, not stuck in a snow drift somewhere."

She had a point.

"Besides, Durango Road is going to be impassable soon," Sinclair warned. "I've just heard a report on the radio. They're calling out dredgers."

"I live on Durango Road," he muttered.

She shot him a sympathetic grimace.

"Is Becca all right?" Barbara asked.

"Yeah, I've just talked to her. She's fine. They're both fine."

The central phoneline rang. Barb hurried to answer it. "Yes?" They all heard her intake of breath. "I'll put you right through."

Savage darted back into his office. "This is Savage."

It was Clearwater.

"Hey, Sheriff. We found your girl's vehicle."

"That was quick."

"Yeah, one of my officers had found it earlier, but didn't know you were looking." Savage hoped they hadn't destroyed any evidence that might be on it.

"Where is it?"

"On Cedar Road, on the rez."

"Any sign of her?"

"Nah, sorry. We're still looking."

"Drop me a pin. I'm on my way." He hung up.

"Was it her?" Sinclair asked. The others looked up waiting for his answer.

"The tribal police found her car," he told them. "I'm heading out to the rez now."

Sinclair got to her feet. "I'll come with you."

Thorpe jumped up. "Me too."

Littleton made to get up, but Savage held up his hand. "Littleton, you hold the fort." The young deputy sat down again, looking downcast. "Let us know the minute anything comes in."

He nodded, straightening up.

Five minutes later, they were driving through the worst snowstorm of the season, on their way to the rez.

TWENTY

THERE WERE no streetlamps or dwellings in this part of the rez, but the pulsing blue halo from the tribal police vehicles showed them the way. Savage pulled over behind Clearwater's light blue Bronco with the orange sun decal on the driver's side door, the insignia of the Southern Ute Police.

They climbed out of the Suburban and looked around. Evie's battered Corolla sat empty on the side of the road, snow piling up around it.

"It's been here for some time," Clearwater said, nodding to the three-inch-deep layer of snow on the hood.

"Probably since this morning," Savage said, grimly. "She disappeared on her way to work."

Clearwater nodded. "Sounds about right. The tire tracks have snowed over. Can't make out any footprints either, but she must have gotten out of the car."

Savage studied the snow around the driver's door. It was undisturbed. Same on the passenger side.

"Can't tell whether she was alone, or someone was with her," Sinclair said, bending down for a closer look.

Savage walked back and studied the ground along the edges of the road. "No tread marks from another vehicle."

"Would she have taken this route from her boyfriend's place to work?" Thorpe asked, scratching his head.

"She might," Savage said. "If she thought Durango Road was closed."

"It wasn't," Sinclair said, opening the car door.

"Anything?" Savage called.

"No. It looks like she took her purse with her when she got out."

Or the killer has it.

Savage met Sinclair's eye. He could tell she was thinking the same thing.

"Did you try to start it?" Savage asked Clearwater.

The Tribal Police Captain shook his head. "Waiting for you to get here."

Savage slipped behind the wheel, noticing the seat position was set for someone with much shorter legs than his. He was pretty sure Evie Stromberg was the last person to drive this car.

"Key's still in the ignition," he called, feeling the hairs on his neck stand up.

"Crap," hissed Sinclair.

"That's not good," Clearwater agreed.

Savage turned it, starting the engine. It chugged a few times, then died out. Savage tried again, pumping the gas. The car wheezed, gave a little cough, then gave up and fell silent.

"Dead," he muttered.

"Could be because it's been out here all day," Thorpe said.

"We need a mechanic to check it out. Let's call a tow truck and have it taken to the auto shop. Doug can take a look." Doug was the town's only mechanic, but he was pretty darn good, so that made up for the lack of competition. He owned Canyon Auto Repair on Durango Road and had serviced almost everyone in Hawk's Landing at some time or another.

"Let's split up and search on foot," Savage suggested.

“Weather’s getting worse,” Clearwater warned. “Storm’s supposed to last most of the night.”

Savage glanced around them at the almost total whiteout. The windchill sent the temperature plummeting into the low teens.

Sinclair, who was blowing on her gloved hands, said, “If she’s out there, we have to try.”

“Sheriff, I don’t mean to rain on your parade, but you know as well as I do that given the conditions, it’s unlikely your girl’s still alive. It’s too damn cold for anyone to survive out here longer than a couple of hours. If she went missing this morning, she’s long gone.”

Savage wanted to argue, to insist they try, but he couldn’t put his fellow officers’ lives at risk. It was late, and they had families to go home to. Visibility was down to maybe ten feet and getting worse by the second.

“Fine,” he agreed, reluctantly. “Let’s pick up the search tomorrow, when the storm’s abated.”

Clearwater nodded. “Wise decision.”

He gathered his men and told them they’d resume at first light.

“What do you want to do?” Thorpe asked Savage, as the tribal police got back into their vehicles and drove away.

Savage stood beside Evie’s car, staring out into the blizzard. The immediate vicinity was lit by the thick beam of his headlights. All he could see were white spears of ice piercing the gloom.

What if she was out there?

“I’m going to take a quick walk,” he said, coming to a decision. “If it were me out there, I’d want to know someone was coming.” While he didn’t expect the others to do the same, he knew he couldn't go back to the station knowing she might still be alive.

“Count me in,” Sinclair said, checking her flashlight.

Thorpe nodded. “And me. Let’s meet back here in an hour. Any longer and we’re at risk from exposure.”

Savage gave a grateful nod, and they set off, each heading in a different direction like the spokes of a wheel, beams from their flashlights stretching out into the night in front of them.

LITTLETON ANSWERED several calls that came through in response to the alert on Evie Stromberg. A man had thought he'd seen the missing woman in fishnet stockings on a street corner in Durango. He'd stopped to ask for directions.

Yeah, right.

The description had been a little off. This woman had long blonde hair while Evie's was just below the shoulder and cut in a layered, fluffy style. The man also reported she had a rose tattoo on her left shoulder, something the caller would not have seen had he been asking for directions. Not in this weather.

Evie didn't have a tattoo.

The next caller said Evie did their hair and she'd seen her three days ago in the salon in Hawk's Landing. The hair stylist had been her usual bubbly self. No, she hadn't said anything strange or out of the ordinary. She didn't appear scared, either, nor did she mention a stalker or that someone was watching her.

Deflated, Littleton kept fielding calls. Then, when Thorpe radioed back and confirmed it was Evie's vehicle they'd found, he relayed that information to Shelby.

"Hope you find her," the Durango Sheriff said. "If not, we can pitch in tomorrow. We're calling it a night."

At eight-thirty, the rest of the team got back to the station, plastered with snowflakes and frozen down to the bone. Barb had left for the day, so Littleton made them all a hot drink and asked them if they'd found anything, even though he could tell by their faces they hadn't.

Savage shook his wet head. "Snow has covered everything. Can't see which direction she went in, or whether she was alone or not."

"Someone could have picked her up," Sinclair grumbled, peeling off her sodden gloves and throwing them on her desk. "But there are no tracks."

"Car's dead too," added Thorpe.

"We gave it our best shot," Savage muttered, although you wouldn't think so given his expression. "Get some rest. We'll pick up the search tomorrow."

If no one's found her by then.

The Sheriff didn't have to say it. Littleton knew it was what everybody was thinking. Tomorrow, they wouldn't be looking for a missing person. They'd be looking for a body.

Littleton was keen to knock off himself. A couple of the guys were meeting at Miller's Walk tonight, a dive bar on the outskirts of town, and he said he'd join them for one on his way home.

He checked his watch. There was still time.

"I'll man the phonelines," Sinclair said, collapsing into her chair. She looked exhausted. Littleton was hit with a twinge of guilt. He wasn't the one who'd been traipsing all over the reservation, and he was going home first.

Still, he'd been on the phone all evening.

"Do you want me to stay?" he asked, giving in.

"Thanks Kev, but that's okay. It's my turn for night duty anyway."

He nodded, relieved. Someone had to be at the station at all times, in case of 911 calls.

"I'll come in early," Thorpe said, picking up his backpack. "Then you can go home and get a couple of hours shut eye."

Sinclair shot him a grateful grin.

"See you tomorrow." Littleton pulled on his jacket. He didn't invite them to come out with him since they didn't know his buddies and would probably refuse. The Sheriff rarely joined them for drinks and definitely not during an investigation. Thorpe might have come, but he looked damp and exhausted, and had only just regained his normal color after the search for Evie Stromberg.

THE BAR WAS HEAVING, despite the abysmal weather. Miller's Walk seemed to be where everybody under the age of thirty had accumulated. Not that there was much choice in the small town. Littleton spotted his friends at the far end. They'd finished a game of darts and were having a drink before heading home.

Grinning, he joined them.

"Glad you could make it," Kent said, slapping him on the back.

"You look like you need a drink," Andy remarked, raising an eyebrow.

"You can say that again. It's been one hell of a week."

The music, the beer, the companionship all helped him relax, and an hour later, Littleton was feeling pretty good. A dark-haired beauty eyed him from across the bar, and he found himself smiling back. Soon, she and her friend sidled over.

"Hey, how are you doing? Can we buy you ladies a drink?" Andy asked, always the confident one.

The ladies agreed, and before long, they'd joined their party. To his surprise, Littleton found himself being chatted up by the dark-haired one.

Andy nudged him in the ribs. "She's a babe. You lucky bastard."

He grinned. It wasn't often he got lucky with women, and almost never got chatted up. Being long and lanky with a thin, earnest face, he was usually the one who got left behind when his buddies paired up. He couldn't count the number of times he ended up going home alone. It made for a nice change.

Izzie – that was her name – put her hand on his arm. "What do you do, Kev?" He liked the way she'd shortened his name.

"I'm a Deputy at the Sheriff's Department." He wondered if being in law enforcement would put her off. Thankfully, it seemed to have the opposite effect.

"Wow, that's so cool. Do you catch bad guys?"

He laughed. "I try."

"Are you after anyone now?" she inquired, her bright eyes fixed on his face.

He hesitated. "We are looking for someone," he admitted, after a beat, "Although I can't really talk about it."

Her eyes gleamed. "How exciting."

"Let's do some shots," her friend said with a laugh. She was one of those bubbly types who got everyone going.

"Sure." Andy winked at him encouragingly.

"Why not?" He glanced at his watch. Eleven o'clock. He had to be at work by nine, which left plenty of time to sleep it off. He'd have one more, then leave.

Izzie's hand was warm on his arm, her smiling eyes just for him. He found himself staring at her mouth as she licked her hand, salted it, then threw back the tequila.

"Your turn." She laughed as he grimaced at the sourness of the lime.

Several shots and suggestive looks later, Izzie leaned over and whispered, "Let's get out of here."

His heart thumped erratically, even as his in-built cautiousness told him this was a bad idea. Tomorrow was Monday, and he had to work. They were in the middle of an important case.

Then again, how often did this happen?

Never.

Not to him.

"I'm supposed to be staying at Anna's tonight." She cast a sidelong glance at her friend who had her arm around Andy's waist. "But I don't think she's gonna want me there. How about we go back to yours?"

He wavered. "That might not be such a good idea. I've got to get up early for work."

"That's okay. Me too."

"Come on, buddy. Live a little," Andy called, bending down to kiss Anna on the neck. Littleton envied his friend's easy charm. Yeah. Why shouldn't he have a little fun? He deserved it.

"You live close by?" she asked, wriggling into her coat.

"Pretty close."

"Good. Let's go then."

Taking his hand in hers, she led him to the door.

TWENTY-ONE

SAVAGE WENT in early after a frantic call from Barb. "We're inundated after the snowstorm last night," she told him. "There are people stranded in their cars, others can't get to work, and Mr. Gibbons' sheep are freezing."

"Where's the rest of the team?" he asked, taking off his jacket and shaking it out. Flakes drifted to the floor, joining the snow left there by his boots.

Barb glanced ruefully at the growing puddle. "Thorpe's towing a stranded vehicle to Doug's, and Sinclair, who isn't due in until midday, has gone to help Mrs. Bennet, who slipped and fell when she took the dog for a walk this morning."

"What about Littleton?"

"I presume he's on his way in, since I haven't heard from him. Must be running late."

"Ask him to check in at the Gibbons' farm," he said, not that he had any idea how his newest deputy would handle the freezing sheep problem. It wasn't an issue any of them had encountered before.

At least the reporters had given up. For now.

"And have Thorpe follow up on Evie's Corolla. I asked Doug to take a look at it last night." Before he was besieged by frozen pipes and stranded vehicles.

"Will do."

Avril arrived, disheveled and covered in snow. She'd walked from the inn, at the other end of town. Even so, you'd have thought she'd be used to these conditions being from Scandinavia.

"You okay?" he asked, as she took off her coat and scarf.

"I've been up all night, reading through my files," she told him. "I wanted to see if your theory about how he's finding the women was true for the other victims."

"Oh? Did you find anything interesting?" He perched against Sinclair's desk.

"I think you might be onto something," she admitted in a tight voice.

"Yeah?" He bet that hurt to admit.

"Ja. I looked at each year in isolation, as if they were separate cases. That's something I haven't done before."

He could understand that. You'd look for a link between all the victims, not just the cluster in each year. "Did you find a link?"

"There were some similarities." Her gaze dropped to her satchel. Reaching in, she pulled out a notebook and flicked to a page covered in her slanting scrawl. "Three years ago, in Billings, Montana, all the victims had done some sort of charity work."

"Like fundraising?"

"Exactly. Not for a single charity, but various ones. I didn't see it before because they held different roles. The first victim canvassed for change on the street, the other hosted a church group, the third was a fundraiser for her son's school, and the fourth wrote grants for a whole lot of different companies."

Savage considered this. "So, he could have got their names from a charity register or social media site?"

"Theoretically, if one existed. I haven't been able to find anything like that, though."

That didn't mean it wasn't there.

"He'd need photographs of them," Savage said.

"I know. That's the problem." She pursed her lips. "How else would he know what they looked like?"

Savage nodded slowly. "What about the other years?"

"The year before was the same thing, except they were all self-employed businesswomen. I presume there is some sort of business group or something they're members of. I'm still looking into that."

Savage felt his pulse kick up a gear. "So there could be a pattern to all of them?"

She gave a reluctant nod. "There could be, yes."

He exhaled. "Avril, this is a breakthrough in the case. You've found the pattern."

She gave a wry smile. "Because of you."

"Actually, it was Becca who first mentioned it." He smiled, thinking of how glad she'd be that Avril had finally made a link, tenuous as it was, after all these years.

"I hope it's not too late," she said, biting her lip.

"It's not too late," Savage said firmly. "That's how we're going to catch this bastard."

The doors hissed open, and Thorpe strode in, bringing a mound of snow with him.

"I give up," sighed Barb, as the snow melted on the floor where she'd just cleaned up Savage's puddle.

"What did you find?" Savage asked.

"At the library or the auto shop?" He took his laptop out of his backpack and set it up on his desk.

Savage had forgotten he'd asked him to talk to the librarian. "Both."

Thorpe took a breath to compose himself. "Well, I looked at the library records and only two historical books were taken out in the last month."

"Yeah?"

"One was by a Freda Morrison, who's eighty-five years old and a long-standing member of the library, and the other—" He paused for effect.

Savage raised an eyebrow.

"The other was taken out by Bob Cullen at the General Store."

"Seriously?"

"He can't have had anything to do with his granddaughter's disappearance," Avril insisted.

Savage frowned. "I don't know. Wouldn't have thought so." The timing was uncanny though. "Maybe we'd better go and have another word with him."

She nodded.

"What about Doug?" Savage turned back to Thorpe. "He have a chance to look at Evie's car?"

"Yeah, that was the other thing," Thorpe said. "Doug took a look last night and said it's an old car, and it overheated."

"That's it? Nothing sinister?"

Thorpe shook his head. "Doesn't look like it."

"Then it was an accident?"

"Do you think the killer was following her?" Avril crinkled her forehead. It seemed too convenient that Evie would break down while she was being stalked.

"Nah." A surge of hope flickered inside him. "Maybe it was just an accident."

"Then where is she?" Avril asked.

Savage glanced at both of them. "That's what we have to find out."

TWENTY-TWO

SINCLAIR RUSHED IN, flushed and out of breath. "Damn, it's chaotic out there. I was at the clinic to get Mrs. Bennet's ankle x-rayed when a truck slid off the road in front of me, nearly causing a multi-car pile-up. After I sorted that mess out, Littleton called, but reception was bad so I couldn't hear him properly – although I'm pretty sure he said something about sheep?"

Barbara shook her head. "The town's gone crazy on account of the weather."

Sinclair shrugged off her jacket and sank into the chair at Littleton's desk, heaving a sigh of relief. "Any news on Evie?"

"It looks like her car broke down," Savage said, stretching his neck. The tension of the last few days was getting to him. "We were just about to go and look for her again."

"I've pinged her phone." Thorpe glanced up from his screen. "Her last known location was two miles from where she broke down. Seems she was walking towards Ignacio." Ignacio was a small town on the Southern Ute Reservation.

Savage grabbed his jacket. "Let's go." He didn't want to think what state she'd be in, if by some miracle, she'd managed to survive the night. Perhaps she'd found shelter at the casino, or in someone's residence.

Savage drove, while Thorpe consulted an app on his iPad. They passed the Ridgewater Casino heading into town, the gleaming building shimmering against the otherwise barren landscape.

"You sure she's not there?" Savage asked.

"Nope, but her location pointed south of here, near the Community Center."

"Maybe she went there for help." Although, he couldn't see how she'd walk two miles in the snow. They'd struggled to expand their search radius to more than a mile, and they had flashlights and adequate protection against the elements. She would have been in her work attire.

They were almost there when Barb's voice punctured through the radio static. "Dalton, come in? Hello, Dalton?"

Savage grabbed the radio. "Barb, what's up?"

"Oh, thank God. I've just had a call from Sam Walking Deer at the Ridgewater Casino. It's too terrible. He says his security team have found a body behind the hotel."

Savage's heart dropped.

Shit.

Please let it not be her.

He couldn't get those laughing blue eyes out of his head.

"Why didn't they call the Tribal Police if they found a body on the res?"

"It's a white woman, Dalton, and she's lying in the snow."

It was her.

"We're too late," he snarled, yanking on the steering wheel. Thorpe clung onto the door handle as the car skidded around in a U-turn, drifting on the icy road.

"We're on our way, Barb," Savage yelled at the radio. "Send the ambulance and get Ray and Pearl down there." He put his foot down.

The glow from the casino lit up the dull sky. It was as if the sun had given up this morning and decided to stay blanketed behind the charcoal-gray clouds.

Savage swung the Suburban around the tight corner and into the driveway that led up to the resort. Landscaped gardens were hidden beneath several feet of snow. Only the frozen sculptures stuck out, glaring at them as they sped up to the entrance.

The security guard at the door looked like he might complain, then stood back when he saw the look on Savage's face.

"Where's Walking Deer?" he barked.

"Here," came a voice from inside.

Savage and Thorpe marched in, hit by the sudden heat, people, and chaos of sounds. Thorpe, who'd never been there before, stopped short, but Savage was so focused on the body, he hardly registered.

"Thank you for calling us." He extended a hand. "I'm Sheriff Savage, and this is Deputy Thorpe."

"You got here fast."

"We were on the reservation anyway."

"Oh?" He looked surprised.

"Yeah, another matter." He waved it away. "Where is the body?"

"Out back. If you'll follow me."

They walked through the plush lobby, ignoring the riot of slot machines, the jarring tunes and the cries of delight. Walking Deer, a long, loping man with black hair pulled back into a sleek ponytail, led them through a service door into what looked to be a utility area. They walked down a corridor and through another door that led outside. The staff entrance.

"It's just beyond the property line." He shot them a defiant look. In other words, not his problem.

"How did your men find her?" Savage asked, blinking against the bitter air that made his eyes water.

"We do regular patrols of the perimeter," Walking Deer told them. At least the snow had abated for the time being. "Every two hours."

Panting, they reached the fence. Savage was glad to see two guards protecting the site. They looked up when Walking Deer arrived. He nodded, and they took off, back to the resort complex.

"Thanks for protecting the scene." Savage ducked through the fence. Like with Stephanie, the victim lay on her back, arms folded across her chest, but so much snow had fallen overnight that he couldn't see her face.

He waited for Thorpe to take a couple of photographs with his phone before – heart hammering – he reached down and gently brushed some of it off. He was wearing thick, winter gloves so he wouldn't destroy any evidence.

His breath caught in his throat. "That's not her."

His deputy bent down beside him. "It's not?"

"No, it's not Evie Stromberg."

Savage gazed at the ashen features of the latest victim. Pale skin, almost translucent. Eyes glued closed with ice. Lips an unnatural shade of violet. It wasn't hard to see she was frozen solid.

The weight and heat of her body had caused her to sink into the snow, forming an icy mold around her. Her blonde hair had turned into a sticky, yellow halo.

"Then who is it?" asked Thorpe.

Savage shook his head. "I have no idea." But this wasn't the girl they'd been looking for.

"Her name is Naomi Madden," said Walking Deer.

They both turned to him.

Madden. As in Matthew Madden, the loner who lived out of town?

"You know her?" Thorpe asked.

"She works in the Casino as a croupier. I hired her myself." He shook his head. "Didn't recognize her, you know, with all the snow on her face."

Savage gave a stiff nod. He'd warned Grace Calhoun, but they hadn't been able to find the Madden descendant.

"We should have warned her."

Thorpe nodded, sourly. “It’s him, though. Right?”

Savage glanced down at the silver chain around her neck. He reached down and carefully pulled the pendant out from beneath her folded arms.

The frigid air seemed to suck his breath away. “Yeah. It’s him.”

TWENTY-THREE

"THE VICTIM'S name is Naomi Madden." Savage told Avril and Sinclair once he'd returned to the office. "She was a trainee croupier at the Ridgewater Casino. The HR department confirmed she'd only been there a couple of months."

"Is that the same Madden that Rex Haverly mentioned?" Avril adjusted her glasses and consulted her notes. "The one with the twin brother who drowned?"

"The same," Savage confirmed. "I'm not looking forward to telling him his daughter's dead."

There was a short silence.

"Naomi lived at the casino during the week," Thorpe said. "On the weekend, she went back to her apartment here in Hawk's Landing. She didn't live with her father on the farm."

"It's more of a smallholding," Barb said, coming in. "I definitely wouldn't call it a farm."

"Why not?" asked Avril.

"You'll see when you get there," Barb replied, rolling her eyes.

"I think I'll head out there now," Savage said. "Might as well get this over with."

"I'll come." Both Avril and Sinclair stood up.

"We don't all need to go," he said, "there's too much work to do here. Sinclair, you follow up with Ray. The autopsy was this morning. Also, Pearl's at the crime scene. I know it's unlikely, but she might have found something."

"Sure. No problem." She sat back down, but there was a definite edge to her voice.

"Where's Littleton?" Savage asked, realizing the young deputy wasn't in yet.

"Tied up at some sheep farm somewhere," Sinclair replied.

"The Gibbons'," Barb supplied. "I'll call him and find out what's happening."

"Tell him to get back here. The sheep will have to wait." Savage glanced out of the window. "Damn reporters are back. News of Naomi's death must have got out."

"How do they find out so quickly?" Sinclair muttered.

Savage shook his head. "Thorpe, we still need to track down Evie. Could you get ahold of Clearwater and ask him to check out her last known location? We never did get there last night."

"Sure. If not, I'll head back out there myself."

Savage gave him a grateful nod, then gestured to Avril. "We'll stop at the casino on our way back and see if Walking Deer will let us view the security footage."

"Can we get a warrant?" Avril asked.

"It won't help," Savage told her. "We have no jurisdiction on the rez."

"So how are you going to get it?"

Savage forced a smile. "Ask him nicely."

They were about to leave when Sinclair said, "Oh, I forgot to tell you. I popped into the general store and spoke to old Mr. Cullen about the library book he took out."

"Yeah?" Savage stopped to listen.

"He said he was thinking about selling some land, and wanted to make sure it didn't have any historical significance."

"Oh, right. Nothing suspicious there, then."

"Doesn't look like it."

Savage nodded, and he and Avril strode out into the cold.

MATTHEW MADDEN'S smallholding consisted of nothing more than a rambling, dilapidated farmhouse, a small patch of fenced-in land, and a shelter that housed some sort of livestock. Pigs, by the sound of it.

"I was expecting more from one of the town's founding families," Avril said, looking out of the window as they bounced up the icy driveway. The farmhouse was in the middle of nowhere. Literally. Miles and miles of unbroken snow stretched around them as far as the eye could see.

"He owns it all." Savage turned off the engine and admired the snow-capped peaks of the distant La Plata mountain range shrouded in mist. "Even though he lives on this one little piece. Barb said he's eccentric. Doesn't like company. Apparently, there was a rumor some years back that he was abusive to his wife, which was why she left."

Avril frowned. "Not much of a homelife.".

"Yeah." It was no wonder Naomi didn't live with her father.

They got out of the car and walked up to the farmhouse. They hadn't gotten far when the front door opened and a scruffy man in dirty corduroy trousers and a mismatched shirt came out onto the porch. He was holding a shotgun.

"Get off my land," he yelled, holding it at port arms with the barrel pointed up in the air.

"I'm the Sheriff." Savage held up his hands. Beside him, Avril froze. "We need to talk to you about your daughter, Naomi."

"Don't have a daughter," he retorted, angrily.

"You Matthew Madden?"

"Yeah."

"Mr. Madden, Naomi's birth certificate lists you as her biological father."

A pause.

"We don't speak."

"I see. Well, we still need to talk to you about her."

"Why? She in trouble?"

You could say that.

"Yes, sir."

"She's always getting herself into trouble." The nose of the shotgun dipped. "I ain't got no money to bail her outta jail. She's got a fancy job, she can sort herself out."

No money with all this land? That was strange.

"She hasn't been arrested," Savage wondered how smart it was to break the tragic news to a father holding a shotgun.

Mr. Madden lowered the gun. "What then?"

"Can we come in, Mr. Madden?" Savage asked, lowering his hands. He didn't want to do this out here.

The old guy must have gotten a sense something bad had happened because his shoulders slumped, and the gun hung loosely in his hand. "Okay."

Savage climbed the steps to the porch, gesturing for Avril to stay where she was. She complied, waiting for his instruction.

"Mr. Madden, do you mind putting the gun down?" He wasn't about to enter a man's house with a loaded gun in the occupant's hands, especially when he could smell alcohol on the man's breath. It rose above the body odor, permeating the air around him. Savage tried not to gag.

"Oh, yeah. Sorry." Madden stood the gun up beside the door. Savage nodded to Avril, who joined him on the porch.

"Thank you."

Madden surveyed them through sunken, bloodshot eyes. "Now, what is it you wanted to tell me about Naomi?"

Savage cleared his throat. "I'm sorry to tell you that your daughter's body was found earlier today on the reservation. She froze to death." They were going with that cause of death for now. It was true, just not the whole truth.

Madden stared at him, his expression blank. The silence dragged out.

"Mr. Madden, do you understand what I've just said?"

The shock had rendered him speechless. Like a puppet, he nodded several times, gulped down some of the icy air, then backed up against the wall of the farmhouse.

"Let's go inside," Savage suggested, nodding to Avril. She took Madden's arm and led him into the warm interior. Like a zombie, he walked to a well-used armchair and sank into it. Savage didn't think he'd even blinked.

"Can I get you anything, Mr. Madden? A glass of water?"

A shake of the head. At least he was cognizant. A fire was burning down in the grate, the coals glowing devilishly in the dimness. It was the only source of warmth.

"She froze?" he croaked, turning to look at Savage. His gaze was empty, like he couldn't find an emotion to settle on. Couldn't grasp what had happened.

"Yes, sir."

"Was it drugs?"

"We're not sure yet." He glanced at Avril who shook her head. None of the previous victims were users. The autopsy report would confirm that, though.

"Did your daughter do drugs?" Avril asked.

"I don't know. Maybe. I really didn't know her anymore. We weren't. . . We weren't close."

"Did she ever visit?" Savage glanced around the threadbare farmhouse. A thin rug lay on the worn floor, with minimal furniture in sight and no electronics. It seemed Madden led a simple life.

"Not really. She has an apartment in town, but she stays at the casino most nights. It's a good gig for a girl like her. Work and board. Money's all right too. I saw her at the farm store last week. She was driving some fancy new car." He was still talking about his daughter in the present tense. Her death hadn't sunk in yet.

It would.

"When was that?" Savage asked.

"Dunno. Last week sometime." He sniffed, but his eyes were dry.

"You don't give her an allowance?" Avril asked.

"Got nothing to give," he muttered with a soft snort.

"But you own all this land," she began, glancing out of the window.

"Land's in a trust," he snarled, the bitterness still apparent. "And they don't think I'm worthy of it."

"I see," Avril said. He could see by her face she was thinking the same thing.

"Who are the trustees?" Savage asked.

Madden gave a rough laugh. "Big firm in Denver." He sniffed. "Don't matter much now, anyhow. I mean, what would I do with all that land? Can't even look after this bit."

"Your parents still alive?" asked Savage, even though he remembered being told they were dead.

"No, sir. Passed on a long time ago. Same as my brother. It's only ever been me and Naomi, and she didn't want to talk to me anymore either." Another sniff. "Now she don't have to." The guy was already at a low. Savage was worried that his daughter's death might push him over the edge.

"Is there anyone you'd like us to call?" he asked.

A shake of the head. "Nobody."

Savage sat down on a footstool. "Mr. Madden, do you know how we might contact your ex-wife?"

"Sheriff, I ain't seen or spoken to that woman in twenty years. I have no idea where she's living now, and I don't wanna know."

"Okay, fine." Savage held up his hand. He didn't want to upset the man any further. They'd find some other way to trace Naomi's birth mother.

He shot a look at Avril. "Come on, let's go. Mr. Madden, thank you for your time. We're very sorry for your loss."

"Knew it was bad news the moment I saw ya," he said, not bothering to get up.

Savage grimaced. Unfortunately, that was usually the case.

"We heading to the casino?" Avril asked, once they were back in the car.

Mr. Madden's unspoken sadness, his obvious depression, drinking, and inability to take care of himself had gotten to Savage. Now the poor guy had to deal with his daughter's death. Avril, however, seemed unaffected.

"Yeah, that's the plan."

She nodded, her eyes bright.

"I think I'll get social services to check up on him," he murmured, unable to stop thinking about it.

"Who?"

He shot her a side glance. "Matthew Madden. The man we've just visited. I don't think he's coping too well."

She looked over at him. "He doesn't seem like a very nice man."

"No, but he's just lost his daughter."

Avril nodded, but he could tell her mind was elsewhere. They drove to the casino in silence. It suited him. He didn't feel much like talking anyway.

It was when they were pulling up in front of the casino that Avril spoke again. "That's three," she whispered.

He glanced at her. That meant one more woman was going to die – unless they could get there first.

The casino was busier than last time. The tables were full, and the noise level had risen from loud to deafening.

"We need to speak to Walking Deer." He had to shout at a member of the security team to be heard. Screams rang out as chips poured out of a nearby machine.

The man beckoned for them to follow him and led them up to the first floor of the hotel to a business suite. "Wait here."

He knocked on a door, then opened it and went inside. A long moment later, Walking Deer came out, a practiced smile plastered on his face.

"Good to see you again, Sheriff." They both knew he was lying. "What can I do for you?"

"We'd like to see the security footage covering the area where Naomi Madden was working," he said. "It might tell us who killed her."

"You have no jurisdiction here."

"I realize that, but we do have a responsibility to the victim's father to find out who murdered his daughter, and that man could be on that video."

"What makes you think he is?"

"We know this guy stalks his victims, and if he came here, you might have caught him on camera."

Walking Deer sighed. "I have nothing to hide. A dead white girl on my property doesn't do the resort's reputation any favors. I'd like you to find who did this."

"Thank you." Savage gave him a respectful nod, even though he knew it was because an unknown cause of death cast the casino in a bad light. A white killer, or someone not connected to the casino, would go a long way to make up for that.

Walking Deer got up. "Follow me. I'll take you to our head of security."

Jonas Half Moon was a thick, stocky man with a square jaw and black, beady eyes. At no more than five seven, he was substantially shorter than Savage, but judging by the size of his hands, Savage bet he could do as much damage.

He regarded them with suspicion when his boss told him to let them see the security footage for the week prior to Naomi Madden's murder. "It's okay," he said, when Jonas looked like he would refuse. "We need to clear the casino of any wrongdoing. This will help us find out who did this."

Jonas nodded and brought up the footage.

"There's a lot," he said. "It's going to take some time to go through it all."

"Can you send it through to us?" Savage asked.

"I'm afraid not," Walking Deer cut in. "I'm happy for you to look at it, but it stays here, at the casino."

"Fair enough." Savage pulled out a chair and sat down, getting comfy. Avril did the same. "Let's get going then. Can we start with last Monday?"

"What shift was she working?" Jonas asked his boss.

"I believe she was on the day shift," Walking Deer said.

"Nine a.m. to five p.m." Jonas said, pressing play. The footage wasn't great, but it was decent enough to see the table Naomi was based at. They watched from above as she took over from a male croupier who'd worked the night shift. They were professional, exchanging only a nod before Naomi picked up where he'd left off.

"I have things to be getting on with, so I'll leave you to it." Walking Deer left the room.

"Can we speed it up?" Savage asked.

"Only one and a half times," Jonas said, clicking a button. The images sped up, the movements became jerky and erratic. After an hour, Savage's phone began beeping incessantly. It was Barb and Sinclair, both trying to get ahold of him. He didn't want to talk in front of the head of security.

"I'll stay," Avril said, nodding at the screen. "You go back to the station."

"Are you sure?"

"Ja. I'll let you know if I find anything suspicious."

He nodded and got up. Avril would know what to look for. She'd been an FBI agent for long enough to spot a stalker when she saw one. She certainly didn't need him to remind her.

"Okay, thanks. Call when you're done. I'll get someone to pick you up."

She didn't answer, her eyes locked on the screen.

TWENTY-FOUR

"THE AUTOPSY CAME BACK," Sinclair said as soon as he walked into the sheriff's office. It was already dark outside. Savage hadn't realized how much time had passed while they'd been at the casino. The constant light and barrage of sounds was an assault on the senses. It made you lose track of time. That was the aim, he supposed.

Savage took off his gloves and rubbed his hands together. It was bitterly cold outside now that the sun had set, and the windchill made it feel even colder. At least the weather seemed to be holding. The radio forecast had said more snow was on the way, but not for another twenty-four hours. They had a brief respite.

"Hey, you okay?" she asked.

"Yeah, just feel bad about leaving Becca at home with Connor." He'd called her on the way back to say it was going to be another late one. She'd said it was okay, that she understood, but her chilly tone meant it really wasn't. Not even telling her she'd been right about the pattern the serial killer was following had warmed her up.

"If you want to head home, we can handle things here."

"Thanks, but every second counts if we're going to catch this monster."

That's three.

Avril's words echoed in his head. They were running out of time.

She nodded. Sinclair didn't have dependents, and as far as he could tell, didn't have a boyfriend right now either. "You'll just have to make it up to her once he's behind bars," she said.

"Yeah." The weight of the case pressed down on him, and he rubbed his eyes. "Let's just hope it's soon. There's another woman out there who he's probably watching."

He saw Sinclair shiver. "I keep thinking that too. He'll be stalking her right now, learning her routines, planning his attack. It's sick. He's sick."

Savage nodded. That much was undisputable. "Got any news on the autopsy?"

"Yes. Ray did the mouth test as you asked."

"Chloroform?"

She nodded gloomily. "Same as the others."

As they'd thought.

"Any news from Pearl on the pendant?"

She shook her head. "Nope. Littleton spoke to her earlier. She's running a fingerprint check on all three but hasn't gotten the results yet."

Littleton, who'd been sitting quietly in the corner, glanced up. "That's right. I'll chase up in the morning."

He looked exhausted. Hair ruffled, dirt smudged on his cheeks, clothes dirty. "How'd it go at the sheep farm?"

"The animals were freezing because the shelter wasn't adequately insulated. I had to find a handyman who would come in and reinforce the barn so the livestock wouldn't die. It took forever because the only guy willing to do it was practically a geriatric, so I had to help."

"Good for you," Savage would have grinned if he wasn't so tense. "Why don't you take yourself home. Grab a shower."

He shook his head. "Not while he's still out there."

Savage nodded, accepting that. They all felt the same way. He walked over to Thorpe's desk. "Any luck with Evie Stromberg?"

He looked up. “That’s why I was trying to call you. I found her at a friend’s house on the rez. When her vehicle broke down, she called her friend to pick her up. Then her phone died. She couldn't get to work, and she couldn’t call to let them know what had happened.”

“Didn’t her friend have a phone?”

“Her parents don’t believe in technology.”

Savage shook his head. “So, it really was a false alarm. Evie’s fine?”

“Seems like it. I gave her a lift home, and Doug said her car will be ready in a day or two.”

“Well, that's the best news I’ve heard all day.” He stretched, feeling his back click.

“That doesn’t mean she’s not a target, though,” Thorpe said with uncharacteristic negativity. Unfortunately, he was right.

“You think he’s going to try again?” Sinclair asked.

“Naomi Madden is the third victim in this cycle. If he sticks to his MO, he’s going to make one more kill, then disappear for a year.”

“You want me to watch her?” Thorpe asked.

“Ideally, I’d like to have a team watching both her and Grace around the clock.” He sighed. “But that’s not realistic.”

“We could call them in,” Sinclair suggested. “Have a private word with them. Let them know the risks.”

Savage thought about that for a moment, then gave a quick nod. “Yeah, set it up first thing tomorrow morning. They’re the only two female descendants left.”

“Actually, there is one more,” Thorpe said. “The Harcourts have another daughter.”

“They do?” How had he missed this? “Where is she?”

“She lives in New York,” Thorpe said. “Her name’s George.”

“Ah, George is a daughter. I assumed it was a son.”

“So did I,” Sinclair admitted.

“She’s a brunette, and is already in her mid-thirties, but she’s still a descendant.”

“As long as she stays in New York, she’s probably safe.”

“We hope.” Sinclair said under her breath.

"Where's Avril?" Thorpe asked. He'd been so busy working, he hadn't heard Savage saying he'd left her at the casino.

"Going through security footage of the week before Naomi was killed."

"You think her killer was at the casino?"

"If he stalked her before he killed her, there's a good chance."

"Let's hope she finds something." Sinclair cracked her knuckles. "I'm losing patience with this sicko."

"Avril won't stop until she does." That was one thing he knew for sure. If there was anything to be found on those cameras, the tenacious FBI agent would find it. "What do we have on the victim, Naomi Madden?"

"By all accounts, she was something of a rebellious child," Sinclair said. "I've been asking around about her. Her teachers said she was always in trouble, lashing out, cutting school, that sort of thing."

"Raised by her single father," Savage said. "Looks like they struggled financially, despite the family holdings being in a trust."

"That's true," Thorpe cut in. "Mathew Madden's parents gave discretionary power to the trustees, a Denver-based law firm, who didn't think Matthew was fit to manage the land. I'm not sure Naomi even knew she could apply to them for funds."

"Such a shame," Littleton said. "She wouldn't have been working at the casino if she had."

Savage gave a grim nod. "Who knows what her father told her? He's pretty bitter about the whole thing, not that I blame him."

"Well, she got a waitressing job out of school," Sinclair continued, "and bummed around for a few years, working in bars and what not. Then last year she applied for the job at the casino."

"Last year?"

"Yeah, but they turned her down. The lady I spoke to in HR said they recommended a croupier's course, which she completed, and when she reapplied a couple of months back, they gave her the trainee position."

"I didn't realize they had a training program."

"It's not run by the casino, but by an organization called 'Get Ahead' out of Ignacio. It's where the Ridgewater send all their recruits for training."

Savage nodded. "Good to know." As he turned for his office, his cellphone rang.

"It's Agent Dahl," he said, answering. "Hey, how's it going over there?" He listened for a while, then said, "Good work. I'm on my way."

"Has she got something?" Thorpe asked. Both Sinclair and Littleton turned around.

"Maybe. Naomi Madden wasn't just a croupier. She was also taking men up to her hotel room after her shift."

Sinclair's eyes widened. "Wow. I didn't see that coming."

"Do you think her boss knew about it?" Thorpe asked.

"Apparently not. Sam Walking Deer denied all knowledge of prostitution at his casino."

Sinclair scoffed. "Of course he would."

"Naomi was earning extra cash on the side," Savage said, thoughtfully. "That explains the new car." They'd had it towed to the lab so Pearl could go over it, but he doubted they'd find any evidence there. Not unless Naomi had given her killer a lift somewhere.

"Do you think the killer—?" Sinclair left it hanging.

"I think it's a possibility," Savage replied slowly. "Don't you?"

Thorpe took a deep breath. "He's a meticulous planner. Maybe he did sleep with her before he killed her. It would be one way to get to know her routine."

"It wouldn't be the same day, though," Sinclair said, thoughtfully. "He wouldn't risk leaving any DNA on her body."

"Agreed, but if he went up to her room, there may be footage of him in the hotel. It would be easier than picking him out of a crowd. I'm going to head over to the hotel now and check."

"Want some help?" Sinclair asked. "That's a lot of footage to trawl through."

"Yeah, thanks."

"I can come too," Thorpe offered. "I'll take my car."

Littleton got to his feet, but Savage gestured for him to stay put. Sighing, Littleton sat down again. "Okay, I'll watch the office."

Driving to the casino, Savage couldn't help the thoughts swirling around in his head. Could the killer really have slept with one of his victims? Had he exposed himself because he hadn't been able to resist? None of the other victims had been prostitutes. There'd never been a chance to get to know them intimately before. Could the Frost Killer have made his first mistake?

TWENTY-FIVE

WHAT WERE they doing back again?

The killer frowned as the Sheriff and his little posse marched into the casino. What were they playing at? The petite blonde FBI agent had been inside all afternoon, and it was now nearly midnight. Late for the whole squad to turn up.

He broke into a cold sweat. They must have found something.

But what?

He hadn't left any clues. He'd been careful, as always. He'd stayed out of sight of the overhead cameras, keeping to the shadows. He'd watched from afar, never once getting close enough for anyone to realize he was stalking her.

Except for that night.

That one night where he'd allowed himself to drown in her arms. He hadn't been able to resist, the temptation was too great.

Soft, sweet-smelling, feminine.

His angel.

His *angels*.

The killer inhaled deeply. He could almost smell her now. That fresh, floral perfume, like a field of wildflowers in the mountains where he grew up. It evoked memories of happier times. Before it was all taken away from him. Destroyed in an instant.

He breathed heavily, fighting for control.

That would never happen again. He was rebuilding what he'd lost, little by little. Soon, it would all be his again. He just had to stick to the pattern.

The pattern was everything.

The killer got out of his car. It was a risk, but he couldn't help himself. He had to see what they were up to, where they were going. He hovered at the entrance, but they'd disappeared inside the flashing, beeping bowels of the casino.

Where are you?

There!

He caught a glimpse of the sheriff as he turned toward the elevators. They were going upstairs. Could it be to the room? To her room?

He scoffed. He was being silly. What did it matter if they went to her room? A hundred men had been in her room, had slept in her bed, had laid on her pillow.

DNA? Ha! Good luck with that.

Feeling more confident, he lingered in the lobby, making his way slowly to the slot machines. He'd hide amongst the one-armed bandits with their neon eyes and steel mouths, coughing up chips when they hit a winning streak. Tempting the weak to play again and again. Until they'd lost it all.

He wasn't weak.

But he did sit at the machine, feeding it chips one at a time, waiting for them to return. When they didn't, he began to worry again. What was taking them so long?

Still, there was nothing he could do but wait.

Eventually, at three in the morning, the tall, slim deputy came down. He was yawning and rubbing his eyes. Shortly after that, the sexy brunette emerged. Her eyes were bloodshot.

Then he got it.

They were looking at the hotel surveillance footage. Above the tables, and in the hallways. They were looking to see whether Naomi had known her murderer. Had taken him up to her room.

The killer felt a moment of panic as he thought about that night. He'd been giddy with excitement, but he'd worn a cap and kept his head down and his face turned away from any cameras. What if there were cameras in places he didn't know about? What if he'd missed one?

Still, she must have taken a hundred johns up to her room in the last six weeks. Too many to identify.

Except, here he was again, in the casino. On camera.

Realizing his error, the killer got up and walked quickly toward the exit. It didn't matter. By the time they got around to looking at all the lobby footage, he'd be long gone.

A nice, long holiday until things settled down.

Florida. He'd go to Florida.

He took a few deep breaths. It was nearly over. His final target was lined up. He'd reserved the next few days solely for *her*.

Soon, he'd know everything about her life, like he did Anita and Stephanie and Naomi. He fingered the silver necklace in his pocket. A special gift for his angel.

Then she would be his, body and soul.

Forever.

TWENTY-SIX

"WHAT THE HELL IS GOING ON?" Savage growled, as he elbowed his way through the large throng of reporters outside the Sheriff's Department the next morning. It wasn't just the obligatory local newspapers. There were a couple of nationals here too, including a TV network van and a well-known news anchor.

How did Stephanie Harcourt really die, Sheriff?

Is this the work of a serial killer?

Is this the infamous Frost Killer?

Is he here, in Hawk's Landing?

They bombarded him with their questions as he marched up the steps to the front door.

The Frost Killer!

How the hell had they found out? Who'd tipped them off?

He strode into the lobby, took one look at Barb's ashen face, and took her with him into the squadroom. She couldn't deal with that lot on her own.

"Nobody is to use the front entrance," he barked. "Leave through the sally port or the door in my office. Keep a low profile."

"Is there a risk to women in the community?" yelled a female reporter, her voice carrying through the glass sliding doors.

He looked around at his team, all of whom were bleary-eyed and run-down after their late night at the casino. Littleton was still here, dirty and disheveled. The poor kid must not have been home yet. "How'd this happen?"

"I don't know. They were here when I arrived," Barb said. "I only just managed to get inside."

"I had to fight my way in," Thorpe said. "It was mayhem."

Sinclair rubbed her arm. "Same."

"They arrived around seven o'clock," Littleton murmured. It was now nearly eight-thirty. Savage had been delayed because he'd taken care of Connor this morning, giving Becca a chance to sleep for an extra hour.

"Oh, my gosh," Sinclair said. "Grace Calhoun and Evie Stromberg are coming in at nine."

"We'll have to warn them," Savage said. "Barb, call them and let them know there's been a change of plans. We'll meet them at the Golden Roast Cafe on the main street, instead of the office. That's far enough away not to attract attention."

"Okay." She picked up the phone on Sinclair's desk. The lobby was out of bounds for now.

"Maybe we should just call them?" Sinclair said.

"I want to talk to them together," Savage said. "It's important they understand the risk."

"We could offer them protection until we've caught this psycho," Thorpe suggested. It wasn't a bad idea.

"I'll think about it," Savage said.

There was a loud yelp from the lobby, followed by frantic pounding on the glass doors.

"Holy crap, it's Avril." Sinclair jumped up and let her in. She had to push back the growing mob of reporters. "Get back. Let her through. No, there's no comment!"

Avril limped inside. Sinclair turned to her. "Are you okay?"

"It's a zoo out there," she complained, straightening her clothes and smoothing a hand over her wayward hair. "I think I broke a heel."

Savage had to admit, the diminutive FBI agent had some guts plowing through that mob.

After she'd composed herself, Avril looked at Savage over her glasses. "I see they've found out about the Frost Killer." She threw a newspaper onto the desk. Emblazoned over the front page was the headline:

THE FROST KILLER IS BACK

SAVAGE STARED AT THE NEWSPAPER.

"They even know about the pendant," Avril said, taking off her coat. "It's right there, in the article."

Savage calmly picked it up and scanned it, but in his head, he was screaming every curse word he could think of.

A moment later, he put it down, his expression grave. "It's all here, including the killer's background. It's like someone's read our files."

Sinclair immediately picked it up and read it, with Thorpe peering over her shoulder. Even Barb came over to take a peek. Only Littleton didn't move from his desk.

"Someone must have leaked it," Barb said.

Savage massaged his forehead. "This is what I was afraid of. Now we've got a media shitstorm on our hands. Every major newspaper will send a reporter to cover the Frost Killer."

To everyone's surprise, Littleton gave a muffled sob. "I think this is my fault."

Savage's head whipped in his direction. "What?"

The young deputy glanced up, his lip trembling. "I met this girl the other night at Miller's Walk. She hit on me big time." He closed his eyes and shook his head. "I should have known it was too good to be true."

"What girl?" Sinclair asked, putting down the newspaper. "Kevin, what happened?"

He sniffed. "Her name was Lila. She and her friend joined our group. We had a few drinks and..." He stopped, flushing.

"She went back to your place?" Sinclair guessed.

He nodded miserably.

"I didn't tell her anything about the case, I swear, but I had the files—"

"You took the files home with you?" Savage could barely hold back his annoyance.

"Yeah. Didn't you guys? I wanted to read through them in my spare time."

"You were just doing your job," Barb said, shooting a warning look at Savage.

He sighed. He'd also taken the files home, so he couldn't berate his deputy for that. In fact, he'd left a copy for Becca to look at. Stuck at home, she'd offered to read through it and give him some additional insight. "You think she read them?"

"She must have. It's the only explanation." He'd obviously been thinking about it. "I got up in the night and found her in the living room. She said she was getting a glass of water, but the next morning, I noticed my bag had been moved." He slapped himself on the forehead. "I'm such an idiot. I fell right into her trap."

"It's not your fault," Savage muttered through gritted teeth.

"Did you get her last name?" Sinclair asked. "Maybe we can find out who she works for?"

Littleton shook his head, close to tears.

"Lila was probably a fake name, anyway," Thorpe said.

Savage put his hands on his hips. "Well, the horse has bolted now. We'll just have to deal with the consequences and hope to hell it doesn't scare the killer off."

There was still one more victim to go. That's how they were going to catch him.

"I'm sorry," Littleton mumbled. Sinclair went over and patted him on the back.

"You didn't know."

"This article is written by a staff reporter at the *Herald*," she said, turning back to the newspaper. "Why don't you go online and see if you can find this Lila person? They may have a photograph of her with a byline somewhere on the website."

Littleton nodded, glad to have something to do.

Avril reached into her briefcase and pulled out the two photographs they'd printed from the cameras last night at the hotel. Laying them out on her desk, she said, "We've got work to do."

"Are those photographs from the casino?" Barb asked. The color had come back into her cheeks. The quality wasn't great, and the subjects were both side-on to the camera. It was hard to make out their features.

"Yeah." Savage glanced at Avril.

She nodded. "We managed to identify several of the men Naomi Madden took up to her room in the last week."

"She was popular," Thorpe added.

Barb wrinkled her nose. "Poor girl, having to resort to *that* to make a living."

"Especially when her family was so wealthy," Sinclair added.

"All the men we identified had alibis for the afternoon of the murder. There were only two men we couldn't name." Avril pushed her glasses up her nose. "I've sent their pictures to the FBI headquarters in Denver so they can run them through facial recognition software. It's a long shot, but they might find a match."

Savage grunted. At least they had access to the FBI's resources. That would help speed things along. "One of these guys could be our killer," he said.

They all stared at the images. The first man was average height, olive-skinned with black hair combed back off his forehead. He was looking down, but they could see he had prominent cheekbones and a bulbous, misshapen nose, possibly the result of too many bar fights.

His suit was cheap, and he wore shoes that were scuffed around the edges.

"He could be Native American," Barb said, picking it up for a closer look.

"Yeah, I'm going to run it by Clearwater later. The Tribal Police might know him."

"What about this guy?" Barb replaced it and picked up the second photograph of a well-built white man wearing jeans and a checked shirt over a white T-shirt. A blue baseball cap covered his head, obscuring his face apart from a thin streak down the side showing an angular jaw. That was it. No other features were visible.

"He's another possibility," Savage said. "We also picked him up in the casino a couple of times during the week. He's always wearing a nondescript cap and similar clothing. There's no clear shot of his face."

"He's careful," Sinclair added.

"Was he there during Naomi's shifts?" Barb asked.

Avril nodded. "He could have been watching her."

Sinclair tilted her head to the side and stared at the image. "It didn't occur to me last night, but don't you think this looks like that ski instructor, Logan Maddox?"

"Not really," said Avril.

"Look at the jaw. Logan had a square jaw like that."

"So do a lot of people," Savage pointed out, but he had to admit, it *could* be him. He was the right height and build too. The photograph wasn't good enough to rule him out.

"I thought we'd already discounted him," Avril said. "Besides, it can't be him, he's been in Hawk's Landing for years."

"We only have his word on that," Sinclair said. "He's a ski instructor. It's possible he travels, working at ski resorts all over the world."

"Always in the winter," murmured Thorpe.

There was a moment of silence as they digested this.

"Go and speak to him again," Savage said, finally. "It'll be easy enough to rule him out if he can provide alibis for both these murders."

TWENTY-SEVEN

TEQUILA-SWIGGING Lila turned out to be Lillian Decker, an investigative reporter for the *Durango Herald*. She had a long and somewhat distinguished career working for the newspaper's crime beat.

"It's too late to do anything about it now," Savage said, when Sinclair came into his office and told him what Littleton had discovered. "The town's gone into a panic. I've just had the Mayor on the line. He said he's been inundated with concerned calls from residents demanding to know what's being done to catch this guy."

He'd spent the last twenty minutes reading the full article, slowly and carefully. The woman wrote well, but the content had been lifted straight from Avril's case notes. The FBI agent would be well aware of this fact too. He admired her stoicism, but then maybe she was used to this type of thing. She'd been chasing this guy for a long time.

"We could get an injunction to stop them printing anything else about the case?" Sinclair suggested.

He mulled it over. "Okay, get on the phone to Judge Cartwright. Let's see what we can do."

"Will do." She hurried out.

If Lillian had read the entire case file, she'd know almost as much as they did about the predatory serial killer. The first article focused on the current crimes, mentioning Anita Cullen and Stephanie Harcourt. Lillian hadn't known about Naomi Madden when the newspaper had gone to press.

He sighed. This was likely to be the first in a series of articles that the newspaper would run. Once the media discovered Naomi Madden's death, all hell would break loose. Three victims. Three women dead in a town the size of Hawk's Landing. It would be mayhem.

The pressure was on.

Outside, the sun tried to break through the clouds without much success. He could see dark, ominous shadows moving in over the mountains to the north. More snow was on its way. He checked his watch. Nearly nine o'clock. Time to meet with Grace Calhoun and Evie Stromberg.

The Golden Roast was a quaint coffee shop with pastel wallpaper, sixties memorabilia, and pretty decent coffee. The best part was it was four blocks away from the Sheriff's Department at the other end of the main street. They'd driven there, leaving from the sally port exit, so nobody had been able to follow.

Savage and Sinclair chose a table at the back, away from the windows. They couldn't take any chances, even though Savage was pretty sure they were far enough away from the office not to run into any caffeine-hunting reporters.

Grace arrived first in a woolen, camel-colored coat and black scarf and gloves. She walked in, looked around, then raised a hand in a tentative greeting.

Savage stood up. "Grace, thank you for coming."

She nodded. "I've had to take a couple of hours off work."

"This won't take long. Would you like a coffee?"

"Yes, but I'll get it." She draped her coat over a vacant chair and headed back to the counter. While she was there, Evie rushed in, more disheveled than Grace, her hair mussed up by the wind, and her old-style bomber jacket unzipped. She must've been freezing.

He got up. "Evie? We're over here."

She hurried over. "Sorry, I'm late, Sheriff. I had to get my car from the shop. It broke down the other day." Then she laughed. "Of course, you know that." She couldn't have failed to see the missing persons alert out for her when she got home. "I'm sorry for causing so much trouble."

She apologized a lot. Becca would say she suffered from low self-esteem issues, probably as a result of her dysfunctional upbringing, but he wasn't here to psychoanalyze her.

"I'm glad you're all right," he said, and meant it. "You scared us there for a minute."

"I know." She sat down. "What's this about, Sheriff? Why is everybody so worried about me? Did I do something wrong?"

"I don't know. Did you?"

She gave a nervous laugh. "Not that I know of."

"Then you've got nothing to worry about," he said, smiling.

She relaxed.

"Can I get you a coffee?" Sinclair offered.

"Oh, yeah. Sure, thanks."

Sinclair got up and went to the counter. When they were all back, Savage cleared his throat. "Okay, the reason we asked you both here today is because we think you might be at risk."

"At risk?" Grace frowned. "Is this about the man you told me about the other day?"

"Yes, but I didn't tell you everything," he admitted.

She fixed her clear gaze on him. "You didn't?"

"No. I'm sure by now you've seen this morning's newspaper."

Evie gasped. "The serial killer dude. Yeah, that's freaky."

He nodded. "I don't mean to scare you, but he's targeting young, blonde women, such as yourselves, from prominent families in the area."

Grace swallowed and wrapped her hands around her coffee cup.

Evie snorted. "Well, that rules me out. My parents are both dead, and I have no money."

"Not quite," he said, turning to her. "I'm not sure if you know, but your family was one of a handful of early citizens who founded this town."

She gave a sad nod. "My grandfather used to tell me stories, but that was a long time ago. There's nothing left. He told me how they lost everything when the taxes came in, and then again in the financial crash. There's no reason anyone would want to go after me."

"What about your mother?" Savage asked.

"My mama left when I was a baby. Took my brother with her. Nobody knows where they are." Her voice cracked.

"Still, we can't rule you out, I'm afraid."

Grace checked the time. "That's grand, Sheriff, but what exactly are you saying? That this guy, this serial monster, is coming after us?"

"I think he might."

There was a pause as his words sunk in. Grace and Evie looked at each other.

"I hope I'm wrong," he added, "but he's got one more kill to make, and you're the only two descendants left. I think he's going to come after one of you."

Grace's hand trembled. She set her cup down on the table a little too hard. "You mean the other victims were also…" She didn't finish.

He nodded. "Yes, blonde and descended from founding families in the area."

"I knew Stephanie," Grace whispered. "Sort of. She was nice."

"Was there someone else too?" Evie asked. She obviously hadn't read the newspaper article yet.

"Anita Cullen was the first victim," Savage told them. "She was a cross-country skier, and we think she was taken from Hawk's Landing in broad daylight last Tuesday."

"That's risky," whispered Grace.

"He's bold," Sinclair warned them. "He studies his targets well in advance and gets to know their routines. Have either of you noticed anyone watching you?"

Evie shivered. "No, not really. I mean, I'm usually rushing from the salon to my boyfriend's house. I don't think I'd notice if someone was following me."

Grace hesitated, but only for a moment. "I don't think so, no."

"Be vigilant," Savage told them. "Keep your eyes peeled, and if you notice anything suspicious, call the Sheriff's Office immediately."

"You're scaring me, Sheriff," Grace whispered.

Evie just stared at him with huge, frightened eyes.

"I'm sorry, but we had to warn you. We can offer you protection, if you want it. I'll assign a deputy to guard you until this is over."

Grace hesitated, but Evie shook her head. "That's okay. I don't want someone shadowing my every move." She glanced at Sinclair. "No offense."

She shrugged. "None taken."

"What about you, Grace?"

"I don't know." She bit her fingernail. "How worried should I be?"

"I think it's almost certain he'll try something in the next few days," Savage said.

She exhaled shakily. "Okay, well I'd like protection, please. I work at a school, and I live alone. I don't want to put the children at risk, and I don't want to be terrified when I'm by myself."

Fair enough.

"I'll get someone to meet you at your place in an hour. His name is Deputy Thorpe, and he's a good man. You can trust him."

"Thank you."

Evie hesitated. Savage could see she was scared but trying not to show it.

"How about you call me when you're leaving work," Sinclair suggested, coming to the rescue. "I'll drive behind you to your house, or to your boyfriend's apartment. Those are the only times you'll be alone, right?"

"Yeah." She put her hands in her lap. "Thank you."

Sinclair nodded and slid a card with her cellphone number on it across the table. “No problem.”

The two women left, and Savage drove Sinclair back to the station. “I feel better,” he told his deputy, as they entered the sally port. “I know it’s not much, but it’s better than doing nothing.”

“We’ll get him.” Sinclair’s eyes flashed with cold determination. “If he tries to grab one of those girls, he’s not going to know what’s hit him.”

Savage hoped she was right.

TWENTY-EIGHT

DEPUTY JAMES THORPE arrived at Grace Calhoun's house exactly one hour later, as instructed. He parked his truck in the wide driveway and turned off the ignition.

Wow. This was a pretty nice house for a schoolteacher. Situated on the outskirts of Hawk's Landing, it was a modern double story with rustic charm nestled in the foothills of the mountain, just where the State Forest began. Thorpe craned his neck to stare up at the tall, snow-dusted trees brushing the silver sky. They surrounded the house, blocking the view of the neighbors, who were at least a football field away on either side.

He inhaled deeply. Pine, clean air, and an earthy smell of decomposing leaves. There was something so fresh and rejuvenating about it.

The front door opened, and Grace Calhoun said, "Deputy Thorpe?"

"Yes, ma'am."

He walked up to the house and showed her his badge. She nodded nervously. "I've never had a protective detail before."

"Don't worry, I'll try not to get in your way."

She gave an uncertain smile. "Please, come in?"

He followed her into an expansive entrance hall with polished wooden floors, high ceilings and expensive chrome light fixtures. Large windows let in plenty of natural light and offered uninterrupted views of the surrounding forest.

She saw him looking around in awe and said, "My parents bought this house for me on my twenty-first birthday. That was nearly ten years ago, and I've lived here ever since."

"It's a big house for a single occupant," he said, without thinking.

"Well, I'm sure they hoped I'd be married with a family by now, but unfortunately that didn't happen."

"I'm sorry," he said, immediately. "I didn't mean to pry—"

She waved a delicate hand in the air. "Don't worry, I know you didn't." There was something warm and easy-going about her, despite her prim manner and reserved demeanor. He wondered fleetingly why she was still single.

He turned his attention to the task at hand. "Do you mind if I look around? I'd like to make sure the property is secure."

"Of course." She hesitated. "Would you like some coffee? I've just put on a fresh pot."

"That would be great. Thanks."

She exhaled, and he realized how nervous she was. What he was less sure about was whether it was because there was a serial killer targeting her, or because she wasn't used to having a strange man in her house.

"I'll be right back." He went upstairs and inspected every window and door in every room. The floor to ceiling windows and sheer drapes meant that if the lights were on inside, anyone looking in would be able to see that she was home.

Even though the windows locked, they weren't the most secure mechanisms in the world and could be forced open at a push. The same could be said for the downstairs ones.

He opened the French doors that led out onto a neat, terraced back garden, and surveyed the perimeter. It was largely open to the wilderness, no fence or wall barring entry to the property. She probably liked it that way. Natural. Blending seamlessly into the mountain. He did too, except it was a security nightmare. Anyone could sneak between the trees into the back garden.

"Everything okay?" She handed him a cup of coffee.

"Yes and no," he said diplomatically.

At her worried look, he elaborated. "It's an amazing place you've got here, but it's wide open. I understand you probably don't want to put a fence up, and quite frankly, that won't stop anyone who really wants to get in, but anyone can walk onto the property without you knowing."

She looked around as if this had never occurred to her before.

"The locks on the windows are flimsy, and the French doors have no bolt or deadlock to secure them," he went on. "A hard kick, and they'd fly open.

She gulped. "I didn't realize it was that easy to break in."

"You should probably get them replaced at some point," he suggested. "Sooner rather than later."

"I'll get on it first thing tomorrow."

He nodded. Good, that was a start.

"You might also want to get some blackout blinds or thicker drapes for the windows, just so nobody can see in at night."

She flushed, grasping his meaning. "Okay."

"Do you have any lights outside?"

"You mean in the garden?"

"Security lights, ma'am."

"Oh. Er, no. Should I have?"

"It would help to deter intruders, yes. You can get automatic lights with sensors that come on if they detect movement. They'd be the best."

"I'll add it to my list." She gave a tentative laugh. "Anything else?"

He gave an awkward smile. "I think that's it for now."

"I'm afraid I've got some work to do, Deputy—" She hesitated. "I'm sorry, I've already forgotten your name."

"It's Thorpe. But you can call me James, if you like."

"Well, I've got some work to do for school, Deputy Thorpe, so make yourself at home. At least, I think that's what I'm supposed to say to the man guarding me."

He gave a grateful nod. "Just pretend I'm not here."

"A man such as yourself? That's not going to be easy, but I'll try."

He wondered what she'd meant. He wasn't that much of an oaf that he'd get in her way. Maybe it was the sheriff's uniform, or the gun. Some people were frightened of weapons.

He got comfortable in the living room and opened his laptop. Things had gotten so hectic, he hadn't had time to properly read the updated case notes. He also had the forensic evidence back from the lab on the pendants. Just because he was on protection detail didn't mean he didn't have work of his own to do.

He took his time and read through the forensic report, not expecting much. The killer had been so careful up until now. Then one line caught his eye.

Partial print.

He jolted upright and fumbled for his phone. Crap, this was huge. A freakin' partial print.

Savage answered after the second ring.

"Did you see the lab report yet?" It came out in a breathless rush.

"No, I was just about to open it. What you got?"

"Pearl lifted a partial print off one of the necklaces."

"Seriously?" The sheriff's voice was raspy with excitement. There was the sound of tapping as Savage brought up the lab report.

"Damn," he muttered. "We might actually have a lead. I'll get Sinclair to run it. Hopefully, it's enough for a match." While they both knew a partial would never be taken seriously in court – there was too big a margin for error – it could potentially point them in the right direction.

"Will you keep me posted?"

"Sure thing. Good work, Thorpe." The line went dead.

Adrenaline whizzed through his veins, making his pulse race. This was the closest they'd ever come to identifying the killer.

Please be in the database.

It would be so easy. A tiny misdemeanor, a domestic abuse case, or a shoplifting charge would do it. Then they could arrest him and put an end to this nightmare.

Thorpe sighed, trying to relax. It was probably best not to get his hopes up. It was only a partial, and in his experience, nothing was ever that easy.

"Everything okay?" Grace poked her head around the door. "I heard talking."

"Yeah. I was calling the Sheriff. We might have a break in the case."

"That's exciting." She ventured further into the room. "Does this mean you know who the murderer is?"

"Not exactly, but we could very soon."

"That's a relief." She hesitated, clasping her hands together. "You're not leaving, are you?"

He could tell she was scared to be alone. "No, don't worry. I'm not leaving."

A relieved sigh. "Thank goodness."

When she didn't move, he asked, "Is there something else?"

"Um, I just wondered if you'd like to join me for supper?"

"You don't have to feed me, Miss Calhoun."

"Oh, I know." She laughed, embarrassed. "But it's the least I can do. After all, you're here, protecting me."

"That's my job, ma'am."

"Still, you have to eat."

He smiled. "In that case, thank you. That would be great."

She gave a pleased nod and disappeared back into the kitchen.

Thorpe was still working when Grace called him to the table half an hour later. "I set places in the kitchen. I hope that's okay. The dining room is so formal, I seldom use it."

"Sounds great."

She wandered over to where he was sitting and glanced down at the photographs he'd scattered on the coffee table. "What are those?"

"Oh, excuse me. You're not supposed to see these. It's part of the case." He made to cover them up, but she put a hand on his arm. He paused.

"Snowflake pendants?"

While he knew he was breaking with protocol, something in her tone made him pause. "Yes. That's right."

"Are they part of the case?" She picked up one of the photographs and studied it.

Thorpe bit his lip. "I can't say."

She lifted her gaze to him. "But it's important?"

He nodded.

She took a deep breath. "I know the lady who makes these."

Thorpe thought he'd misheard. "Excuse me?"

"These paper snowflake cut-outs. I know the artist. She lives in Durango. I hired her to give my fifth-grade art class a lesson one time. They loved it." She smiled.

He stared at her. It took a while for his brain to catch up with what she was saying. "You know the person who made these?"

"Uh-huh."

"How do you know it's the same woman?"

"They're very specific. I recognize the design. Wait here." She dashed out of the room. Thorpe was rooted to the spot. All he could hear was the pulse throbbing in his head.

Grace reappeared carrying a large version of the snowflake. Handing it to Thorpe, she said, "Look. Isn't it the same snowflake?"

He inspected the design, then compared it to the one in the photograph. It was much bigger, but the snowflake was identical to the one in the pendant. Out of the millions of snowflake variations in the world, this one was exactly the same as the killer's calling card. He stared harder, until his eyes burned. There was no difference. Grace was right. It was the same artist. It had to be.

"Could you give me her details?" he croaked, his voice hoarse.

She glanced up. "Deputy Thorpe, you've gone white. Are you okay?"

"I'm fine. If you could just write her details down for me, I'd appreciate it."

She seemed flustered. "Um, yes. Of course."

Picking up his pen, she scribbled an address down on his notepad. "I've got her number in my phone. Give me a moment."

"Thank you."

She left the snowflake on the table and went to get it.

With shaking hands, Thorpe took out his cellphone and snapped a couple of photographs of the enlarged snowflake.

Then he called the Sheriff back.

TWENTY-NINE

"YOU MEAN he didn't make them?" Savage paced up and down his office on the phone. "He *bought* them?"

"It looks like it," Thorpe said. "I took a closer look at the other pendants from previous years, and they are different."

"How different?"

"Well, the design is different, and they're not as intricate. They seem rougher around the edges."

"He could have gotten better at it," Savage thought out loud. "Or used the woman's snowflake as a pattern."

"He could have," Thorpe agreed. "But if he copied her design, he must have been in contact with her."

"Send me the address," Savage barked. "I'm heading over there now."

"Will do."

Savage stopped pacing and looked out the window. The snowy street was littered with press. Reporters, photographers, news anchors. The network vans had formed a snaking line down the side of the road. He sniffed. At least the Bouncing Bean Café was hopping. "They're the only shop in town who actually benefits from this drama," he'd snapped earlier, when Barbara had brought him a coffee. Now he felt bad. Damn Lillian Decker and damn the *Durango Herald.*

He pulled open his office door. "I'm going out," he said. "Grace Calhoun thinks she recognizes the snowflake design. Said there's a woman in Durango who makes them. I'm going to check it out."

Avril stood up. "What? That can't be right."

"Thorpe swears it's the same design. Take a look." Savage handed her his phone, and she stared at the two images, flicking between them. Then she removed her glasses and looked again.

"They're the same."

"Exactly. He got them made."

"But he couldn't have." Avril's lip trembled. He could tell a thousand conflicting thoughts were flying through her brain.

"Look, I don't know how it relates to his previous MO, but this looks to me like it's the same artist."

She nodded, dully. "I'm coming with you."

He looked across at his deputy. "Sinclair?"

"I'm going to talk to Logan Maddox again," she said. "We need to get his alibis for the last two murders."

He nodded, then turned back toward his office. The side door was the only option here. "Okay, then let's go."

Avril pulled on her oversized coat and rushed after him, but before they could make it more than a few steps, there was frantic banging on the front door. Savage stopped so suddenly, Avril bumped into him.

"Barb, what is it now?"

"Commissioner Albright is here."

Savage turned around. Avril scuttled out of the way.

A harassed Albright strode into the squadroom. "It's madness out there."

"Tell me about it. What can I do for you, Commissioner?"

"You know damn well what you can do for me, Sheriff. You can find the bastard responsible for murdering these young women. The body count has gone up to three. How many more are going to die before you catch this guy?"

He squared his shoulders. "We're trying, sir."

"Not hard enough. When we spoke last, I asked you to call me if you needed any help. I'm still waiting."

"We're chasing down several leads," he began.

"This looks to me like you need help." He gestured toward the window. "You've lost control of this investigation."

"Details of the case were leaked to the press," he bit out. Littleton cowered behind his computer, making himself as small as possible. "This is not our fault. It was only a matter of time before it got out."

"Who leaked it?"

"Three women murdered in the span of two weeks. You think the media aren't going to be all over that?" He deflected the blame away from Littleton and the department.

Albright shook his head. "The press is going crazy. Helicopters are flying in correspondents from all over the country. Hotels are filling up. Even the ski resorts are at capacity. The casino has never been this busy."

Savage took it back. The Bouncing Bean wasn't the only one profiting from this.

"You owe me an update," Albright said. "I need to know how close we are to catching this monster."

"I'm actually on my way out." Savage jingled his keys to make a point.

"I've got a duty of care," Albright snapped, the stress showing. "People are scared. There's a killer on the loose, and they want answers."

"I'm trying to get them answers," Savage retorted, his voice growing in volume. "All you're doing by berating me is holding me up."

That made the other man pause.

"You're going to see a suspect?" he asked, unable to disguise the hope in his voice.

"A possible witness," he said.

Avril cleared her throat. "The FBI is trying to identify photographs of two possible suspects from the casino security footage, sir. And we also have a partial fingerprint we're running."

Savage had to admire her confident tone. He guessed it had come from years of answering to superiors. The effect on the Commissioner was immediate.

"Well, why didn't you say so," he huffed.

"We should have some answers soon," Savage added, shooting Avril a grateful look.

"Good. Be sure to keep me updated."

"I will, sir."

The Commissioner nodded, then looked reluctantly at the front door. The lobby was still swarming with reporters who wanted first dibs at whoever came out and were sick of standing in the snow. "You don't have a back door, do you?"

Savage kept a straight face. "Only the sally port, sir, and that's locked up. We use it to bring in suspects."

Albright took a deep breath, then pressed the button to open the automated doors and disappeared into the fray.

"Nicely done," Sinclair said, once he'd fought his way through the crowd.

Savage managed a grin. "You too, Avril."

She gave a tiny smile. "We have lots of people like that in the FBI. Are we going now?"

"Yeah, but come this way. I'm not going anywhere near them."

THE PAPERCUT ARTIST, a woman called Celia Swanson, lived in a rustic cabin 20 miles north-east of Durango. It appeared to be on sprawling ranchland but was situated some way away from the main ranch house, near a frozen lake.

"I think she's a tenant," Savage said, as they pulled up in front of the quaint wooden dwelling. Bamboo wind chimes jangled outside, and he spotted several crystals glued into the paving stones on the path leading to the front porch.

A large brass knocker on the door gleamed at them. Avril raised it and knocked three times.

A short while later, the door swung open.

"Mrs. Swanson?" asked Savage.

The lady nodded. Mid-fifties, long, silver hair in a messy bun, and wearing paint-smattered clothes, she looked every bit like an eccentric artist.

"Thank you for seeing us."

Mrs. Swanson rubbed at a mark on her cheek, then beckoned them inside. "I must admit, I was surprised by your phone call. I don't often get visits from law enforcement." She smiled, but Savage was too uptight to return it.

"Mrs. Swanson—"

"Please, call me Celia."

"Celia, do you recognize this pendant?" He took the evidence bag containing the silver chain and pendant out of his pocket. He drew it out and handed it to her. The forensic tests had been completed, so there was no risk of contamination.

Curious, she took it and turned it over in her hand. "Yes, that's one of mine."

Avril inhaled sharply.

"You made this?" Savage asked. They had to be absolutely sure.

"I made four of them just last month. It was a private order. I don't usually make such small ones, but the buyer was specific about the size."

Avril clutched his arm. He could feel her quaking as she clung to him.

"Did you speak to the buyer?" he asked, gently shifting Avril toward a chair. She sat down, her face pale.

"Not directly, no. He sent me an email with instructions. Said he'd seen my website. I gave him a quote for the work, and he sent an envelope with the cash. I admit, it's a little unorthodox, but some people don't like to pay online. You know how it is – so many scammers these days."

He gave a distracted nod. "Can I see the email?"

"Sure, give me a second to pull it up."

Avril had moved a hand to her mouth. He understood her shock. After more than a decade of searching, they may have found the clue they were looking for. Was this woman the link to the killer?

Celia turned around. "Here it is."

Savage bent down to look at her screen. She had a Hotmail account, and the email had been sent to info@silvermoonbeams.com.

The sender's address was frosty463201@gmail.com.

The killer had a sense of humor.

"It's a generic Gmail account," he told Avril, who still hadn't moved. "We'll trace the IP."

"Do you want to see the envelope?" Celia asked.

"You still have that?"

"Oh, yes. I haven't gotten around to entering it into my invoice ledger yet."

He gave a nod of his head. "If you don't mind."

"Not at all, Sheriff." She glanced at Avril. "Is your colleague okay? She looks like she's seen a ghost."

Avril didn't respond. Her eyes were fixed on the computer screen, her expression unreadable, but he could guess what she was thinking. Is this for real? Did the killer really order the pendants from this woman? Would they find anything here that would lead them to him?

"She's fine."

Celia came back with an open envelope containing money. "I charged him four hundred dollars. I know it seems like a lot, but the snowflakes are very time consuming. The work is extremely detailed."

"I can see that." Savage took a forensic glove out of his pocket and pulled it on. Gingerly, he extracted the four hundred dollars and handed it to her. "Celia, do you mind if we take the envelope to the lab for analysis?"

Her eyes widened. "Oh, okay. Sure, if you want to."

Savage slipped the envelope into an evidence bag and then into his inside jacket pocket. “We’ll need to take your prints for elimination purposes.”

She gave a nervous nod.

Maybe they could pull a print off it. Maybe the print would match the partial on the pendant. And maybe they’d be able to match it on the database. A lot of maybes, but with a bit of luck, they could finally put a name to their killer.

THIRTY

"WE DROPPED the envelope off at the lab," Savage told Sinclair and Littleton when he got back to the station. "Pearl is going to put a rush on it."

"Why is he outsourcing now?" Sinclair asked. "When he made his own in the past."

"We don't know that he did," Savage said.

"Yes, we do." Avril spoke for the first time. She hadn't said anything on the way home, and he'd left her alone with her thoughts. She reached down into her shirt and pulled out a silver chain. At the end of it was a snowflake pendant, similar to those left on the victims' bodies. "This was his first one, the one he left on my mother."

Sinclair stared at her in horror. "You kept it?"

A tiny nod. "It reminds me of why I'm doing this."

Savage exhaled under his breath. Shit, she was messed up.

"What about it?" he said, looking down at the ornament. The silver frame had rusted slightly, and the snowflake was yellowing with age, but other than that, it was in good condition.

"See how the edges are uneven, how it's torn in places?"

Savage agreed it looked like it was done by an amateur. "Okay, so he made that one."

"Here are the others." She reached into a folder and took out a pile of photographs. Some of them were taken at crime scenes, the others in a lab. "They're all pretty rustic, but he's getting better at it."

Savage nodded.

"You can see the improvement." She pointed to the photographs. "These are home made."

"Then why buy them now?" Savage asked.

Avril collapsed against the back of her chair. "That's what I don't understand. He wouldn't."

"Maybe he was short of time," Littleton suggested. It was a good theory.

Avril shook her head. "He plans these kills weeks, if not months in advance. There's no way he wouldn't be ready."

There was a long pause while they thought about this. Finally, Savage said, "I can't answer that, Avril. All I can tell you is we have a potential lead with the online order, and we're going to follow it. Hopefully, it checks out and we get a name."

Avril tucked her chain back into her shirt and gathered up the photos. "It doesn't make sense, that's all."

Nothing about this case made sense.

He turned to Sinclair. "What happened with Logan Maddox?"

"He checks out," she said. "He's got an alibi for the time frames in which Stephanie and Naomi were murdered."

"I'm listening."

"On the morning Stephanie was killed, he took a group of skiers to the Hesperus Ski Area. They set off at eight and were gone for most of the day."

"According to her father, Stephanie leaves for her run at seven," Savage pointed out.

"Yeah, but she would have gotten to the creek closer to eight, and there's no way he'd have made it back in time to meet the group."

"And he wasn't late?"

"Apparently not. I spoke to a woman in his group who said he was right on time. He's in the clear."

"What about Naomi?" Savage asked.

"Similar story. Naomi was last seen on the casino cameras at five o'clock when her shift ended. Maddox was seen socializing with the guests in the West Mountain ski resort bar. It's called the Snow Plough. His boss vouched for him."

"His boss?"

"Yeah, the owner of the resort. Austin Lambert."

"I guess we can rule him out then."

Avril looked up from her phone. "I've just heard back from the FBI office in Washington. They ran the photographs of those two men at the casino and got a match for one of them."

"Which one?" asked Sinclair.

"The Native American. His name is Felix White Feather."

"How come he was in the system?" Savage wanted to know.

"He's got a record. He served time for assault. Punched a man in a bar. Got four years and served two. He's just been released."

"Two years," murmured Savage. "Didn't you say the killer had been dormant for two years?"

"Yes, but—"

"But you don't think the Frost Killer could be a Native American?"

"Not really. The first murders occurred in Scandinavia fifteen years ago."

Savage had to admit, that did make it more complicated. "Okay, well let's bring him in anyway. Got an address?"

She nodded. "He lives on the reservation, not far from the resort."

Savage beckoned to Littleton. "You go with Sinclair and bring him in."

The young deputy jumped out of his chair so fast it nearly fell over. "No problem."

. . .

AN HOUR LATER, Savage sat opposite Felix White Feather in the station's interrogation room. The man wasn't any prettier close up, and by the smell of him, he hadn't showered in a few days either.

Savage slid the photograph across the table. "Is that you?"

The man glanced down at the picture. "Yeah, that's me. What of it?"

"What were you doing at the Ridgewater Casino?"

"Gambling. What do you think I was doing?"

"You go there often?"

"Fairly often. I live less than a mile away." His dark eyes flickered from Savage's face up to the camera mounted on the wall, and back again.

"Win anything?" Savage asked.

Felix White Feather frowned. "Why you askin' me that?"

"This photograph was taken by one of the hotel security cameras. Would you like to tell us what you were doing when this photograph was taken?"

Felix didn't answer.

"I can remind you, if you like." Savage tapped the photograph with his forefinger. "You were on your way back from paying a lady a visit. Room 213. Does that sound about right?"

He swallowed.

"Need some water?" Savage asked.

Felix shook his head.

"So, what were you doing in room 213?"

Felix's eyes darted to the door, then back at Savage. There was no way out of this one. He sighed. "You obviously know what I was doing there."

"I want to hear you say it."

"Why, so you can arrest me?"

Savage didn't reply.

"Since when is sleeping with a beautiful woman a crime?"

"It's not. Paying to sleep with her is."

Felix gave an angry shake of his head. “I’ve been inside for two years, damn it! All I wanted was a little human contact. Is that so bad?”

Savage fixed his gaze on Felix’s face. “I’m not interested in how you spend your free time, Mr. White Feather.”

“Then what do you want?” He looked genuinely puzzled.

“Did you know the woman you slept with that night?”

“No, I just met her. I mean, I played blackjack at her table a couple of times. She seemed nice. I didn't know she was a wh—um, soliciting, then.”

“How did you find out?”

“One of the bartenders told me. I said I was looking for some company, and he recommended Naomi. Said she was into making some extra money after hours.”

“So you propositioned her?”

“Hey, careful now. Don’t go putting words in my mouth. I had a friendly chat with her, that’s all. She invited me up to her room.”

“Okay, we’ll go with that for now. What happened when you got there?”

His eyebrows shot up. “You want me to be explicit?”

“No, Felix. I don’t want the details. I just want to know if you had sex.”

He grinned. “Yeah, we did. It was good. She’s a pretty lady.”

“Did you argue with her at all?”

“Argue? No.” He shifted in his chair. “We didn’t do much talking.”

“You see her again?”

“No, just the once.”

“You didn’t go back another night hoping to get invited up to her room?”

He shook his head. “If you don’t believe me, just ask her. She’ll tell you.”

“We can’t ask her, Felix,” Savage said. “Because someone drugged her and left her out in the snow behind the hotel. She froze to death.”

Felix White Feather stared at him. “Naomi’s dead.”

“Yeah, Naomi’s dead.”

The gambler blinked at him, registering the news.

Savage let the silence drag out.

Suddenly, Felix jumped up. “Oh, no. You ain’t gonna pin this on me. I didn’t have anything to do with her death, I swear. I only ever saw her the one time.”

“Sit down.”

“I just got out of the slammer, man. I’m not going to murder anyone. Do you think I’m crazy? She was a good time, that’s all.”

“Okay, I believe you. Sit down, Felix.”

The big man lowered himself into the steel chair, suspicious eyes glued to Savage.

The Sheriff studied the man across from him. The Frost Killer was an organized, meticulous multiple murderer. He hadn’t been caught in over a decade. They knew he spent time stalking his victims, which meant he would know where the security cameras were in order to avoid them. After years of not being caught, he’d be more confident than ever in his abilities.

None of that described Felix White Feather.

“Okay, just for the record, where were you last Monday night?”

He frowned. “I don’t know.”

“Think. It’s important.”

“I reckon I was at Mac’s Roadhouse,” he said, after scrunching up his forehead for a long moment.

“On a Monday? You a member?” The Roadhouse was a biker bar on Durango Road, farther out past his place. They’d had a few run-ins with the members in the past.

“Not officially, but I ride. Or I used to, before I went away.”

Savage nodded. “Will the bar staff vouch for you?”

“Yeah. I was there till closing.”

That would be easy enough to check out.

“Okay, Mr. White Feather. Thanks for your time.”

“I can go?”

“Yeah, you can go.” Savage opened the folder and slipped the photograph back inside.

Felix glimpsed down in time to see the second photograph, the one of the white guy in the baseball hat. "I remember him."

"What?" Savage narrowed his eyes. "You remember who?"

"That guy. In the other photo."

"This guy?" He moved Felix's picture out of the way. "You're sure?"

"Yeah, man. He was sitting at the slots for hours, acting kinda weird."

"In what way?" Felix had his full attention now.

"He was playing slowly, feeding in one chip at a time, almost like he didn't wanna be there. Most people play in a hurry, you know? They wanna win, not waste time like he was doin'."

"You noticed him because he was playing slowly?"

"Yeah, and 'cause he was looking over at the blackjack table all the time. I thought he was staring at me. Like he knew me or something, but I ain't never seen him before."

"You think he was watching Naomi?" Savage found he was holding his breath.

The man nodded. "I think he was. Yeah."

THIRTY-ONE

"I'M SORRY," Savage said, going straight over to Becca and giving her a hug. He'd left Avril at the office with Littleton, who was making up for his blunder by offering to do another night duty.

Sinclair had left around five to give Evie Stromberg a lift home, and then take her to her boyfriend's house where she was staying the night. He hoped Evie would be safe there. Sinclair had promised to have a word with Richie Vines so he was aware of the potential threat to his girlfriend's life.

Thorpe was still providing protection for Grace Calhoun in addition to working the case. Thanks to his tip-off, they now knew their killer had commissioned the snowflake pendants, rather than made them himself. It had been an odd turn of events, and something none of them had been expecting, but it did open up a potential lead.

Becca hugged him back, but she felt stiff and reserved. Afterwards, she handed Connor to him and disappeared into the bathroom with a glass of wine and a book. He didn't blame her. If their roles were reversed, he'd be mad too.

But there wasn't much he could do other than apologize. Three young women had died, and he was going to do all he could to prevent a fourth death.

Whatever it took.

It was his job. His responsibility. Given the choice again, he'd do the same thing.

He took Connor into the living room and sat down on the couch. Immediately, the baby started crying. After checking his diaper, which was clean, he asked, "You hungry?" It was nearing supper time. "I know I am."

Going back into the kitchen, he made Connor a bottle. That's when he noticed the folder. It was open, his case notes scattered all over the table. Becca had been busy. The folder contained all of Avril's notes that he'd managed to print off, including her research into the previous murders dating back to the first one in Sweden in 2007.

It was a long litany of kills. Four women murdered each year for thirteen years, if you included this one. And the worst part was there was no actual evidence, hardly any witnesses, and very few leads.

Until now.

Savage put Connor in the cot they kept in the kitchen and called Ray. The ME was at home and sounded like he was eating supper. "I hope you don't have another body because I'm halfway through a pot roast, and I'm not getting up."

Savage grinned. "Don't worry, there's no body. Just calling to find out if there's any news on the envelope."

"No prints other than the woman's," he replied. "Sorry, I know that's not the news you were looking for. Was gonna wait until tomorrow to break it to ya."

Savage heaved a disappointed sigh. "You sure?"

"Yep. Whoever handled the envelope wore gloves."

Of course they had. This wasn't a stupid killer. It had been foolish to hope he'd leave a print. "Okay, thanks, Ray." He hung up.

That left only the partial on the pendant itself. They'd run it through AFIS, but it hadn't been enough to render any results. Avril had passed it on to her colleagues at the FBI in Denver. Maybe they'd have more luck.

With Becca in the bath, and Connor dozing in his little bed, Savage decided he'd make himself useful and prepare supper. Opening the refrigerator, he explored the contents. Slim pickings, but then Becca hadn't been to the store in days.

He knew she didn't want to drive in the icy conditions. Earlier that year, she'd had a particularly bad accident when she'd been pushed off the road by a drug-dealing outlaw biker, and she'd been nervous ever since. The recent snow dump had made the roads even more treacherous.

Grimacing, he took out some eggs and cheese. Tonight, it was going to be omelets. That would do until he could get to the store tomorrow. Just to be sure, he knocked on the bathroom door. "How does an omelet sound?"

"Fine with me."

"Fifteen minutes?"

"Okay."

He could tell by her voice she was still upset. Grabbing a beer, he set about making the best damn omelet he could. Connor slept through the entire process, including beating, frying and flipping the eggs. Savage stifled a yawn.

Moving the documents to the side, he set the table. As he was tidying up, he noticed Becca had sorted them into little piles. He'd thought it would be year by year, but instead, she'd taken all the photographs of the pendants out and stacked them together. In a second pile, she'd put all the crime scene photographs, the women posed in situ. Pale and pristine in the snow.

A piece of paper containing questions lay on top of Avril's notes.

Becca's handwriting.

The top few caught his eye.

- Craftsmanship?

- Chain?
- Location?
- Last two years?

HE FROWNED, wondering what she meant. Something about the pendant had piqued her interest, as well as the location of the crimes, and the period the killer had been absent. Well, he'd have to wait until she got out of the bath to find out.

He plated the omelets, then checked Connor, and sat down to wait for Becca. The food was growing cold by the time she emerged from the bathroom in a robe.

"You shouldn't have waited."

"I wanted to."

She raised her eyebrows and sat down. He caught a waft of lavender soap and freshly washed hair.

"I'm sorry this case is so consuming." He reached for her hand, but she pulled it away. "I know it's hard being with Connor all day. I hope you understand that I want to be here, it's just—"

"It's just that this case is important."

He nodded. "It is."

"That's the thing." She sighed. "They always are."

"But this one in particular, it's—"

"I know. I read all about it." She nodded to the documents he'd placed on the countertop.

He hesitated. "What did you think?"

"Are we talking about the case now?" She picked up her knife and fork.

"No. I mean yes. Only if you want to."

"You want to, though."

"I want to hear what you think."

She put her cutlery down again. Savage sensed something big was coming and steeled himself. "When I was pregnant, I told you I didn't want to raise this child alone. You said I wouldn't have to. You said you'd be there for me."

He nodded, remembering that discussion all too clearly. It haunted him. It left him wracked with guilt. "I have to work," he said quietly.

"I know you have to work, Dalton. I'm not asking that you give up your job. All I'm saying is that spending all night at the station isn't good enough." Her eyes filled with tears. "I can't do this on my own. It's too hard."

He took her hand, vaguely alarmed at the tears. It wasn't like Becca to cry. She must be overwrought. "It's only temporary. I know I made you a promise, but I have to stop this guy, Becs, before he kills again. You understand that, don't you?"

She withdrew her hand. "I do, but it doesn't make it any easier. I haven't even been able to go shopping. There's nothing in the house."

More tears. This time they ran down her face.

"I'm going to handle that," he said. "Make me a list, and I'll go shopping later."

She sniffed, wiping her eyes. "Thanks."

"I saw your notes," he said, once she'd recovered and had picked up her knife and fork again.

Becca ate a few mouthfuls, then said, "This is not a bad omelet."

He grinned. "Thanks."

She pointed to the handwritten note on top of the folder. "Pass me my notes?"

He reached over, picked up the handwritten questions, and handed them to her.

She looked down. "About the pendants—"

"Actually, we were discussing them today."

"So, you would have noticed that the first few years are really basic. The snowflakes are jagged and simple in design. You can see they're homemade."

"Agreed."

"After that, he gets a little better at it. He's learning a new craft, refining his skill."

"Yeah, that's what we figured."

"He gets better and better at it. Each year the snowflakes are more intricate, more complex shapes. I think he's enjoying it."

Savage watched her, waiting for what he sensed was coming next. He knew there'd be a 'but' somewhere along the line.

"But then we get to this year."

He smiled.

She stopped. "What?"

"I knew you'd found something."

She shook her head. "I don't know if I have. They just seem different, that's all. The style is different, the shapes are bolder, more flamboyant. Almost like they were made by someone else. That's the only way I can describe it."

"You're incredible, you know that?"

She flushed.

Time to come clean.

"We discovered that he outsourced the snowflakes this year."

Becca stared at him for a long moment. Her reaction was similar to Avril's. "No way."

"Yep. There's an artist in Durango who received the commission. Four snowflakes. One for each of his victims. He emailed her the order and sent the cash in the mail."

"This guy?" She prodded the folder.

"Yeah."

Becca was shaking her head. "Uh-uh."

Savage frowned. "What's so strange about that?"

"This guy"—she picked up the folder–"would *never* outsource the pendants."

Again, her reaction was just like Avril's. "Why not?"

"Why not?" She laughed. "Because he's a perfectionist. He spends months planning for this one season. He researches his victims, studies them, maps their movements. He cuts out his own snowflakes, glues them into the pendant, and attaches it to a silver chain. It's a process. A ritual."

Savage hung on to her every word. It made sense.

She took a photograph out of the folder and passed it to him. “See this chain link? It’s good quality, real silver. He’s been buying chains from the same supplier for years.”

She fished out another photograph. This time of Stephanie Harcourt. “Look at this one. The chain is inferior. Cheap, stainless steel. The chain link pattern is different too. Can you see?”

He squinted at the fragile weave in the chain, a growing sense of unease building in the pit of his stomach.

“There’s more,” she said.

“More?” He inhaled deeply through his nose.

“Look at the locations. First Scandinavia, which is where he’s from, I’m guessing. Then he disappears and re-emerges in the United States, probably because the Scandinavian police got too close.”

“I don’t know about that. They didn't have any viable leads.”

“Well, something made him move here,” Becca said. “Maybe he tried to quit. Make a fresh start. Get away from the person he was.”

“You mean he wanted to stop killing?”

“Possibly.” She shrugged. “Who knows?”

Savage rubbed his stubbly chin. “But he didn’t stop.”

She shook her head. “He couldn’t. The first murders in this country were in Wyoming. That’s where he settled when he came over from Sweden.”

Savage had had the same thought when he’d gone through Avril’s notes. “It gets cold there in the winter.”

“He likes the cold. It reminds him of home.”

Savage stared at her. “How could you possibly know that?”

She shrugged. “Human nature. Actually, it’s an educated guess, but I’m willing to bet I’m right.”

He wouldn’t bet against her. Becca was extremely good at her job. Hell, she’d even got him to open up, and that was saying something.

“The next murders are in Washington, then Minnesota. After that, he moved to Oregon, then New Hampshire. You get my drift?”

“Not really. He’s jumping around.”

"Exactly. He thinks he's being clever by not sticking to a pattern, but that's exactly what's causing the pattern. He's jumping around, going from the west of the country to the east, and then back again."

Savage had to admit, it made sense in a crazy kind of way. "Okay, so he's jumping around, choosing cold climates where there's plenty of snow."

"To preserve the bodies."

"You think that's what he's doing? Preserving them?"

"I'm almost sure of it. The way he poses them, the arms in the funereal position, the pendant. He's taking care of them, worshipping them."

"Now you're being freaky."

She smiled for the first time since he'd walked through the door, and it made him feel slightly better. Everything was going to be all right.

"Except for this time."

Savage frowned, distracted. "What do you mean?"

"Well, he disappeared for two years, right? No sign of him. No murders."

"Right," drawled Savage.

"His last killing spree was in Montana, so by rights, his next should be on the east coast."

"But he's in the west," Savage said, frowning.

She arched an eyebrow. "It goes against the pattern."

Savage processed this while he stared at the picture of Stephanie Harcourt lying in the woods. Her closed, frozen eyes glued shut. Her lips glistening with icy gloss.

Suddenly, he knew what Becca was getting at.

No way.

An arctic chill swept over him.

Was she right?

Was it possible?

He exhaled slowly. "Are you saying what I think you're saying?"

She gave a short nod. "This isn't your original killer. It's a copycat."

THIRTY-TWO

SUPPER WAS NICE.

Rather than being awkward, Thorpe found Grace to be an interesting, articulate person. They talked about her job, teaching at the local high school, and he could tell she loved what she did.

"It makes me feel useful," she admitted, a slight blush to her cheeks. "My family never intended for me to get a proper job. My father wanted me to work for the Foundation, like my mother did, but that never really appealed to me. I know it's charity work, and maybe I'll get more involved one day." She sighed. "But sitting on an executive committee and lunching at the country club every day isn't what I want."

He liked that she had values. Her family's wealth and heritage hadn't skewed her thinking. She was still a hard-working, normal person, despite it all.

In return, he found himself telling her a little bit about his background, and how he came to be in Hawk's Landing. "I was born in Nashville," he said, declining a glass of wine. "No, thanks. I'm on duty."

"I could tell you weren't from here by your accent." She smiled, pouring herself a small glass. "It's softer than ours."

He found himself grinning.

"What was it like? Nashville?"

"Loud, vibrant, musical. My parents were both musicians, so my childhood was full of sounds, instruments, and—" He rolled his eyes. "Band practice. There was always something going on, always people around." He shrugged. "I was a nerdy kid, more interested in math and computers than anything else. My parents didn't understand. They devoted all their time to my sister, who was more like them. She's a singer now." Winona Thorpe was becoming a household name in Nashville. She loved the limelight. He'd always shied away from attention.

"How come you joined the police force?" Grace asked. He liked that she didn't fixate on his musical heritage. Most people found that way more interesting than law enforcement.

"My grandfather. He was a retired sheriff and used to tell me stories about his days on the force. It sounded so exciting, and with the way the world was going, I knew there was a need for a logical, data-driven approach to crime-solving." He grimaced. God, that sounded boring, even to himself.

Thankfully, she didn't seem to mind. "How did you end up here, in our little backwater?"

"I joined the Nashville Sheriff's Office, but they didn't share my approach to policing. The Sheriff was very traditional, and he thought I was wasting time analyzing data to solve cases."

"He sounds like a narrow-minded man."

Thorpe smiled. "Yes, he was. Anyway, we were butting heads the whole time, and it created a toxic environment. Eventually, I decided to leave. Sheriff Savage ended up following a case out to my neck of the woods. We connected on it. Found we worked well together. At the end of it, he offered me a job. Figured Hawk's Landing might be a better fit. And, as they say, the rest is history."

She waved a hand around. "You swapped the vibrant city lights of Nashville for space, snow and silence."

He chuckled. "It hasn't been that quiet."

"No, of course not. I'm sure you see a totally different side to our town."

Since he'd arrived, he'd hunted down two serial killers, a ruthless gang leader, and a mob boss out for vengeance. Life definitely had not been dull. "I see more action than I ever did in Nashville."

"It's a dangerous job, Deputy. I think you're very brave."

He tried to look modest. "Nah, not really."

She gave a rueful smile.

There was a brief pause, then she said, "I feel so much safer with you here – and it's nice having someone to cook for. It's been... it's been a while."

He felt himself getting hot. "Same for me."

They gazed at each other for a moment, then Thorpe cleared his throat and looked away. "I'd better get back to work. Thank you for this." He gestured to their empty plates. "It was delicious."

"Oh, it was nothing, really." She got up to clear away the dishes.

"Here, let me help."

Together, they loaded the dishwasher, and she poured herself another small glass of wine. "I'm going to take a bath," she said, after they were done. "So, I'll say goodnight."

He wished he hadn't just pictured her naked in the bathtub.

Swallowing his awkwardness, he said, "Okay. I'll be down here. Sleep well."

She flashed him a shy look. "Goodnight, Deputy."

"You can call me James."

"Okay. Goodnight, James." She smiled as she said his name.

"Goodnight, Grace."

The house was dark. Thorpe walked around downstairs, peering out of the windows at the street outside, and then the forested slopes beyond the property. The lights were out, the bottom part of the house in darkness, other than a small lamp he'd left on in the living room.

He'd been reading the case files, going back to 2007 and marveling at the level of detail in Agent Dahl's research. She really had put everything into hunting this man, the Frost Killer.

It was an appropriate name, even though he didn't approve of giving criminals nicknames, as the media were so fond of doing. Killing at the start of every winter, after the first snowfall. Regimented, like clockwork.

He imagined the killer to be someone like himself with great attention to detail, driven by data. A planner. Leaving nothing to chance. That's what made this last spate of murders even more puzzling.

The Sheriff was going by the theory that the killer had slept with one of his victims, Naomi Madden. They had CCTV photographs of a potential suspect leaving her room, head down, looking furtive. Clearly not wanting to be seen by the cameras.

That seemed messy to him. Risky. Not a chance this killer would take.

Thorpe pondered this as he checked the French doors to make sure they were locked. Why now? Why had the killer breached protocol and had sex with his target?

Had he always wanted to, but resisted? For twelve years?

He scowled into the darkness. There was no sexual motive for these attacks. None of the victims were sexually assaulted. Quite the opposite. They were made to look beautiful, laid out in the snow like angels, their hair positioned around them, their arms folded over their chests.

Peaceful.

Preserved in ice.

The sex thing didn't make sense. It didn't add up. Thorpe made a mental note to bring it up with Savage and the team in the morning.

He'd just sat down again when a faint scraping sound made him freeze. He listened hard.

There it was again.

A quiet clanging, like someone fiddling with a lock.

Drawing his weapon, he crept through the house toward the sound. It was coming from the kitchen. The window maybe?

Entering the darkened room, he heard the gentle whirring of the dishwasher and smelled lemony detergent from the pot Grace had cleaned before going to bed.

There it was again.

Scrape. Scrape.

He strained his eyes to see through the darkness. Was that a shadow at the window?

There was a soft grunt as the lock gave out and the window creaked open.

Thorpe gripped his gun. Standing behind the kitchen door in the darkest part of the room, he waited until the figure had entered the house. If he arrested him now, it would be breaking, but not necessarily entering. Crooks did everything in their power to get off these days. He had to be certain when he nabbed this guy that he would go down for good.

Was this the Frost Killer?

Had he come for Grace Calhoun, his fourth and final victim?

The dark shape glided over the window ledge and jumped down onto the tiled floor. Thorpe flicked on the light and pointed his firearm at the intruder.

"Freeze! Put your hands up where I can see them."

THIRTY-THREE

"JEFF?" Grace, alerted by the noise, darted into the kitchen. "What are you doing?"

"You know this guy?" Thorpe hesitated, then when she nodded, he lowered his gun.

The intruder glared at Thorpe. "Who are you?"

Five ten, a hundred and sixty pounds, very little muscle. He could take him, easy. Thorpe holstered his weapon. "Deputy Thorpe. Who are you?"

"I'm Grace's boyfriend."

Boyfriend.

Hang on a minute.

He turned to Grace. "Is this true?"

Her hands balled into little fists. "Jeff is *not* my boyfriend. We broke up over a year ago."

"Then why is he here?" Thorpe frowned as his brain went into overdrive. This wasn't the killer. There was someone else after Grace.

What were the chances?

"I just want to talk to you," Jeff pleaded, turning to Grace. "You won't answer my calls."

"So you break in?"

"It was the only way to see you."

"I told you to leave me alone," she fumed, eyes blazing.

Thorpe hadn't realized she could get so angry. He kinda liked it.

"What part of 'leave me alone' don't you get?"

"Has he been bothering you?" Thorpe tried to read the situation, but he didn't know how much of a threat this guy was. Grace was obviously afraid of him.

"No!" cried Jeff.

Grace nodded.

Thorpe turned to her. "Grace, what's going on?"

She gave an exasperated sigh. "He took our breakup really badly and began following me around, harassing me. He wouldn't leave me alone, so I took out a restraining order against him."

Thorpe's eyebrows shot up.

Restraining order? They hadn't picked up on that.

"I thought that was the end of it, but the other day, I saw his car parked outside the school, and I knew he was still stalking me."

"Are you seeing someone else?" Jeff scowled at Thorpe.

"This is my bodyguard," she retorted, her gaze flicking to Thorpe's. "He's protecting me, not sleeping with me."

Thorpe wished she hadn't said that.

Jeff took in the uniform, badge and gun, then said, "What do you need protecting from?"

"You, for one." She shook her head.

"Is that why you agreed to this?" Thorpe asked quietly. "Because you were afraid of him."

She gave a shameful nod. "I'm sorry. I didn't mean to lie. I mean, I am worried about that serial killer, obviously, but I knew Jeff had been watching me. I could sense it. He'd been in my house, gone through my drawers. I could smell him in the bedroom." She wrinkled her nose.

"I have not been in your house," Jeff blurted out.

"I know it was you."

"How?" asked Thorpe. "How do you know it was Jeff?"

She seemed surprised. “Who else would rifle through my underwear? Use my perfume. I could smell it, hanging in the air. You used to comment on it all the time.”

“Grace, I did not break into your house,” he repeated.

“I just caught you,” Thorpe reminded him.

“This wasn’t breaking in. I just wanted to talk.”

Thorpe took out his handcuffs and attached them to Jeff’s wrists. “You’re under arrest.” He read him his rights.

“Hey, man, you can’t arrest me!”

“Sure, I can. You just committed a criminal offense. I’m taking you down to the station to book you.”

Jeff shot a pleading glance at Grace, but she looked away. “You know what, Deputy Thorpe. You do what you’ve got to do. I’m glad this happened. I’m glad it’s finally over. Now, maybe he’ll leave me alone.”

“I’m sorry, Grace,” Thorpe said, “but you’re going to have to come with me.”

“Me? Why?”

“Well, you’ll have to give a statement, for one, but I also can’t leave you alone in the house. My job is to protect you.”

“You’ve caught the intruder. I’ll be fine now.”

Thorpe grimaced. “We can’t be sure it was Jeff who broke into your house those other times. You asked who would rifle through your things, use your perfume? Well, the killer might. That's just the sort of thing a man like him would do.”

She turned pale. “I think you’re overreacting, James.”

He paused at the intimate use of his name. “I don't think so. We know he stalks his victims, gets to know their routines. That feeling you had about being watched, that might not just have been Jeff. It could have been him.”

“What killer?” Jeff asked, but both Thorpe and Grace ignored him.

She stared at him for a long moment, her gaze raking his face. After a beat, she said, “Okay, I’ll get dressed.”

Thorpe exhaled, quietly relieved as she ran upstairs to change.

"What killer?" Jeff asked again.

"I can't discuss an active case," Thorpe snapped.

Jeff gasped. "Holy shit! You mean that psycho that's freezing all those women? The one in the newspaper."

Thorpe's heart sank.

Here we go.

"Is he after Grace? Hey, man. If he's after Grace, you gotta let me go. I can protect her."

"You have the right to remain silent," Thorpe reminded him. "I suggest you use it before you get yourself into even more trouble."

He shut up after that.

Grace came downstairs in jeans and a cream turtleneck with a thick, navy fleece over the top. She'd brushed her hair, and it hung straight and blonde over her shoulders. She looked very pretty, in a casual kind of way. It was a far cry from the prim schoolteacher image. He wondered which persona was the real her.

"Let's go," he said, leading Jeff out to the police vehicle.

Grace followed after locking up behind them.

Thorpe secured Jeff in the backseat.

Grace climbed into the passenger seat. As they drove away, Thorpe noticed a dark SUV parked farther down the road. It hadn't been there when he'd arrived this afternoon, nor when he'd done his rounds earlier that evening.

As they passed it, he thought he saw a dark shadow duck down out of sight, but he could be mistaken. It may have been a reflection of the streetlight. An uneasy feeling settled over him, and he mentally noted the car's number plate as they drove off. It was probably nothing, but then again, this had been one helluva strange night.

THIRTY-FOUR

THE KILLER DUCKED down as the deputy drove past, swearing under his breath.

Shit.

Not. Good.

Had they made him?

He'd been sitting there patiently, waiting for his chance to act, but it had been snatched away from him by some overweight buffoon breaking in via the kitchen window.

What an idiot.

The killer had spent days on this, hovering in the shadows, watching Grace Calhoun, learning her schedule. He'd enjoyed it too. She was an enigma. So prim and proper on the outside, but soft and sensual on the inside. When she thought nobody was watching, she let her hair down. Dancing around the kitchen to classical music, opening the patio doors and staring out into the night, listening to the wind blowing through the trees. In the middle of winter, too.

Who did that?

He liked that she was quirky, complicated, not all she seemed.

Under normal circumstances, she was exactly the type of woman he'd be interested in romantically.

It was a shame, really, that he had to kill her.

He'd nearly taken her then, through the open patio doors, but the timing hadn't been quite right. It was too soon. Too soon after Naomi.

While he didn't mind the killing, he didn't enjoy it. Not like his namesake, the Frost Killer. That man had a penchant for murder. Patience, attention to detail, obsessive behaviors. But then the Frost Killer had killed all of those girls because he was sick. He couldn't help it.

No, for him this was all a means to an end. His agenda didn't involve a sick need to snuff out a life, or to preserve the bodies in a certain way, forever etched in his fucked-up memory. Oh, he'd read the news reports and the psychobabble. He even agreed with some of it. There was no doubt about it, that guy was disturbed.

Not like him.

One thought bothered him. How had the Sheriff's Department been so sure he was going after Grace? He'd been so careful.

Then again, it didn't take a genius to figure out how he'd selected his victims. He'd hoped the Frost Killer's MO would confuse them for a while, but they were cleverer than he thought. That Sheriff Savage was a smart guy. Or maybe it was that FBI agent, Dahl. No flies on her.

He snorted.

The Frost Killer's first victim's daughter. All grown up and an FBI agent, hunting the man who'd destroyed her life.

What a cliché.

It was kinda sad, actually. She wasn't bad looking, if you looked past the oversized clothing and nerdy glasses. Come to think of it, she was like her mother. She fit the profile.

But he was done here.

Grace would be his last victim.

As long as they still thought he was the Frost Killer. If they'd figured out these murders weren't related...

A chill passed over him.

Then he was in more trouble than he thought.

He clenched the steering wheel, the frustration of the botched evening getting to him. Tonight was supposed to be *the* night. He'd steeled himself, mentally prepared for what was going to happen. Despite what the press wrote about him, it didn't come easily, taking a life. It wasn't as hard as it should've been, either, but it wasn't easy. He was proud of that. It meant he was still human. On some level.

At one point, not so long ago, he'd thought life had knocked all the emotion out of him. That there was no empathy left. His crappy upbringing, his mother's drug habit, the men she'd brought around to the hovel they called a house. Her overdose, the social services, the abuse.

He could keep a psychologist in business for decades.

It was amazing he hadn't turned out to be some sick serial killer like his nemesis. Then he smiled at the irony.

He couldn't be fixed. There was no cure for what he had. Life had dealt him a bad hand, and the only thing that would ease his pain was making it right. And to do that, he had to go back to the beginning.

Yet this fat bastard had messed all that up. Now the lawman had glimpsed his car. He'd seen his quick look in the rearview mirror. The white face glancing back at his vehicle. Had there been enough time to take down the number plate?

He slammed a hand onto the wheel. Why hadn't he covered it up? Because he'd thought he was safe, that's why. Never in a million years had he expected some other dude to break into Grace Calhoun's place and for that Sheriff's Deputy to come out with the guy in cuffs.

It should have been him. *She* should have been his. It had been planned down to the finest detail. While he'd been waiting, he'd bitten his nails down to the quick. Now he picked at the inflamed stumps.

What to do?

He had to get out of here and ditch the car. That was the first step. If the deputy had clocked his plate, it wouldn't be long before they came knocking.

The killer started the SUV, performed a U-turn, and drove silently down the street. The neighborhood was dark and quiet. Once he was out of the immediate area, he put his foot down and gunned it toward the reservation. He'd leave the car there. Anyone who asked would assume it had been stolen.

The casino was lit up like a Christmas tree, an oasis in the barren desert of the reservation. He wasn't against it. It provided jobs for the indigenous people and temptation for the desperate and the weak.

He wasn't weak.

Gambling held no enticement for him. The killer had no intention of throwing his money away. He'd worked too hard for it. Nope, he had bigger plans. Much bigger. If only he could pull off this last kill. Then the pattern would be complete. Then he could get on with his life.

Damn the Sheriff's Office for putting a protective detail on Grace. Damn that idiot for breaking in.

Now he had to wait.

Again.

He exhaled noisily. It didn't matter. He'd been waiting most of his life for this. A few more days wouldn't make any difference.

THIRTY-FIVE

SAVAGE SLIPPED in through the side door, avoiding the mob of reporters who'd doubled in size. It was all over the news, too, how the Frost Killer was hunting girls in the southern Colorado town of Hawk's Landing. The bit that irked him the most was the insinuation that the sheriff's department didn't seem to have any leads.

What did they know?

Expecting to find his team hard at work, he was surprised to find Grace Calhoun asleep on the sofa in his office and Thorpe grilling a suspect in the interrogation room.

"What's going on?" he asked Sinclair.

"Beats me. I've just got here."

"Same," said Littleton, who'd gone home to catch a few hours of sleep before coming back to the office.

"Is that Grace Calhoun?" Barb whispered, coming out of his office. He'd forgotten he'd given her the spare key.

"Yes, and before you ask, I've got no idea what she's doing there."

Thorpe finally emerged from the corridor leading to the interrogation rooms. "Mornin'," he said.

"You look like hell," Sinclair said.

"Thanks."

He clearly hadn't slept and had dark shadows beneath his eyes, stubble almost as long as Savage's, and a wrinkled uniform.

"Thorpe?" Savage raised an eyebrow.

He collapsed at his desk. "You won't believe the night I've had."

"Who's in the cell?" asked Sinclair. "Is it him? Did someone try to break in?"

"Yes, but it's not what you think."

Savage shook his head. "You'd better explain."

"It's Grace's ex-boyfriend." He coughed. "I mean, Miss Calhoun's ex-boyfriend. He's been stalking her. Last night, he broke into her house, violating a restraining order. Also, I think I may have seen our killer."

Thorpe paused to take a breath.

Savage turned his thoughts from the copycat theory to what Thorpe was saying. The last bit jumped out at him. "You saw the killer. How?"

"The ex-boyfriend noticed a black SUV parked outside her house on more than one occasion. I saw it too, on the way here. I thought there was someone inside, but I could be wrong."

"You get the plate?" Savage asked.

"Yeah. I'm running it now."

"Good job. Let me know what you find."

"Will do. Um, what do you want me to do with Jeff?"

"Who?"

"Jeff. The ex."

Savage shrugged. "You caught him breaking and entering. Book him."

Avril came in through the front, once again pink-faced and disheveled. He ought to give her a spare key too, just while the press was camped outside, but first, he had something he needed to say.

"Listen up." He closed the door to his office. Grace Calhoun was still fast asleep on the sofa. "There's something I want to run by you."

They turned to face him. Avril took off her coat and sat down, folding her arms across her chest.

"This might come as a shock," he began, "but I spoke with Becca last night, and she thinks we've got a copycat."

There was a stunned silence.

"A copycat?" Sinclair was the first to react. "You mean this isn't the Frost Killer we've been chasing?"

"I don't believe it is, no. The thing with the pendants, the way he painstakingly makes his own then suddenly goes out and buys them, it doesn't make sense."

"You're right," said Thorpe. "I was thinking about that too. This guy is meticulous, he plans everything to the nth degree. There's no way he'd buy the pendants just to save himself time. Then, there's the way he slept with the third victim, Naomi. The real Frost Killer has never slept with a victim before. Has he?" He turned to Avril, who shook her head.

"Then there's the two-year absence. What happened?" Savage looked around the room. "My guess is the original killer is either in prison or dead. A man like that doesn't stop. He can't. It's an obsession. Something happened to make him stop."

Avril still hadn't said a word.

"But the MO," Littleton stammered. "The way he poses the bodies, the snow, the pendant. It's identical. How did he know?"

"There are news articles online about the original Frost Killer," Sinclair said. "I've been reading them. A couple of true crime podcasts too, you know those ones on serial killers. It's not hard to dig up information on him if you really want to. His MO, the pendants, how he kills his victims, it's all there if you know where to look."

Avril stared bleakly ahead of her.

"Avril, are you okay?" Savage shot her a worried look. She'd gone incredibly pale. Her lip was trembling too, which wasn't a good sign.

"I—I need some air." She got up, grabbed her coat and stumbled toward the door.

The reporters, sensing someone was coming out, surged forward, their cameras ready.

"Avril, don't go out that way," he called, but it was too late. She'd slammed her hand down on the buzzer, and the doors hissed open.

"For goodness' sake."

Avril fought her way through the barrage and out into the street.

"Avril!" he yelled, but she kept going.

He was besieged by questions.

Sheriff Savage, do you know who he is yet?

Do you have a man in custody?

Is he the Frost Killer, Sheriff?

Savage marched forward and bulldozed into the front line of journalists.

"Get out!" he yelled at them. "Out of the building. Nobody is allowed into the lobby. Is that clear?" He kept going, shepherding them out with his arms spread wide. Enough was enough. They stumbled backwards in their haste to get out of his way. One reporter tripped and fell onto her backside. Cursing, Savage reached down and helped her up.

"I'll issue a statement when I'm ready," he told them. "Anyone who steps foot into this building is going to be arrested for trespassing."

When the last reporter was outside, he slammed the door shut, and marched back inside. "Avril's gone."

"Poor dear is upset," said Barb. "But then, I'd be too if I'd spent ten years chasing a serial killer only to find out it wasn't him."

"It's got to be tough for her," Savage said.

"Embarrassing too," added Sinclair. "She came all this way, adamant it was the man who'd killed her mother, and all the time it was just a copycat."

"But why?" asked Thorpe. "Why would anyone emulate the Frost Killer? If he got caught, he'd go down for all those other murders too."

Savage had thought about this. "Maybe because he wants to disguise the real reason for murdering Anita, Stephanie, and Naomi."

Sinclair tilted her head toward him. "Which is?"

He sighed. "I don't know yet, but I think it's got something to do with their families."

"A historical connection?"

"Yeah. It must be. Something to do with their legacy, their land or their status. That's the one thing the victims have in common."

There was a pause as they pondered this.

"What's going on?" came a voice from behind them, making them jump.

Grace.

Savage had forgotten she was still here.

Thorpe smiled at her. "You're up."

"Yes, I feel much better. Thank you, Sheriff, for letting me take a nap on your couch."

"You're welcome."

Now she was here, he wasn't quite sure what to do with her. They couldn't send her back home, not with the killer still on the loose.

"Did you arrest Jeff?" Grace asked Thorpe.

He nodded. "Yeah, we had to."

"Good. He deserves it, the stupid idiot. Hopefully this'll teach him a lesson."

Savage raised his eyebrows.

"Okay, so what now?" Sinclair asked, steering them back to the investigation. To Savage's surprise, Grace wandered over to Thorpe's desk and sat down on a spare chair.

Savage decided he'd deal with her later. "Now, we look at the crimes in isolation. Treat them like a new investigation. Victim backgrounds, partner checks, bank accounts, cellphone data, the works." He turned to Thorpe. "I'm going to need you on this one, Thorpe. There's a lot of data to crunch."

"Yes, sir."

It felt good to be doing something proactive again. "Any luck on that partial print?"

"Avril didn't mention anything," Sinclair said, with a wry grimace.

He'd give her some time to process, then call her. They still needed her FBI contacts, even though he was pretty sure they were finally on the right track. Thanks to Becca.

"I've got a hit on that plate," Thorpe said as his computer beeped.

Grace looked up. "Was that the SUV parked outside my place last night?"

Thorpe nodded.

"Who does it belong to?" Savage asked.

"You won't believe this," he said quietly, looking up from his screen.

"Who?" urged Sinclair.

Thorpe's eyes widened. "Logan Maddox."

THIRTY-SIX

"LOGAN MADDOX?" Savage stared at him.

"Yeah, if can you believe it. The bastard was sitting outside Grace's house."

"But I checked out his alibis," Sinclair interrupted. "He was in the clear."

"Are we saying he's the killer?" Littleton asked, confused.

Sinclair was shaking her head. "Someone must have lied."

Savage pulled up a chair. "Let's go through them one by one."

"Okay." Sinclair brought up the report on her computer. "For Anita Cullen's murder, he told us he was at the West Mountain Ski Resort. He had lunch with the victim, and after she left, at three fifteen in the afternoon, he took the ski lift up the mountain to do some free skiing."

"Free skiing? So, nobody can vouch for him?" Savage narrowed his eyes.

"Also, we only have his word that Anita Cullen left the resort at three fifteen," Thorpe pointed out. "What if she left earlier?"

"I was going to check with the restaurant," Sinclair said, looking downcast, "but Agent Dahl arrived, and suddenly, we were looking for someone different."

Savage cringed. Avril's insistence that they were looking for a serial offender meant they'd ruled Logan Maddox out. He was in his early thirties, at most, which meant he could never have committed those murders in Scandinavia fifteen years ago.

"Don't worry, it's not your fault," Savage reasoned.

"We know she was in the Bouncing Bean at around three thirty," Littleton said.

Sinclair exhaled. "Yes, that's right. The timing fits with what Logan told us, but I'll get on to the restaurant now, anyway, just to check." She reached for the phone.

Thorpe brought up a map of the West Mountain. "This is interesting," he said, leaning in to take a closer look.

Savage turned to study his screen.

"There's a run that goes down the back of the mountain to the Thompsons' ranch."

Sinclair put down the phone while Littleton stared at him. "You mean he could have got there by skiing down the mountain?"

"Satan's Spine," Grace said. "I've heard of it. That's a dangerous run, especially at this time of year and with the snowfall we've had. I doubt anyone could have made it down there in one piece."

"He is a ski instructor," Sinclair argued. "If anyone could make it, he could." It was no secret she didn't like Logan Maddox.

Grace shrugged. "Maybe. If he's very, very good."

Savage frowned. "If he made that run, he would've skied to the barn and then somehow got back to the resort."

"The resort has snowmobiles," Sinclair pointed out. "I saw them when Avril and I went back to question Maddox."

Savage pondered this for a moment. "Anita was taken in broad daylight off the main street. We found her abandoned vehicle in the parking lot."

"Maybe she went for a cross-country ski," Littleton suggested. "She could have had a second set of skis."

"Her parents would know." It was a good idea. "Littleton, call and ask them."

They waited while he made the call. Savage found it hard to marshal his thoughts given the new information they were considering.

"Yes, sir," Littleton said into the phone. "That's good to know. Thank you."

"So?" asked Savage, when he'd hung up.

Littleton nodded. "She kept her best skis in her car, that pair at the resort was her backup."

Sinclair exhaled. "Holy crap."

"Then her skis are missing," Savage murmured. "They weren't in her car, and they weren't at the barn, which means the killer must have them."

"Should I get a search warrant for Logan Maddox's chalet at the resort?" Sinclair asked.

Savage nodded. "Yeah, but first, let's go over his alibis for Stephanie Harcourt and Naomi Madden's murders? I want to be sure about this. And Barb, see if you can get hold of Agent Dahl. That partial might belong to Logan Maddox."

Sinclair took a deep breath. "He took a ski group up the mountain at eight o'clock on the morning Stephanie was found. I spoke to that woman who confirmed he was on time."

"A woman," said Savage, raising an eyebrow. "If he asked one of his floozies to lie for him, do you think they would?"

Sinclair colored. "I feel so stupid. Of course. He's probably slept with half the women he's taught."

"See if you can talk to the rest of the group," Savage said. "He can't have slept with all of them."

Sinclair bit her lip and nodded.

"What about Naomi?"

She cleared her throat. "He said he was in the bar at the resort all evening. His boss vouched for him."

"Oh, yeah. That Lambert guy. Is he trustworthy?"

"He owns the resort," Sinclair said. "Why would he lie?"

"Talk to him again," Savage said. "If he's covering for Logan, we need to know why. In the meantime, Littleton, get that search warrant."

IT WAS midday when Sinclair pulled up in front of the West Mountain Ski Resort clubhouse. She was still kicking herself. How could she have been so dumb? Every one of Logan's alibis was bullshit, and she'd fallen for all his lies.

Of course, they hadn't seriously considered him a suspect until now, so she hadn't been as diligent as usual, but that was thanks to Agent Dahl's curveball that threw them all off course.

The poor woman had been so desperate to catch her mother's killer that she hadn't stopped to look at the murders in isolation. To be fair, the MO had been exactly the same. Sinclair could see how she'd been fooled. How they all had.

Despite her initial dislike of the FBI agent, she'd come to realize Avril wasn't a bad person, just very single-minded in pursuit of her goal. Her entire life had been dedicated to finding her mother's killer, and as a result, she didn't have time for anything else.

It was also very sad. To come all this way, to get your hopes up, only to find out you're chasing the wrong guy.

"Deputy Sinclair, isn't it?"

Sinclair had been so lost in her own thoughts, she hadn't heard anyone approaching. "Yes?" She spun around, nearly tripping over a mound of snow.

"I'm sorry," came the laughing reply. "I didn't mean to startle you."

"Oh, Mr. Lambert."

The handsome boss of the ski resort smiled at her. "Yes, can I help you with something?"

"Actually, I'm here to see you. Do you mind if we go somewhere and talk?"

He seemed surprised. "Sure, we can go to my office. Is everything all right?"

"Yes, just a few questions. It won't take long."

She followed him past the reception area, through the pub-style restaurant, and down a long corridor that led to the administrative offices.

"This is me." He held open the door for her.

"Thanks." She walked into a wide, spacious office with lovely big windows overlooking a muddy carpark. Pity about the view.

"Take a seat." Once she was seated, he said, "Now, how can I help you, Deputy?"

"It's about Logan Maddox," she began.

He sighed. "Haven't we already had this discussion?"

"Yes, we did, but I need you to clarify something. Do you remember when you said you saw Logan in the bar, last Monday?"

"Yes." He drew out the word.

"What time was that? I'm going to need you to be as precise as possible."

His forehead crinkled as he thought back. "It was about five o'clock," he said. "I can't be absolutely sure about the time, but it was after he'd finished his last lesson of the day. The guests like to have a drink with the instructors after their session. Après-ski, as the French say."

Five o'clock was when Naomi Madden was last seen at the casino. "Was he here all evening?"

"Yes, I think so. I saw him later that night."

"Do you remember when?"

"Oh, gosh. It gets so busy in the bar, it's hard to tell."

"It's important, Mr. Lambert. Was it seven or eight o'clock, or more like ten or eleven?"

"I'd say more like ten or eleven. I had some work to do, so I came to my office, and then went back for a nightcap, before heading to my cabin."

"You live here at the resort?"

"Yeah, of course. Most of the permanent staff do. It helps to be on hand."

"I see. Okay, well thank you, Mr. Lambert. You've been very helpful." Sinclair got up, her mind whirling. If Lambert had only seen Logan again after ten o'clock, that meant their suspect had enough time to drive to the reservation, kill Naomi, and get back to the bar in time to make sure his boss saw him, thereby giving him the perfect alibi.

"I'd say it's a pleasure, but I must be honest, Deputy Sinclair, I don't like what you're insinuating. I've seen the newspapers, and I know all about your Frost Killer. Logan Maddox is a good guy, not some psychopathic murderer. It's a ridiculous notion."

"We're just ruling him out." Sinclair flashed him a bright smile before leaving his office. "Thanks again for your time."

THIRTY-SEVEN

SAVAGE STOOD outside Logan Maddox's apartment, Sinclair beside him, search warrant in hand. The suspect stared back at them, confused and disheveled.

"What is this about?" He wore sweatpants and a long-sleeved top with a ski logo on it. His hair was ruffled, and it looked like he'd just woken up despite it being three-thirty in the afternoon.

"We're here to conduct a search of your premises," Savage said, handing it to him.

Logan glanced at it, then frowned. "I don't understand."

"It's simple," Sinclair said. "This gives us the legal right to search your apartment, which is what we're going to do right now." She brushed past him.

"Hey!"

"Wait here," Savage ordered, following her in.

"Not bad for resort accommodation," said Sinclair, looking around. The living room was modern and spacious with large steel-framed windows looking out onto the jagged mountain peaks and sweeping ski runs.

"I'll take the bedroom," Savage said, while Sinclair went to work in the living room.

"What are you looking for?" Logan was still standing by the front door. At least he could follow instructions.

Nobody answered him.

"Got any skis?" Savage asked, coming back. There was nothing incriminating in the bedroom. Nothing belonging to Anita Cullen; no jacket, no phone, no skis. But then, he doubted the killer would be so stupid as to keep them in his apartment.

"Yeah, sure."

"Where are they?"

"Outside, in the rack."

"Show me."

Logan leaned around the door and pointed to a wooden ski rack standing against the wall. "Those are mine, the yellow Backcountry ones."

"Who do these belong to?" He pointed to the various other sets of skis and snowboards in the rack.

He rubbed his eyes. "You want me to tell you who they all belong to?"

"If you could, yeah."

Logan shook his head. "You guys are nuts." But he rattled off several names that Sinclair wrote down in her phone.

"Where can I find these people?" she asked.

"Here." He blinked at her. "They all live here."

"Okay, thanks." She looked at Savage. "See you later."

He nodded.

While she was checking up on the skis, he searched the bathroom and kitchen, not that he expected to find anything. And he didn't. The place was clean.

"Okay, we're done here," he said, hiding his disappointment.

"You sure?" mocked Logan. "You don't want to search my car too?"

Savage's eyebrows shot up. The search warrant didn't cover his vehicle. "Actually, now that you mention it."

"I'm kidding." Logan gave an annoyed shrug. "Anyway, my car was stolen two nights ago. They found it out on the rez. Can you believe that?"

Savage stopped what he was doing. "Stolen? Two nights ago?" That was when Thorpe had seen it outside Grace Calhoun's house.

"Yeah. Taillight's busted, so it's in the shop. I'm getting it back tomorrow."

"Did you report it stolen?" he asked.

"No, because I got a call from a guy called Tomahawk at the Tribal Police before I'd even realized it was missing. No point in reporting it after it's been found, is there?"

"Guess not."

Savage studied Logan, trying to work out whether he was telling the truth. Was it possible someone had stolen his vehicle to watch Grace, and to commit the next murder? Or was he just a phenomenally good liar?

"Where were you when your SUV went missing?"

"Halfway up a mountain, I imagine. Like I told you, I didn't even know it was missing until I got the call. Sometimes I don't leave the resort for days."

"Where do you keep your vehicle?"

"In the resort parking lot, behind the club house. That's where we all park."

"I see." He paused. "Have you ever skied Satan's Spine?"

Logan took a moment to processes the change in direction of the conversation. "Yeah, once or twice, why?"

"Could you do it in this weather?"

Logan looked at him as if he were nuts. "No way, man. Not even the crazies attempt Satan's this time of year. You'd be signing your own death warrant."

. . .

"LOGAN MADDOX IS NOW our primary suspect," Savage announced, when he and Sinclair got back to the station. "He claims his car was stolen two nights ago, which is just too convenient for my liking."

"It's what I'd do if I were caught watching someone and my license plate was clocked," Thorpe said, earning himself a sideways glance from Grace, who was sitting quietly in the corner, reading a book. Every now and then she'd glance up, they'd discuss something, and she'd go back to reading. Savage had given up trying to persuade her to leave. In fact, her quiet presence was reassuring. At least if she was with them in here, he knew she wasn't out there being murdered.

"Hypothetically, speaking," he added hastily.

"I spoke to several members of his tour group," Sinclair said. "And he was late the morning Stephanie Harcourt died. The woman who covered for him had a crush on him." She shook her head. "I should've seen that coming."

"What about Anita Cullen's death?" said Thorpe. "Did you check if he was telling the truth?"

"Hard to tell," Savage said, gnawing his lower lip. "I asked him about Satan's Spine, and while he admitted to doing it before, he said it was madness to attempt it this time of year."

Grace nodded in agreement.

"But he could have done it," said Sinclair. "That's the point here. Every one of his alibis has a hole in them."

"Why would he want to kill all these women?" Littleton asked. "I mean, what's his motive?"

It was a good question, and one Savage had been battling with since he'd executed the search warrant. "That's what we've got to find out," he said, quietly. "There was no evidence at his apartment. We didn't find Anita's skis, or any of her other personal belongings."

"Which, if you were dating someone, is kinda odd," cut in Sinclair. "You'd think she'd have left something there."

"According to Logan, they weren't really dating," Thorpe pointed out.

"Yeah, she was just another one of his conquests." Sinclair pulled a face.

"Are we sure he's after me?" Grace said, speaking directly to Savage for the first time since he'd been back.

He gave a curt nod. "Pretty sure. It's either you or Evie. There's nobody else."

"It's your house he was watching," Thorpe reminded her. "It's also possible he was inside, going through your things."

She shivered, then straightened her shoulders. "What if I were to go home?"

"Out of the question," Thorpe said, straight away. "Not unless I come with you."

She shot him a grateful smile. "Hear me out. He's not going to come after me if I'm here, is he?"

"That's the whole point," Thorpe said.

"Then how are you going to catch him?"

Savage began to see where she was going with this. "We're going to get evidence of his last three murders and arrest him for those. We're not going to use you as bait. It's far too dangerous."

"Isn't that what you've been trying to do all day?" She looked from Savage to Thorpe and then across to Sinclair. "There doesn't seem to be any real evidence against him."

"We have the footage from the Ridgewater Casino," Sinclair said.

"Won't hold up in court," Savage barked.

"What about his car?" Thorpe tried.

"He's already told us it was stolen," Savage replied. "It's not enough."

"We could bring him in for questioning," Sinclair suggested. "Ask him face to face."

"We could, but what if he doesn't break? Then we've achieved nothing. We'll have to let him go after twenty-four hours."

Sinclair shook her head. "So he can try again?"

"Exactly," Grace burst out.

Savage and Sinclair turned on her at the same time.

She gazed back at them, lifting her chin in defiance. "The only way you can be sure it's him is if he tries again."

"No way," snapped Thorpe. "The Sheriff already said we're not using you to get to him."

Grace rose out of her chair. "If you want this to be over quickly, it's the only way."

There was a heavy pause as they all contemplated the scenario.

"She might have a point," Sinclair concluded after a moment.

Savage studied Grace. Standing with her head held high, her blue eyes battling with his own, she was confident in her own conviction. "You could get hurt," he said softly.

"I know the risks, but you'll be there, right?"

Savage nodded.

Thorpe took her hand. "Grace, I don't want you doing this."

She gently pulled it back. "I *want* to do it, James. Three women have died, and I'm going to be next unless we catch him. You can't protect me forever. This is the only way."

Thorpe stared helplessly at Savage.

"I think it's worth a shot," he said evenly.

"Sheriff—"

But Savage was already trying to figure out how it could be done.

THIRTY-EIGHT

AT FIVE THIRTY, Grace Calhoun walked into the Snow Plough. She'd dressed carefully in jeans, a pretty floral top that brought out the lavender in her eyes, and a pair of heeled cowboy boots. When she took off her coat, she saw more than a few heads turn in her direction.

A few minutes later, Becca walked in. Sheriff Savage's partner looked around, spotted Grace, and waved. The two women embraced like they were old friends. Beaming at the bartender, Grace ordered them both a drink, then they went to sit at a corner table to catch up. The weathered voice of the country singer lamenting about missed opportunities hovered just above the normal vocal level, so they had to raise their voices to be heard.

"Is he here?" Becca asked.

"Not yet. That's his boss, though, Austin Lambert. I remember Sinclair describing him." She admired the man in the suit, which he wore with more than a touch of disdain. "I see what she means. He is rather good looking in a James Bond kind of way."

"I can't disagree with you there," Becca said, and they both laughed.

It felt good to release some tension. Even though she'd insisted on doing this, Grace felt anything but confident. In fact, she was downright terrified – just not as terrified as being knocked out with chloroform and left to die in the snow. The thought made her shiver with dread. This way, that wouldn't happen. At least, she hoped not.

Thorpe was out in the parking lot in an unmarked car, watching the entrance to the bar.

Thorpe.

What a steady, reliable man. Without him, she wouldn't be doing this. She'd never felt so safe as when she was with him.

Deputy Sinclair was covering the back. There was no other way in or out.

"That's him," she hissed as a tanned man in jeans and a checked shirt strode in. He made a beeline for the bar and ordered a shot of something, followed by a beer. Logan Maddox was in a party mood tonight.

A group of young women sidled up to him, preening and flirting, clearly hoping to catch his attention. They watched as he said something, his eyes crinkling at the sides. One of the women burst out laughing. Too loud, almost raucous. Logan looked around, his attention already diverted.

"You ready?" Becca whispered.

Grace took a deep breath. "Let's do it."

They got up and approached the bar. Grace smiled demurely at Logan and saw his gaze roam over her body. A warm molten smile lit up his face. "Can I buy you ladies a drink?"

"Actually, I have to dash." Becca flashed Grace an apologetic look. "I'm sorry, Grace, it's been great catching up, but I've got to get home. You know how Mike gets when I'm late." She pulled a face.

"Sure, I understand." Grace slung her purse strap over her shoulder. "I should go too."

"No, stay," Logan pleaded. "Just for one drink."

"See you later," Becca said. "Call me tomorrow." After giving Grace a quick hug, she left the bar.

Grace hesitated. "I shouldn't. I don't know you."

"Logan Maddox, ski instructor." He held out a hand.

She shook it.

Logan grinned. "See, now you know me."

Grace laughed. He was very charming. "Okay, just the one."

His grin broadened. "Great."

"Good snow today?" he asked, conversationally.

"Actually, I don't ski. I was just meeting my friend here. She lives nearby."

"Ah, well maybe I could show you sometime."

Grace smiled politely.

"Seriously, you ever thought about taking lessons?"

"Not really. I'm not much of a thrill seeker."

He went out of his way to make eye contact. "You might surprise yourself."

She held his gaze, ignoring the flutter of nerves in her belly. "Maybe."

He leaned in. "Is that Valentino?"

Her perfume.

She stiffened. "Yes, how did you know?"

Was it you who broke into my house? Went through my things?

Her skin crawled to think he'd held her underwear in his hands.

"An ex-girlfriend wore the same perfume."

"Oh, right." She hesitated, wondering how far to push it. She knew how to flirt, she was just out of practice. Jeff's creepy behavior had turned her into something of a hermit. A smile played at her lips. "Is that a good or a bad thing?"

He chuckled and placed his hand on her back. "Good, definitely."

His hand burned through her top into her skin. She had to fight not to shift position.

"So, what do you do, Grace?"

Her eyes flew to his. "How'd you know my name?" Suddenly she felt shaky, uncertain. Her legs were wobbling, so she anchored herself against a barstool.

"Your friend said it before she left."

She exhaled. Of course.

Keep it together. You can do this.

"Oh, yeah. Sorry, I forgot." She pulled herself together. "I'm a teacher." There was no point in lying. If he was the man who'd killed those three other girls and was stalking her, he'd know exactly who she was and where she worked anyway.

"A teacher. Wow. What subject?"

"Math and biology."

"I knew you were smart. Too smart for me."

She laughed, pretending to be flattered. "Why'd you say that?"

"I'm just a lowly ski instructor. Didn't go to college."

"Doesn't mean you're not smart. Some of the most successful entrepreneurs in the world didn't go to college."

"True." He grinned. The gleam in his eye told her he was full of shit. There was no shortage of self-esteem here. He didn't for a moment regard himself as stupid. Not after planning and executing all those murders.

She shivered involuntarily.

"You cold?" he asked, feeling her tremble.

It was very warm in the bar. "No, I'm good."

His gaze lingered on her face, unnerving her. What was he thinking? How best to get her alone? How to administer the chloroform?

Suddenly, Grace found it hard to breathe. His hand was still pressing into her back, making her feel trapped. She broke into a sweat, and nausea rose in her throat.

"Excuse me," she murmured. "I'm going to the restroom. I'll be right back."

She had to get away from him, if just for a moment. To breathe, to regroup. Gasping for air, she made her way through the bar to the door that led to the bathroom. The band had broken into a rambunctious, twangy rock number, and at the front, people were dancing.

She pushed through the crowd and made it into the clear corridor. Thank goodness. There was a window open at the end, and she moved toward it, desperate for some fresh air.

At the window, she paused, letting the chill wash over her, waiting for her heartbeat to return to normal.

It's okay. You're safe. There's law enforcement all around. Nothing is going to happen to you.

Then a strong hand over her face made her jump. She tried to shrug it off but couldn't. Acrid fumes assaulted her nostrils, and within seconds, she felt herself falling... falling.

Then there was only blackness.

THIRTY-NINE

THORPE COULDN'T EXPLAIN IT, but he sensed something was wrong. Turning to Savage in the surveillance van, he said, "I don't like this. I'm going in to make sure she's okay."

"She hasn't come out," Savage confirmed. "We've had eyes on all the exits."

"I know, but something doesn't feel right. Nobody will recognize me in there, and I've never met Logan Maddox before."

"Okay." Savage agreed. "But make it quick."

Thorpe, dressed in plain clothes, looking like any other guest at the ski resort, entered the bar. Loud music assailed his senses as he peered around, looking for Grace. It was warm inside, thanks to the indoor heating and mass of bodies.

She wasn't at the bar. That much he could see immediately. Neither was Logan. A throng had gathered on the dance floor, a giant pulsing crowd of people. They could be there, but he thought it unlikely.

He moved around the periphery, scanning the tables, but they weren't there either. His breath quickened. Where the hell were they?

Climbing onto a chair, he surveyed the dance floor. Maybe he'd asked her to dance, and she'd gone along with it, to make him think she was interested. A blonde head bobbing up and down caught his eye. Jumping down, he moved quickly through the crowd in the direction of the blonde.

"Grace, thank Go—" He froze. The woman turned around, and his heart sank. It wasn't her. It wasn't Grace.

Shit.

Panic set in.

Had Logan somehow managed to get Grace out of the bar without them seeing?

Thorpe pushed open the back door and raced into the parking lot. Sinclair, who was sitting in her unmarked vehicle, wound down the window.

"What are you doing?" she hissed. "I'm supposed to be undercover."

"Did you see Grace come out?"

Her eyes hardened. "No. Why?"

"I can't find her. She's not inside."

"She must be."

"She's not. I looked."

"Did you check the restroom?"

Thorpe relaxed slightly. "No, I didn't." That was it, she'd gone to the restroom.

But then where was Logan?

"I'll check," Sinclair said. She climbed out of the car and walked up the few steps into the bar.

"What if he sees you?" Thorpe said, knowing her cover would be blown.

"Can't be helped."

Thorpe followed her in, across the dance floor, and down a wide corridor to the restrooms. It was cooler here, thank goodness. Perspiration poured off him, but it had nothing to do with the heat. It was cold fear. He couldn't help but feel something terrible had happened.

He waited while Sinclair barged into the ladies' room, leaving the door swinging on its hinges. Thorpe held his breath.

A few seconds later, she reemerged frowning. "She's not in there."

God, no.

"Where the hell is she?"

"You check the men's?"

It didn't take long. The stalls were empty.

Thorpe felt sick. "How could we have missed her?"

"I don't know, but we gotta tell the others."

They moved quickly back into the bar, then Sinclair clutched Thorpe's arm. "Look! It's Logan Maddox. He's still here."

"Thank God." Thorpe felt weak with relief.

Sinclair marched up to him. "Logan, where's Grace?"

He stared at her, blinking. "Grace? How do you know Grace?"

"Where is she?" demanded Thorpe, his hands balling into fists.

Logan recoiled at the breach of his personal space. "Who are you?"

Thorpe took out his silver star and shoved it in Logan's face. "What have you done with Grace?"

"Thorpe," warned Sinclair.

"Done with her? Nothing. She went to the restroom ten minutes ago and hasn't come back. I think she ran out on me." He scoffed. "That's never happened before."

"I can't understand why," Sinclair shot back, then turned to Thorpe. "You search out front, I'll go out back. We need to find her. Now."

They split up. Thorpe's heart thumped like a drum.

Please let her be okay.

"Something wrong?" asked Savage. He'd climbed out of the van as Thorpe charged back outside.

"Yeah. Grace's gone."

Savage stared at him. "What? How?"

"I don't know, but she's disappeared. Vanished into thin air."

"Logan Maddox?"

"He's in there." Thorpe pointed back to the bar. "Hasn't seen her since she went to the restroom ten minutes ago."

Littleton climbed out of the van, looking scared. "What do we do?"

"Secure Maddox," Savage barked. "We want to keep him in our line of sight while we figure this thing out."

Littleton ran inside.

"We need to lock this place down."

"CAN I HAVE YOUR ATTENTION," yelled Savage, holding his Sheriff's badge in the air. The band had stopped playing, and guests were standing around, confused expressions on their sweaty faces. "This bar is now closed. Please make your way to the front exit and give your name to one of my deputies."

There was a communal groan, as people shuffled to the main exit.

"Except you." Savage grabbed Logan Maddox by the arm. Littleton had him in handcuffs.

"This is harassment," the ski instructor demanded. "Why am I under arrest?"

"I need to talk to you about Grace Calhoun."

"Like I told your deputy, Grace went to the restroom and didn't come back. That's the last time I saw her."

"You didn't go look for her?"

"No, why would I?"

"To check if she was okay?"

"Hey, man. I thought she'd run out on me. I wasn't about to go after her. I'm not that desperate." Savage supposed that was a fair assumption. They had just met, after all.

He bit his lip. Logan's apartment was a good ten-minute walk from the clubhouse bar. There wasn't time for him to get there and back.

"Your car still in the shop?" he asked.

Logan nodded. "Yeah. I told you, I'm picking it up tomorrow."

Without a car and his apartment out of reach, there wasn't anywhere else he could have stashed an unconscious Grace Calhoun.

"Okay, take him to the station," he told Littleton. He wasn't ready to release their prime suspect just yet. "I'm holding him until I know what the hell went down here."

Littleton nodded, then led a protesting Logan Maddox away.

Savage joined Sinclair at the front door. She was recording everybody's name as they left. That way they'd have a record of who was here tonight if they had to appeal for witnesses or double-check any details.

"You seen this girl?" Sinclair asked, holding up a picture of Grace. She was asking everyone in the hopes that someone had noticed what had happened to her.

"Nah."

"No."

"Uh-uh."

A pretty inebriated woman in her forties grabbed his arm. "I think I saw her, yeah."

Hope surged. "Where?"

"Near the restrooms. She was leaning against the wall like she was sick or something."

Savage frowned. "What time was this?"

"I don't know." She shrugged. "Maybe an hour ago."

"Was she with anyone?"

"No, she was by herself."

"Okay, thanks."

The woman gave him a drunken smile as she stumbled past.

He beckoned Thorpe over and told him what the woman had said. "She was pretty drunk, though. I'm not sure how reliable a witness she is."

"Let's check it out." Thorpe ran back to the restrooms, Savage on his heels.

"This might be a dumb question, but have you tried calling her?" Savage asked as they dodged customers coming out of the restroom.

"Yeah. Her phone's on, but she isn't picking up."

"Keep trying."

"There's a window at the end of the hallway, but it's too small for anyone to climb through," Thorpe said. "She may have been here, but she didn't leave this way."

"What's behind these doors?" Savage asked a passing waitress. Apart from the two restroom doors, there were several others on the opposite side that were locked.

"Those are the offices," she replied.

"You got a key?"

She shook her head. "No, sir. Only the managers have keys."

He nodded, and she hurried back down the corridor toward the bar.

"We need to search them," Savage growled. "These are the only places he could've dumped her body. Maybe he was planning to go back for it."

"I'll call her again. If she's in there, her phone will ring."

He dialed her number. Both Savage and Thorpe listened hard.

"Nothing," mouthed Thorpe. They moved to the second door. Savage put his ear against the wood. It was silent.

As they approached the third door, they heard a faint humming sound.

"That's it!" Thorpe nodded at Savage. "That's her phone, I'm sure of it."

They both listened, and sure enough, the hum was louder right outside the third door.

"We're going in," Savage said.

Thorpe nodded, and they took a step back. Together, they kicked the door, which sprung back with a loud crack and fell off the top hinge. Before it had stopped ricocheting, both men had darted into the office.

"Where's it coming from?" Thorpe looked around.

"Over there, near the window." Savage reached down and picked it up. He handed it to Thorpe.

"It's Grace's." His face was ashen. "She was here."

"Whose office is this?" he barked.

"It's Austin Lambert's," said Sinclair, staring at the broken door. "Why?"

Thorpe held up Grace's cellphone. "She was here."

"Holy shit. Do you think Logan stashed her here?"

Savage shook his head. "Not Logan, no."

Sinclair gasped. "You think it was Lambert?"

The blind rattled, and Sinclair pulled the cord to release it, letting in a frigid blast of cold air. The window was wide open.

"He was here earlier," Savage said. "Becca saw him."

"Not when I came in." Thorpe stared at the man's neat, organized desk. "He'd left by then."

"He followed her to the restroom," Savage deduced, staring at the open window. "He must have grabbed her either going in or coming out. It would have been quick. Chloroform acts fast. Then he dragged her in here."

Sinclair let out a shaky rush of air. "I can't believe it. He seemed so... normal."

"He lives on the resort, right?"

Sinclair nodded.

"Same as Logan Maddox."

"Yeah, but—" Then Thorpe's eyes widened. "You mean he could have taken Logan's car the other night?"

Savage gave a grim nod. "This is how he got her out."

All three peered out over the ledge.

"There are scuff marks in the snow," Savage said briskly. "Let's check outside."

They ran back through the bar and around the building.

"It's this window!" Thorpe, glasses misting up, aimed his flashlight at the ground. It had started snowing again, and the flakes danced through the beam as they fell toward the ground.

Savage bent down to take a closer look. Sure enough, the snow was messed up, like several people had trampled over it in the last few hours. Tufts of hardy grass stuck up between the thinner patches, visible in the yellow beam of light.

"Looks like drag marks." He followed the striations in the snow, heading away from the window to the parking lot. "This is where the staff park their vehicles. Logan told me this was where his SUV was stolen."

"I noticed the parking lot this morning, when I was talking to Lambert," Sinclair said, frowning. "I remember thinking, what an unfortunate view."

Thorpe stared white-faced at the drag marks.

"She's gone, isn't she? He's got her."

FORTY

THE SNOW WAS COMING down in large drifts by the time they got back to the sheriff's department. The commentator on the radio announced another storm warning.

Stay indoors, folks. This is going to be a bad one.

Great, that's all they needed. The only upside to the weather was that it had sent the reporters scurrying back to their hotels.

Savage refused to beat himself up. Thorpe was right. They shouldn't have used Grace as bait, but if they hadn't, they wouldn't have discovered who the real killer was.

Austin Lambert.

He frowned. Why? That was the bit nobody could understand. What the hell compelled a seemingly well-adjusted young man, who owned a ski resort, to stalk and murder four women?

Three, he corrected. Grace wasn't dead yet. They still had time.

Barb, who'd been manning the office, looked up as they marched in. "Any luck?"

Savage shook his head.

The admin secretary wrung her hands. "Dalton, there's something I need to tell you."

"What?"

"It's about Agent Dahl."

"Go ahead?"

"Well," she glanced at the others before saying, "I couldn't get ahold of her on her cellphone, so I tried the FBI offices in Washington to see if they knew where she was."

"Yeah?" He tapped his foot impatiently.

"They said she was on leave."

He stopped tapping. "What?"

"Yeah, she took leave two weeks ago and isn't due back until the new year."

He frowned. "Maybe she had to take leave to come here."

"There's more. The FBI shut down the Frost Killer case two years ago. She was reassigned, and nobody at the Washington office knew she was here."

There was silence in the squad room.

"You're telling me she came here in a personal capacity?" Savage croaked. There'd be hell to pay if the Commissioner found out about this.

"I knew there was something strange about her," Sinclair muttered.

"She's obsessed," Littleton said.

Thorpe shook his head. "And she threw us way off course. This case had nothing to do with the original killings. If we'd—"

"We'd never have known about the Frost Killer's MO without her," Savage reasoned, although he was seething inside. "The chloroform, the pendant, that was all her."

Why didn't she just come straight with them? Because he'd never have worked with her, a voice whispered in his head. And she knew that.

"How did she run those photographs through the FBI database, then?" asked Barb.

"She must have contacts," Savage muttered. "Anyway, it's not important now. We've got to focus on finding Austin Lambert and rescuing Grace. Every second counts."

"I'll put the coffee on," Barb said, heading to the tiny kitchen.

"Littleton, put out a BOLO on Austin Lambert's vehicle and call Clearwater at the Tribal Police. Ask him to send out patrols on the reservation. He may have taken her there, thinking it was out of our jurisdiction."

Savage watched as Littleton nodded his head and scurried back to his desk.

"Sinclair, call Shelby at the Durango Sheriff's Office. We're going to need his help, and I'll call the Commissioner. I want as many cops out looking for her as possible."

"I've got Lambert's phone number," Thorpe said, his fingers flying over the keyboard. He'd gone into full data-crunching mode. "Pinging it now."

Savage went into his office and called Albright on his direct line. The Police Commissioner answered straight away. "Sheriff, if you're calling this late, I can only assume you need my help. What can I do for you?"

Savage explained the situation, and that they now had an ID on the killer. "We need officers out looking for his vehicle," he said. "He's not at his apartment on the resort, so he's taken her somewhere else. My guess is it'll be somewhere isolated."

"Hell, Dalton, he could be anywhere."

"I know, that's why we need your help."

To give him credit, he didn't hesitate. "Okay, I'll make some calls. Stand by."

"Thank you, sir."

There was a knock on the side-door. Soft, but insistent. Savage frowned and got up. Nobody ever came in that door. Nobody knew it was there, which was the whole point of having it. Cautiously, he unlocked and opened it. A shivering Avril Dahl stood outside, snow blanketing her coat and hair.

"Avril, what are you doing here? I thought you were supposed to be on leave."

She glanced down at her hands. He noticed she wasn't wearing gloves. "So, you know?"

"Yeah, Barb called the Washington office looking for you. Why didn't you tell me?"

"You know why."

He sighed. "Well, come in before you freeze to death."

He held the door open for her as she scampered through. "I saw the lights on and knew someone was here. I came to collect my laptop." She'd left in such a hurry earlier, she hadn't taken it with her. "And to apologize for storming off. I needed to process what you'd said. You were right, of course. It couldn't be the Frost Killer."

"We know who it is," he said, impatiently. "It's the ski resort owner, Logan Maddox's boss."

Her eyes widened. "How did you—"

"We arranged a sting," he said. "We set Grace Calhoun up with Logan Maddox, and Lambert grabbed her. He's in the wind. I've got every law enforcement agency this side of the county looking for them."

"Oh, that reminds me," she said, pulling her phone out of her voluminous coat pocket. "I've got something for you."

"Avril, I don't mean to be rude, but I really don't—"

"My contact at the FBI found a match for that partial. It's only a sixty percent match, so I didn't think it was important, but now that you've got a suspect, you might be able to use it."

She handed him her phone.

Savage read the email, scanning the words until he came to a name.

Hugo Stromberg.

FORTY-ONE

"HUGO STROMBERG?" Littleton said, looking up. "Isn't that Evie Stromberg's brother?"

"I remember looking him up," Sinclair said. "He left Hawk's Landing with his mother when Evie and he were babies. The parents got divorced and split them up."

"Why is his fingerprint on the pendant?" Thorpe asked, pushing his glasses up his nose.

Savage exhaled slowly. "Because I think Hugo Stromberg is Austin Lambert."

There was a long pause.

"Evie's the only descendant that hasn't been targeted," Littleton said, with surprising insight.

"She told me she'd never met her brother." Sinclair said. "After her father died, she tried to find him, but didn't have any success."

"Maybe that's because he changed his name," Savage said.

"Or his mother did." Sinclair bit the end of her pencil.

Savage nodded to himself. "Get Evie in here. If Lambert is Hugo, he may have made contact with her."

"On it." Sinclair picked up her phone and began dialing.

"I'll look into Stromberg's background," said Littleton, turning back to his computer.

"Any luck with Lambert's cellphone?" Savage asked Thorpe.

"Not yet. It's off, but the last lookup was at the Snow Plough at twenty-three minutes past six this evening."

"That's about the time Grace disappeared."

"Evie's at her boyfriend's place. Shelby's bringing her in," Sinclair said, putting down her desk phone.

"Good. Sinclair, go talk to our guest, Logan Maddox. See if he knows anything about his boss that might help us locate him. Favorite haunts, properties, places he likes to go, that sort of thing."

"My pleasure." She got up and was about to go through the connecting door that led to the cells, when Avril stepped out of Savage's office.

There was a lull as they stared at her.

"I'm just here for my things," she said in a soft voice. "I won't get in your way."

"I think you've already done that," Sinclair bit out.

"I know. I'm sorry for misleading you. I really thought it was him."

Barb, unable to help herself, came over and gave Avril a hug. The FBI agent froze. Then Savage saw her blink furiously. "Don't you worry, dear. We understand, don't we Dalton?" She flashed him a stern look.

Savage cleared his throat. "It did look like the Frost Killer's agenda," he admitted. "And we wouldn't have known we had a copycat if it wasn't for you."

"I know, but that doesn't excuse—"

"It's done now," Barb said, interrupting. "Do you want a cup of coffee before you go?"

"No, thank you, Barbara. I'll get my things and be on my way."

Sinclair left the room, closing the door behind her. Littleton and Thorpe turned back to their computers while Barb went back to her desk, shaking her head.

"Avril, come in here before you go," Savage said.

A few moments later, she entered his office, backpack over her shoulder.

"I'm sorry it wasn't him," he said, gesturing for her to sit down. She didn't.

"It's not your fault. I should have seen it myself. There were too many things that didn't add up."

He nodded.

"Your victims are all connected," she continued. "None of the others ever were. I tried to find a link between them, I even thought there was a charity connection, but I was grasping at straws. There weren't any real links, nothing to tie them together."

"He must have some way of selecting his victims," Savage said rationally. "There's always a pattern."

"If there is, I haven't found it yet." She paused, gathering her thoughts. "Then there's the pendants. You were right about that, but I wanted so badly to believe that he was the same killer, I failed to see what was right in front of me."

"What are you going to do?" Savage asked. She looked so lost, standing there in her oversized coat, her backpack hanging off her arm.

"Go home, I guess."

"To Washington?"

"No, I think I'll go back to Sweden for the rest of the year. I'm on leave, remember?" She gave a brittle laugh.

"You could always stay and help us catch this guy," suggested Savage.

She managed a wry smile. "I'd just get in your way."

"Okay, well take care, Agent Dahl." He held out his hand. "It was... interesting working with you."

Her lips turned up as she shook his hand. "You too, Sheriff."

AFTER AVRIL LEFT, Savage ran Hugo Stromberg's name through the DMV database. To his surprise, it came up with a hit. He printed out the driver's license and took it into the squadroom.

"DMV has him registered in Denver, but his last known address was in Breckinridge. He appears to have worked at a ski resort there, pretty much consistently all the way through his twenties."

"Is there a photograph of him?" asked Thorpe.

Savage held it up. "This looks a lot like Austin Lambert, to me."

"It's definitely him," Sinclair confirmed. "Although he's filled out a bit now that he's in his thirties."

"So, Hugo Stromberg is Austin Lambert. I wonder where he got his money from. He owns the West Mountain Ski Resort, doesn't he?"

"Yeah, he bought it from a failing corporation two years ago," said Littleton, who'd been looking into the purchase. "They wanted to consolidate and were looking to off-load the resort. He got a deal."

"He was married in 2016," Thorpe said, scanning the article on his screen. "To a German heiress called Sonja Fleischer. They divorced two years later, but there was no prenuptial agreement, and he got millions in the settlement."

Sinclair whistled under her breath. "What happened to her?"

"It looks like she went back to Germany. Apparently, they met on the slopes. He was her ski instructor."

"Big mistake," murmured Sinclair.

"He bought West Mountain with the money from his divorce?" Savage paced up and down the room. He didn't know why, but it always helped to clear his mind.

Littleton nodded.

"Why is he killing these women?" asked Barb, coming back in with the coffee. "He's got money. Why is he targeting Grace and the others?"

"I think it's revenge," murmured Savage.

Thorpe frowned. "Revenge?"

"What do you mean?" asked Sinclair.

Savage paused, scratching his head. "Remember Rex Haverly told us that the Strombergs specialized in forging and blacksmithing, crafting the tools needed for mining. When the mining shut down, they moved into agricultural equipment, but it wasn't the same. They ran into hard times and had to sell a lot of their land. Fast forward a couple of generations. Evie and Hugo's parents split, and each took a child. Hugo left with his mother, while Evie stayed in Hawk's Landing with her dad." He looked at Sinclair. "What happened to him again?"

"He died from alcoholism nearly a decade ago, leaving Evie to support herself."

"They went from being a wealthy founding family to having nothing," Savage said, pacing again. "I think Hugo Stromberg is trying to take back what he feels is his family's land."

"I don't get it," Sinclair said. "How is killing Anita, Stephanie, and Naomi taking back his family's land?"

"Because they bought it up," Thorpe said, catching on. "I looked into the land deeds earlier on in this case, and when the Strombergs sold their land, it was bought up by the Harcourts, the Cullens, and the Albrights."

"As in Commissioner Albright?" asked Littleton.

"Whose son Stephanie was engaged to," added Thorpe.

"What about the Maddens?" asked Barb. "They didn't have that kind of money."

"Matthew Madden didn't, because it was held in a trust, but I'll bet if you look up the holdings of the trust, you'll find some of the assets were purchased from the Strombergs."

Sinclair hissed out a long breath. "Holy smokes. Do you really think that's what all this is about? Revenge?"

Savage shrugged. "Maybe."

"I'll look into the trust now," Thorpe said, turning back to his screen.

"But why mimic a known serial killer?" Sinclair asked. "What's the point in doing that?"

"To disguise his real intentions. To throw suspicion onto someone else."

"Onto a ghost," Thorpe muttered.

"Someone we'd never find," added Littleton.

For a second, Savage wondered what Becca would say about that.

"Okay, so given what we know, where would he take Grace? I mean, he must know we're onto him by now."

"Not necessarily," Savage said. "He doesn't know we used Grace as bait. He doesn't know we linked Logan's missing car to him, and he doesn't know we know who he really is."

"He thinks we suspect Logan," Sinclair said, getting excited. "I questioned him about Logan's alibi."

Savage gave a quick nod. "That means he's going to be careful, but not too careful. He's not going to disguise his vehicle or get off the roads. He'll think he's got time."

"Time for one more kill," said Thorpe with a gulp.

FORTY-TWO

"WEATHER'S GETTING BAD AGAIN," warned Barb, looking out of the window. The temperature was dropping too. Savage didn't want to think what that meant for Grace Calhoun.

Thorpe kept pinging Lambert's phone, desperate for a read. "Nothing," he muttered, slamming his fist down on the desk. "It's been two hours."

"There's still time," whispered Sinclair, although they all knew it was running out fast.

There was a rap on the door. Looking up, they saw Sheriff Shelby standing there with Evie Stromberg. Barb let them in.

"Thanks, Shelby." Savage shook his hand. "Appreciate you bringing her in."

"Anything to help."

Smudged eyes, messy hair, ripped black jeans. Evie stuffed her hands into her pockets and stared at them. "What's wrong, Sheriff? What have I done?"

"Evie, we need to talk to you about your brother."

Her eyes widened. "My brother?"

"Yes, come with me. We'll talk in my office."

Evie glanced at Sinclair, who she knew better than the other deputies, with pleading eyes, but followed Savage into his office.

Sinclair stood. "I'll come too."

Savage gave her a grateful nod as she joined them. He closed his office door so they wouldn't be disturbed. As he did so, he heard Barb offering Shelby a cup of coffee before he headed back to Durango.

Evie sat on the couch that Grace had been sleeping on earlier that day. He pulled up a chair and faced her. Sinclair sat down next to her.

Savage cleared his throat. "Evie, did you know your brother was back in town?"

She gasped. "No, I had no idea."

"He hasn't tried to contact you at all?"

"No. Why would he? I haven't seen him since we were children."

Savage rubbed his jaw, thinking. "Didn't you try to find him once? When your father passed away?"

Her lip wobbled, just a little. "I did, yeah, but I couldn't find him. I traced him to a house in Denver, but the realtor said the family had moved out years ago and left no forwarding address." Her shoulders slumped. "So, I gave up."

"I'm sorry," Sinclair said, placing a gentle hand on the woman's arm.

Evie gave a tiny nod. "I always wondered what he was like, you know? My mother left when we were very young and took him with her. I've always wondered what it would have been like if..." She shrugged. "Well, it is what it is. You can't change the past, right?"

She turned her smudged blue eyes up to Savage. He gave a rough nod. "Yeah, unfortunately you're right about that."

"So, where is he?" she asked. "Can I see him?"

"He's going by the name of Austin Lambert," Savage said, handing her the DMV printout. She stared at it for a long time.

"This is Hugo?"

"Yeah, does he look familiar?"

She nodded, and a little sob escaped her lips. "I met this guy a couple of months back. He tried to speak to me in the Bar-T. I thought he was hitting on me, so I shut him down."

"He did?" Savage frowned. "What did he say?"

"He asked if I worked there, and I said no. Richie was working, and I was there with some girlfriends."

Savage nodded, encouraging her to continue.

"We were having a good time, when this guy"–she scanned the sheet of paper– "Austin, came up to me. He was casual, you know? Like making conversation. He asked if he could buy me a drink. I said no, thanks, and that I was with someone, and he shrugged, and said another time maybe, and he left."

"He left?"

"Well, he left us alone after that, but he was still there. I felt like he was watching me. It was a bit creepy." She sniffed. "I never knew he was my brother." Her eyes filled with tears. "Why didn't he come and tell me that?"

"He probably didn't know how," Sinclair said.

Evie nodded and wiped her eyes with the back of her hand, smudging her makeup even more.

"You didn't see him again after that?"

"No, not since that night."

Savage hesitated. "Evie, why do you think he's come back to Hawk's Landing now?"

"I don't know," she whispered, clearly upset. "Why are you looking for him? Has he done something?"

Savage leaned forward. "You know that man we were worried about, the one hunting blonde women in town?"

She gasped. "No way!"

He nodded. "We think it's Austin."

"Hugo wouldn't do that." She squeezed her eyes shut as if she didn't want to think about it. "Why would he do that?"

"We think he's angry about your family losing all their land," Savage said. "This is his way of getting revenge on the families that took it."

Evie stared at him, horrified. "Those other girls, they were from rich families? I remember you saying that."

"They were descendants of the families that founded Hawk's Landing," Savage explained. "Back in the late eighteen hundreds during the gold rush."

She shook her head. "It seems impossible. All that time ago. Why would he be angry about that?"

"Because he had a bad life," Sinclair said.

Evie turned her stained eyes to the deputy. "What happened to him?" It was a whisper. "I want to know."

Sinclair glanced at Savage, who gave a quick nod. It was better Evie knew the truth.

"From what we can gather, your mother had dependency issues. They stayed in hostels and squats all over Denver while he was young, often not very nice places."

Savage had been shocked at some of the residences she'd dragged her young child to. His contact in the Denver PD had told him they were crack houses and hostels that prostitutes operated from. He could only imagine what damage it had done to the poor kid.

"How do you know this?" she stammered.

"She was collecting social security payments," Sinclair said. "To do that, you need an address."

Evie put her hand over her mouth. "That's terrible. I had no idea." Her eyes filled with tears. "I used to dream of my mother. I pictured her as this pretty, blonde woman, with hair like mine, and a bright smile who used to come to me in dreams and tell me everything would be all right." She scoffed. "And all this time, she was some burned-out druggie."

"I'm sorry, Evie," Sinclair said, giving her a sad smile.

"Where is she now?" Evie asked, turning to Savage.

"She died a long time ago," he said, grimacing. It was tough to hear. Evie was handling it better than expected.

She gave a stiff nod. "What happened to Hugo?"

"He went into care."

She cringed. "Poor Hugo. Why didn't he come home? Why didn't they send him back to us?"

"I don't know," Savage said honestly. They should have, but maybe they couldn't find his real father. Perhaps child protective services had screwed up. "From what we can tell, he was put with a foster family for a couple of years." What he didn't say was that Hugo had jumped around, from home to home, not settling, acting out, and often getting into trouble. They'd found juvie records of minor infringements and antisocial behavior. His sister didn't need to know that.

Tears ran down her face. "Where is he? I want to see him."

"He's disappeared," Savage said. "That's why we need your help. We need to find him."

Her eyes glistened. "How can I help?"

"He might respond to you, if you call him and ask to talk."

"He'll know you've told me to get ahold of him," she said, and she wasn't wrong. "I don't have his number."

"You could say you tracked him down, just like we did. You contacted the DMV who gave you his drivers' license, and you recognized him from the photograph."

"Is that what you did?"

He nodded.

She blinked several times, the tears staining her cheeks. "Okay, I'll try."

"Thank you."

Savage went back into the squad room while Sinclair sat with her. "Thorpe, she's going to call him now. Keep pinging his phone. We might get a read."

Thorpe gave him a thumbs up.

Savage went back to the office. "Evie, here's his number. Could you call him now?"

She took the notepad he'd jotted the number on and reached into her pocket for her phone. Her hands were shaking.

Licking her lips, she dialed his number. "What do I say?" she whispered.

Sinclair squeezed her arm. "Just be natural. Say you want to meet up, that you recognized his picture and realized he was the man from the bar."

Savage nodded.

"Okay."

She made the call. Savage held his breath, waiting to see if it would connect. He was hoping Austin Lambert had Evie's number, even if he'd never used it. Maybe he'd been planning to at some point, building up the courage, but hadn't gotten round to it.

"It's off," she said, holding up the phone.

"Leave a message," Savage said.

Biting her lip, she did as she was told. In a wavering voice, she said, "Hi, Hugo? This is Evie. I'm sorry to call out of the blue, but I got your driver's license from the DMV and recognized the picture. Are you the guy who spoke to me in Bar-T a while back? Was that you?" A sob. "Are you my brother?"

Overcome with emotion, she hung up.

"I'm sorry, I can't go on." She bowed her head and cried. Sinclair put an arm around her.

"You did good," Savage said. "That was perfect."

If Lambert turned his phone on, he'd see the message. It might slow things down. He might even contact her before he left Grace out in the cold to die.

FORTY-THREE

THE RADIO BUZZED.

"Come in, Hawk's Landing Sheriff's Department. This is Durango Search and Rescue. That BOLO you put out, one of our patrols spotted the vehicle heading north on state road 36."

Savage threw open his office door.

"Did I hear that correctly? They've spotted Lambert's SUV?"

"Yeah." Thorpe had jumped out of his chair and was already reaching for his jacket. "He's heading to the mountains."

"Barb, tell them to head to the sighting. We're going to need their help."

"Will do." Barb reached for the radio and relayed the instructions.

"We'll try," came the operator's brusque voice, "but we're currently involved in a search and rescue operation over at Perjury. A couple of skiers have gone missing. I'll send the patrol over who spotted your suspect, but he's not in a snowmobile. Over."

Shit.

"Send him anyway," barked Savage. "We need all the help we can get."

"I'm coming too," said Sinclair.

"Someone should stay with Evie."

"She'll be okay with me," said Barb.

He nodded.

"What about me?" asked Littleton.

"Keep pinging Lambert's phone," Savage ordered. "Let me know the minute you get anything. It'll help pinpoint his location."

"Okay."

"You can use my computer," Thorpe said. "I've got it up."

Littleton moved over to Thorpe's desk and sat down.

"Where's Shelby?" asked Savage.

"He left before the roads got too bad."

"If we get a read on Lambert's position, call him back and send him after us. We might need back-up."

Barb nodded.

"Please don't kill him," Evie begged, coming into the room. Her face was wet with tears. "Please."

Unfortunately, that was a promise Savage couldn't make.

"It's going to be freezing up in those mountains, Dalton," Barb warned, giving him a worried look.

"I know."

Savage took his shotgun from the gun safe and pocketed a box of rounds.

Sinclair tied up her hair, then checked her service weapon. "Roads are pretty bad."

"We can get as far as he can," Savage said grimly. "Don't forget he's carrying an unconscious woman, which means he's weighed down. Let's go."

They followed the northbound road until it split into two separate roads. Both led up into the mountains, but one was more of a service road, while the other led to a wealthy suburb bordering the State Forest. "Which way?" asked Thorpe, who was driving. The guy had a way with cars and could handle almost any condition. Way better than Savage could.

"The service road," said Sinclair. "He's going to leave her out in the snow."

Thorpe turned the wheel just as the radio blared to life. "Sheriff, it's Littleton. Come in, Sheriff?"

"Littleton, what've you got?"

"He switched his phone on for a second," the deputy said, excitedly. "I managed to get a reading." He read out the coordinates.

Thorpe checked the map on his iPad, which he always took with him. "He's on the edge of the forest," he said before pointing toward the other road. "That way!"

Spinning the wheel, he headed toward the wealthy area.

"Thanks, Littleton, we're in pursuit. Let us know if you get anything else."

"Yes, sir."

Thorpe sped along the icy street, as fast as he dared. Savage trusted his driving implicitly. "That was lucky," he said, his hands on the dash.

"We need some luck," Thorpe muttered. He wasn't wrong there.

They raced through the suburb, to the forest line, going up the steep incline. "Thank God for the streetlights," muttered Savage, as the snow reduced visibility to a few feet. They went into a skid, and Thorpe was forced to slow down.

"It's getting icy," he gritted, knuckles white on the wheel.

"Easy," said Savage. They didn't want to end up in a ditch and need rescuing themselves.

Crawling along now, they kept going until the road ended. There was nothing ahead but trees.

"What now?" Thorpe turned to Savage.

Savage stared into the frozen wilderness but couldn't see anything. It was a near total whiteout. He opened the passenger door and climbed out.

"Let's take a look around. He must be here somewhere."

After pulling on woolen hats and gloves, Thorpe and Sinclair climbed out of the Suburban. Their flashlight beams hardly penetrated the blizzard. Spreading out, they explored the tree line.

"Over here!" yelled Thorpe.

Savage and Sinclair followed the sound of his voice. There was another service road, partially hidden by a mound of snow, but through it was the tread of thick SUV tires. "These are recent," Thorpe said. "He went this way."

"Can the Suburban get over there?" Sinclair asked, studying the mound.

"If he can, we can," Savage growled, his voice filled with determination. There was no way he was letting Lambert get away now. Not when they were so close.

"Let's go," said Thorpe, hurrying back to the car.

Savage braced himself as the SUV growled over the icy mound, its tires screeching as it fought for traction. In the backseat, Sinclair clenched her gloved hands onto Savage's headrest.

They bumped over the top, then skidded down the other side, until the chains on the tires gripped the frosty gravel. "Well done," hissed Savage.

"We're not done yet," murmured Thorpe, as the SUV's engine screamed as it shifted to a lower gear. The winding service road grew increasingly treacherous as they ascended, first through the forest and then into the mountains. The tracks of the suspect's vehicle were still visible in the snow, but only just.

Thorpe's mouth was in a thin line as he concentrated on navigating the uneven surface, keeping the SUV on track. Another ten minutes, and he came to a stop. "I can't go any farther."

Savage peered through the frosted glass windshield. The service road had become impassable, buried beneath a drift bigger than their own vehicle.

"Damn it!" he hissed.

Thorpe tried to go around, but the tires spun against the deep snow. They didn't move an inch. He shut off the engine, and a deafening silence enveloped them, broken only by the relentless howling of the wind. "What now?" His face was drawn and tense.

Sinclair peered out into the swirling snowflakes, her brow

furrowed in frustration. “We can't just sit here."

They could wait for backup, but what they really needed was a snowcat, and the search and rescue team were hours away. Grace would be dead by then. Hypothermia wouldn’t take hours in these conditions. It would take minutes.

“We can’t wait,” Savage said, reaching for the shotgun at his feet. “We’ll have to follow him on foot.”

“He can’t have got much farther,” Thorpe said. “Not in these conditions.”

“And he’s got Grace with him,” Sinclair added.

Savage checked the shells in his shotgun, then opened the door. The biting cold punched him in the face, and immediately, his eyes teared up. He blinked furiously and pulled down his woolen hat. Thorpe and Sinclair followed suit, their breath forming frosty plumes in the frigid air.

Clambering over the snowdrift, they proceeded up the service track in pursuit of Lambert’s SUV. It didn’t take long to find it.

“There!” Thorpe’s words were snatched away by the wind. The dark shape of a car materialized out of the snowstorm.

Savage hurried over and checked it out. There was nobody inside. “It’s been abandoned,” he shouted. “But the engine’s still warm. He can’t be far.”

“He went this way!” Sinclair pointed to a set of deep footprints in the snow. Only one set. Savage knew he was carrying Grace by the depth of them. He’d once tracked a criminal through the State Forest with Tomahawk, the Tribal Police’s best tracker, and he’d learned a thing or two.

“He can’t have gone far. Let’s go.”

They trudged forward, through knee-deep snow, sometimes sinking into drifts up to their waist. It was slow going, and before long, Savage’s breath was coming in hot, burning gasps. His deputies weren’t faring much better.

Each step they took higher into the mountains brought them closer to their quarry, but also deeper into the heart of the storm.

FORTY-FOUR

"HE CAN'T HAVE CARRIED Grace far in this," yelled Thorpe, helping Sinclair up. Not as tall as the men, she was struggling to get out of waist-deep snow.

"He's not planning to." Savage looked around. "He's going to leave her somewhere around here."

"Should we split up?" Thorpe asked. "We'll cover more ground that way."

"Yeah, but if you find him, don't tackle him alone. Text your location." He checked his phone, they still had reception. But just barely.

"You going to be all right?" Savage asked Sinclair, who was back on steady ground.

"Yeah," she panted, her cheeks flushed from the exertion. "I'll go west, the snow's not as deep there."

Thorpe headed east along the road, every step an effort in the knee-deep snow.

Savage went farther north, into the mountains.

He'd been walking for a good half hour, the wind howling, whipping the snow up around his legs. Before long, he was grunting and panting with the effort. He'd just reached the tree line when his phone buzzed. The signal was faint, but he had a text from Sinclair.

HELP!

HEART RACING, he turned and ran. Sprinting as fast as he could, he cut through the forest toward the west. The trees loomed like shadowy giants, their branches heavy with snow.

Was she still alive?

Had they found her in time?

Was Lambert still there?

As he pushed through the dense forest, his phone buzzed again. It was another message from Sinclair, her words typed out in haste.

HURRY!

HEART POUNDING IN HIS CHEST, he pushed harder. His first priority was Grace, but if Lambert was there, he'd do what needed to be done. He gritted his teeth in determination. The trees closed in around him, their heavy branches obscuring his path. The fading light made it increasingly difficult to see, but he didn't slow down.

Finally, he burst through the trees into a wide, hilly expanse of snow. There, he saw Sinclair, her breath visible in the freezing air, desperately trying to keep Grace warm. She'd placed her own jacket over the still figure and was in the process of pulling on her hat and gloves.

"Is she alive?" Savage yelled.

Sinclair nodded. "Yes, I can feel a pulse, but it's faint. She's in the beginning stages of hypothermia. I'm going to need an external heat source."

"Where's Lambert?"

"He went that way." She pointed up the hill directly in front of them.

Thorpe came charging around a rocky outcrop. "Have you found her? Is she alive?"

Sinclair nodded.

Thorpe dropped to his knees and felt her pulse. "Thank God."

"Get her back to the SUV," Savage said.

Sinclair glanced up. "What about Lambert?"

"I'll go after him."

"Alone?"

"It's going to take both of you to carry her back. If we don't get her to the SUV, she'll die."

They hesitated, knowing it was risky letting him pursue the killer by himself in this blizzard.

"That's an order!"

"Okay, let's go." Thorpe hauled Grace to her feet, but she was a dead weight. He tried slinging her over his shoulder but fell to his knees. The snow was too deep.

They each took one of her arms and dragged her forward, one step at a time. Savage watched them head off in the direction of the service road, then turned to face the mountain. It didn't take him long to find Lambert's tracks. Lighter now, he was moving faster than he had before, over the rugged terrain into the hills.

Lambert was fit, a ski instructor, and younger than Savage. He was used to the terrain. Savage was from Denver and hadn't experienced snow like this before he took the job in Hawk's Landing.

Still, he wasn't about to let the guy get away. Not now. Not after what he'd done.

Anita.

Stephanie.

Naomi.

He would never forget their frost-bound bodies, as white as the snow that encased them. The killer had let the life seep out of them, minute by minute, until they'd literally frozen to death.

That monster was going down.

The wind whipped up plumes of snow that danced before his eyes, but he kept going, concentrating on the fresh tracks. A surge of adrenaline shot through him. He was gaining on him.

Savage felt his heart pounding as he crunched through the snow. It was a steep ascent into the hills. Almost there. He couldn't be far off now.

Lambert's tracks led to a narrow ridge overlooking a steep ravine. Panting, Savage came to an abrupt halt. Shining his flashlight into the darkness, he could just about make out the figure of a man. The killer was trapped. There was nowhere else to go.

"Hands in the air, Lambert!" Savage's command cut through the icy air. The clouds separated, and silvery moonlight flickered down, temporarily lighting up the landscape.

Lambert, trapped between Savage and the ravine, turned to face his pursuer. Desperation made his eyes gleam with defiance, but he didn't reply. Silence hung between them, broken only by the wailing wind. Savage watched every move, every twitch, as Lambert weighed his fate. In an instant, Lambert made his choice, and raised a pistol.

The shot whizzed past Savage's ear, sending him diving into the snow. Turning off the flashlight, he lay still. There was a clicking sound as the spent round was ejected and another slotted into place.

"Hugo?" he called.

Silence. Only the wind spraying snow in his eyes.

He tried again. "Hugo. It's over. We know who you are."

Nothing.

"I spoke to Evie," he said, wondering if mentioning his sister would make him talk. "She begged me not to shoot you."

"You shouldn't have done that, Sheriff." There was angst in his voice.

At least now he had some sort of dialogue. Evie had begged him not to shoot Lambert. He was giving the man a chance to walk out of here alive. "Give yourself up. It's the only way this will end without you in a body bag."

A brittle laugh. "Nice try, Sheriff."

"My deputies are behind me. You're trapped. You've got nowhere to go."

"Bullshit. I know they took Grace back down the mountain."

Well, it had been worth a try.

Savage crawled closer, moving toward the voice. He kept his gun pressed out in front of him, ready to fire.

Shuffling sounded from dead ahead. Footsteps in the snow. Lambert was getting nervous. He didn't know where Savage was. A shot rang out. It flew harmlessly over Savage's head, clearing it by at least four feet. Had he been standing, that would have been a different matter.

"You know, we're not that different, you and I," Hugo said.

Savage doubted that.

"We're both hunters. Look at you now. You're stubborn, I'll give you that much. Most men would have given up by now."

"I don't kill innocent women."

"Well, you see enough darkness, and it consumes you." A harsh chuckle. "There is no light anymore. Only redemption."

Savage wasn't buying that. Slowly, inch by inch, he approached the shadowy figure. The blizzard made it easy to move around without being seen.

"Sheriff, you there?"

Savage didn't reply. To do so now would reveal his position. He kept crawling forward.

"Sheriff, I know you're there!" Another shot, desperate and in the wrong direction.

"What about your family's land?" Savage stood up. He was three yards behind Lambert, pointing his gun at his head.

Lambert, caught off guard, swung around.

"Drop it." Savage warned.

The killer hesitated, then lowered his hand but didn't drop the gun.

Savage glared at him. "Drop the gun, or this is going to end badly."

"You don't know what it's like to lose everything," Lambert spat. "My mother was a junkie and a whore. I grew up in a Denver squat. You wouldn't believe some of the things I saw. Things no child should ever have to see."

Savage cringed but didn't budge. He'd been a homicide cop in Denver for ten years. He knew what Lambert was talking about. "I get it, you had a shit childhood. Doesn't mean you need to take it out on these women."

"I only wanted what was mine – and Evie's."

"Why didn't you just talk to Evie?"

"I wanted to. Several times. But I never found the right moment."

"How do you tell someone you're a serial killer, right?"

"Right." He scoffed, but there was no humor in it.

"You thought you'd wait until you'd bought your family's land back." Lambert's eyes widened, surprised Savage knew so much. "It wasn't hard to put together once I knew who you were."

"You think I did all this for land?" Lambert's breath smoked out in front of him.

"You wanted to avenge your family, take back what was yours."

"Please." Lambert laughed. "Give me some credit."

Savage frowned.

Lambert gave a slow swivel of his head. "Look around you, Sheriff. These mountains are full of quartz rock, and you know what comes from quartz rock?" When Savage didn't reply, he said, "Silicon."

Lambert gave a quick, dry laugh, and Savage realized he'd misread the situation. This wasn't about revenge. Lambert was a psychopath. He didn't bother with vengeance. It meant nothing to him. Not even Evie could penetrate that lack of empathy. That had been drained out of him years ago. This was about something infinitely more useful.

Money.

"Silicon is found inside nearly every cell phone and computer chip in the world."

Savage kept his rifle locked on Lambert. "Money? You did all this for money?"

"It's not just *money*," Lambert said. "It's *billions* of dollars. The rocks around here are unique. High in silica, low in contaminants. Every producer's wet dream."

"You want to mine these mountains," Savage deduced, keeping his gaze locked on Lambert's. His finger rested on the trigger, ready for whatever came next. The man looked happier than he should be given the situation.

"I *am* going to mine these mountains," he retorted.

"See, that's where you're wrong." Savage gestured for him to put his hands back up. "You're going to prison. For murder."

"No, *you're* wrong!"

Lambert spun, bringing the handgun up as he did so. Savage pulled the trigger, but Lambert had already got a shot off. It hit Savage in the shoulder, and his own went wide.

Shit, that hurt.

His shoulder was on fire. Pain radiated down his arm, burning like hell. He'd forgotten how much he hated being shot.

Lambert raised his arm, ready to fire again. With a furious yell, Savage dropped his shotgun and closed the distance between them. The killer fired, but Savage was too close. The pistol discharged into the air, and there was no time to reload. He knocked the gun out of Lambert's hand.

Damn Lambert. He should have shot him when he had the chance. Instead, he'd listened to his story, trying to understand why, but it all boiled down to greed. The commonest and most petty of motives. Savage was disappointed.

He punched Lambert in the face, but the killer swung at him, stunning him with a decent right hook. Savage stumbled backwards, momentarily disoriented.

Sensing weakness, Lambert slammed into him, sending them both flying. Savage hit the ground, the air leaving his lungs in a *whoosh*. They rolled, a tangle of limbs and naked aggression, each trying to gain the upper hand in the slippery terrain. Snow swirled around them as they grappled. Savage, severely handicapped by his bullet wound, landed punches when he could, his breath coming in ragged gasps.

Lambert managed to pin Savage down, his hands closing around his throat. Savage gasped, scrabbling at the murderer's wrists, but Lambert was strong, and Savage's strength was ebbing with every second that went by. He was losing blood, the snow was stained with it. No, he couldn't go like this, not by the hands of this greedy madman. He wasn't about to check out just yet. With a surge of adrenaline, Savage bucked his hips, throwing Lambert off balance.

Seizing the opportunity, Savage flipped their positions, now pinning the murderer beneath him. His fist came down like a hammer, pummeling Lambert's face until it was a bloody mess, but he couldn't keep him down. Not with one arm. A brutal knee in Savage's ribs sent him sprawling to one side.

Both men staggered to their feet, battered, bloodied, and breathing hard. Savage locked eyes with Lambert and saw such hatred there, it made his skin crawl.

With a guttural roar, they collided once more, fists flying, each blow landing with a thud muffled by the snow around them. It was a brutal dance, and one Savage wasn't winning.

Between one ragged breath and the next, the killer landed a solid punch to Savage's temple. The Sheriff crumpled, his body sinking into the snow, vision blurring.

Lambert stood over him, breathing hard. "I don't have time for this."

The snow fell softly on Savage's face. How easy it would be to close his eyes, drift off to sleep and never wake up.

Lambert was looking around for his gun. He had mere seconds to act. Savage groaned and rolled onto his side, his shoulder numb. It dulled the pain but rendered it useless. With his good arm, he reached for his own Glock. It had fallen just out of reach during the fight. He had no idea where his shotgun was.

It was a race to see who could get to their weapon first. Lambert lunged for his. Savage's mind ran the time distance equation in a heartbeat. No chance of beating him to the punch. But no way would he give up, not when his life depended on it.

Becca. Connor. He couldn't abandon them. Not now. Not out here.

Savage torpedoed himself at the Glock, praying he'd get there in time. His good arm stretched beyond its limit. He felt the cool polymer grip, the familiar ridges seating into the palm of his hand. Rolling onto to his back, he swung the pistol upwards, but he was too late. The barrel of his enemy's weapon was bearing down on him.

With a sinking heart, Savage weighed the slim list of options as he lay sprawled on the ground. His mind readied for the bang, his muscles tensing in anticipation of the searing bullet. If Lambert made the mistake of taking a body shot, Savage planned to unleash a torrent of violence once the gunfire started. If he took aim for the head, the game would end. One shot, and lights out.

Lambert committed. His finger pulling back the trigger. Savage froze, teetering on the paper-thin edge of life and death.

Click.

For a heartbeat, Savage wondered if it was his mind playing a trick. What had just happened? He should be dead. It took only another fraction of a second for him to realize no muzzle flash followed the trigger squeeze.

Misfire. In Savage's tunnel vision, he hadn't noticed the stovepipe. The casing from the round Lambert fired hadn't properly ejected and was now sticking out from the port. Savage didn't think, he reacted before Lambert had a chance to clear the weapon.

With a burst of adrenaline, he brought his Glock up and locked on the target. Desperation lined Lambert's face as he racked the slide. The casing sailed into the air as the next round entered the chamber.

This time, Savage had the advantage. He felt the kick and watched as Lambert fell backwards, taking the bullet center mass. There was a look of disbelief on the killer's face as he clutched his chest.

"You shot me—"

Savage got to his feet and stumbled over to where Lambert lay.

"How does it feel?" he growled, kicking the man's gun out of reach. Lambert wasn't dead, but he was dying. The blood seeped out of the hole in his chest and onto the snow, melting it and forming a fuchsia stain beneath his body.

Before Lambert died, there was one thing Savage wanted to know. "How did you get Anita Cullen to the barn?"

A groan. "What barn?"

"On the Thompsons' Ranch."

"I didn't. We went skiing together. I left her in the snow, not far from the barn."

"Unconscious."

A smirk. "Of course. That was the Frost Killer's MO."

"You decided to pretend to be a renowned serial killer to terrorize the town?"

"Why not? It worked, didn't it?"

Savage stood there for a long time, watching the life drain out of the killer, making no effort to keep him warm or tend the wound. There was nothing he could do, anyway. The man would die, regardless. Savage shot to kill. There was no coming back from this.

Lambert knew it too. He glared at Savage, his eyes burning with hate, then pain, and finally there was nothing.

The blizzard. The cold. The bed of snow. It seemed strangely fitting.

It didn't make up for what Lambert had done, not by a long shot, but as the snowflakes fell on the killer's body, covering it in a soft, white shroud, Savage felt a strange sense of peace.

FORTY-FIVE

"HOW'S SHE DOING?" Savage strode into the urgent care ward at Animas Surgical Hospital, ignoring the shocked glances from the staff. Wet, dirty, and bleeding from the wound in his shoulder, he knew he looked a sight. Luckily, it was only a graze.

"You're bleeding!" Sinclair rushed over. "You need to see a doctor."

"I'm fine." He nodded at Grace, so pale and still in the hospital bed. "How is she?"

"She's fine," Thorpe said, looking up. He sat at Grace's side. She was still unconscious, but the machine she was hooked up to beeped in rhythm. "Her blood pressure and other vitals are stable."

"That's good." He stumbled, and Sinclair grabbed him by the arm and made him sit down.

"Stay there, I'm going to call a doctor."

He didn't refuse.

"What happened to Lambert's body?" Thorpe asked. They'd been in radio contact since Savage climbed down the mountain and called for help, so the rest of the team knew what had happened.

"The Search and Rescue team are retrieving it and taking it to the morgue," he said.

Thorpe nodded. "I'm glad he's dead. After what he did to those girls..."

Savage leaned his head back against the wall and closed his eyes, overcome with exhaustion. Now that he was sitting still, his adrenaline had dropped. He could feel every stiff joint and bruised area of his body.

"Sheriff, are you okay?" Thorpe's voice roused him.

"Yeah, just tired."

"You've lost a lot of blood," came a sterner voice, one he didn't recognize. Opening his eyes, he saw a man in a white coat staring down at him, alongside Sinclair's worried pale one.

"I'm fine," he tried to say, but it sounded garbled, even to his own ears.

He was moving. The ground seemed to tilt, and he felt himself being wheeled along a bright corridor. He squeezed his eyes shut against the bright lights.

"I'm going to need two units of blood," came an urgent request.

There was a tight squeeze around his good arm. He tried to shake it free but couldn't. "His BP is dropping."

"We need a transfusion, now!"

"I'm fine," he tried to say again, but couldn't get the words out. Sparks twinkled at the sides of his vision, even though his eyes were closed. That was weird. Maybe he wasn't fine.

He was so tired. If he could only sleep for a moment, he'd feel better. It was all the exertion in the snow. It had worn him out. Unable to fight the exhaustion, he let himself drift off.

THE FIRST FACE he saw when he opened his eyes was Becca's. "Thank God," she said, leaning in to give him a hug. "You had me worried sick."

He inhaled her scent, warm and familiar. "I told them I was fine."

"You got shot," she admonished. "You are not fine."

"It's just a graze."

"You lost a lot of blood," the nurse told him. "We had to do a transfusion."

"Really?" He hadn't thought he was that bad.

"Yes, really."

He looked down to see his shoulder was professionally bound, his arm in a sling.

Becca shook her head. "I told you not to take any unnecessary risks, and what do you do? Go off after a killer by yourself in a blizzard."

"Can we not do this now," he murmured, dropping his head back on the pillow.

She gave him a stern look. "All right, but you scared me."

"I know. I'm sorry."

Thorpe came in, smiling. "Good to see you awake, Sheriff."

He managed a grin. "Takes more than a bullet to kill me. How's the patient?"

"You mean other than you?" Sinclair shot him a wry look. He hadn't even realized she was in the room.

"She's fine," Thorpe said. "The effect of the chloroform has worn off, and she's conscious."

"That's great." He tried to sit up, forgetting he couldn't use his left arm. "Goddamn."

"It'll take a while to heal up," the nurse said. "The doc said it grazed a nerve."

That explained the lack of feeling.

"Thorpe just gave a statement to the press," Sinclair told him. "Along with the Police Commissioner, who's claiming a lot of the credit."

Why wasn't he surprised. "At least they'll be satisfied." He snorted. "We got them a killer."

"But not the Frost Killer," said Sinclair.

"Let's leave them to figure that one out," Thorpe said with a chuckle.

Barb rushed in, carrying a boxed treat of some sort. The hospital room was getting crowded. “I bought this for you.” She glanced furtively at the nurse before setting it on the side table. “It’ll boost your strength.”

He grinned. “Thanks, Barb.”

“Only when he’s off the IV,” the nurse said.

Savage looked around at his team. “It’s good of you all to come.”

“We’re not just here for you,” Sinclair said. “We want to know what happened with Austin Lambert.”

“I shot him.”

“We know you shot him.” She rolled her eyes. “But did he say anything? What happened before that? Do you know why he killed all these women?”

He told them what Lambert had said when he’d been holding him at gunpoint. About the silicon in the mountains, billions of dollars’ worth.

Sinclair’s eyes were huge. “He wanted the land so he could mine the mountains?”

Savage nodded. “He thought if he killed off all the descendants, he could buy the land on the cheap. There’d be no one to leave it to, I guess.”

Barb gasped and put a hand over her mouth. “Mr. Harcourt called the station. He said he’d been made an offer and was selling up. He didn’t want to be here anymore, not after what happened to his daughter.”

“Come to think of it, old Mr. Cullen at the general store said he was also thinking about selling some land. That’s why he took out that library book, to see if it had any historical value.”

“Find out who the offers were from, Barb,” Savage said. “I’ll bet it was Lambert.”

She hurried out of the room to make the call.

“What about Anita Cullen?” said Sinclair. “How did he lure her out to the barn?”

“They met for coffee,” Savage said, recalling the look in Lambert’s eyes when he told him. "Lambert suggested they go skiing, and of course, Anita agreed. After all, he was Logan's boss."

She scratched her head. "And I suppose he was lying in wait for Stephanie Harcourt. If he'd been watching her, he knew where she went running every morning. It would be easy for him to drive out there ahead of her and wait until she came along."

"Yeah, he didn't have an alibi. Didn't need one. We didn't even suspect him."

"We managed to identify him on the lobby cameras at the casino," Thorpe told him. "He was sitting there for hours, watching Naomi. It was creepy."

"What a sicko." Sinclair took a steadying breath. "Then it had nothing to do with revenge?"

Savage shook his head. "He was too far gone for that." He shuddered as he remembered the naked hatred in Lambert's eyes. It was pure greed.

"What should we do about Evie?" Sinclair asked. "She's still at the station. Littleton is guarding her."

"You can let her go," Savage said. "I owe her an explanation, but that'll have to wait until I get out of here."

"Now you're talking sense," said Becca.

Barb returned, still holding her phone. "You were right. Both the offers came from Lambert's company. The same one that bought the resort."

"He killed three women just to get his hands on that land," Becca mused, shaking her head. "Even going so far as to pretend he was an infamous serial killer."

"That way he'd scare the families into selling out," Savage said.

"It's diabolical," Barb whispered.

No one disagreed.

SAVAGE WALKED INTO HIS HOUSE, glad to be home. Becca, Connor in her arms, came in behind him. Two days in observation, and he was itching to get out. The inactivity and hospital food were driving him crazy.

"Welcome home," she said, putting a sleepy Connor down in his crib.

Savage embraced her. "Thank you," he said.

"For what?"

"For putting up with me during this investigation. Not only that, but you helped us solve it. We'd never have realized it was a copycat if not for you."

She nodded. "I won't say you're welcome."

"I know, but it's over now."

"You scared me."

"So you said." He smiled at her, but she didn't smile back.

"I need you, Dalton. *We* need you. Working too hard is one thing, but getting yourself shot is quite another. What would we do if you weren't here?" She glanced down at a sleeping Connor.

He didn't want to think about that.

"Nothing's going to happen to me," he said.

"You can't say that." She walked away to make a bottle. Connor would be hungry when he woke up.

"I promise I'll be careful."

She turned around. "That's the problem. I don't believe you anymore. You put your life at risk to catch that guy. A killer. Someone who isn't worth the air that he breathed. You risked all this." She waved her arm in Connor's direction.

"It's my job," he said, quietly. "You know that."

"Well, maybe I don't like your job." She went back to what she was doing.

He sighed. "Becca, there's nothing I can do about that. I'm the Sheriff. Catching bad guys is what I do."

She dropped her gaze. "I know, and I'm sorry for giving you such a hard time. It's just... I'm terrified of losing you."

"All I can say is that I'll do my very best to make sure that doesn't happen."

She managed a small smile.

"Okay?"

"Okay."

He took her into his arms, holding her close, and they stayed that way until Connor let out a powerful cry.

"He's hungry." She laughed, wiping her eyes.

"I'll feed him."

Becca nodded her thanks and went to the bedroom. He knew he'd put her through hell these last couple of weeks.

"Here you go," he said, giving Connor his bottle. Hungry hands reached up to grab it. Savage smiled down at his son. Becca was right. His family was too precious to risk losing his life. He had to be more careful.

Savage made himself a coffee and sat down at the table to drink it. His shoulder burned now the painkillers were wearing off, and he didn't have all the feeling back in his left hand, but it was getting there. Becca had put a pile of mail on the table, and the top one caught his eye. It was postmarked Stockholm.

Curious, he picked it up. It was addressed to Sheriff Savage, at his home address. He tore it open and turned it over to take out the letter. A snowflake fell out. It wasn't attached to a pendant, just by itself, but it looked just like the ones the Frost Killer used to make.

He stared at it for a minute, puzzled, before pulling out the post-card that was included. His breath caught in his throat. In a neat, precise hand was written:

THIS ONE'S FOR AGENT DAHL

***

Dalton Savage returns soon in ***CRIMSON MOON***! Click the link below to pre-order your copy now!

https://www.amazon.com/dp/B0CRK4K8BB

COMING SOON! A new series featuring Avril Dahl!

Want to be the first to know when it is released? Join the L.T. Ryan reader family & receive a free copy of the Rachel Hatch story, *Fractured*. Click the link below to get started:
https://ltryan.com/rachel-hatch-newsletter-signup-1

Join the L.T. Ryan private reader's group on Facebook here:

https://www.facebook.com/groups/1727449564174357

LOVE SAVAGE? Hatch? Noble? Get your very own L.T. Ryan merchandise today! Click the link below to find coffee mugs, t-shirts, and even signed copies of your favorite L.T. Ryan thrillers! https://ltryan.ink/EvG_

ALSO BY L.T. RYAN

Find All of L.T. Ryan's Books on Amazon Today!

The Jack Noble Series

The Recruit (free)

The First Deception (Prequel 1)

Noble Beginnings

A Deadly Distance

Ripple Effect (Bear Logan)

Thin Line

Noble Intentions

When Dead in Greece

Noble Retribution

Noble Betrayal

Never Go Home

Beyond Betrayal (Clarissa Abbot)

Noble Judgment

Never Cry Mercy

Deadline

End Game

Noble Ultimatum

Noble Legend

Noble Revenge

Never Look Back (Coming Soon)

Bear Logan Series

Ripple Effect

Blowback

Take Down

Deep State

Bear & Mandy Logan Series

Close to Home

Under the Surface

The Last Stop

Over the Edge

Between the Lies (Coming Soon)

Rachel Hatch Series

Drift

Downburst

Fever Burn

Smoke Signal

Firewalk

Whitewater

Aftershock

Whirlwind

Tsunami

Fastrope

Sidewinder (Coming Soon)

Mitch Tanner Series

The Depth of Darkness

Into The Darkness

Deliver Us From Darkness

Cassie Quinn Series

Path of Bones

Whisper of Bones

Symphony of Bones

Etched in Shadow

Concealed in Shadow

Betrayed in Shadow

Born from Ashes

Blake Brier Series

Unmasked

Unleashed

Uncharted

Drawpoint

Contrail

Detachment

Clear

Quarry (Coming Soon)

Dalton Savage Series

Savage Grounds

Scorched Earth

Cold Sky

The Frost Killer (Coming Soon)

Maddie Castle Series

The Handler

Tracking Justice

Hunting Grounds (Coming Soon)

Affliction Z Series

Affliction Z: Patient Zero

Affliction Z: Abandoned Hope

Affliction Z: Descended in Blood

Affliction Z : Fractured Part 1

Affliction Z: Fractured Part 2 (Fall 2021)

ABOUT THE AUTHOR

L.T. RYAN is a *Wall Street Journal*, *USA Today*, and Amazon bestselling author of several mysteries and thrillers, including the *Wall Street Journal* bestselling Jack Noble and Rachel Hatch series. With over eight million books sold, when he's not penning his next adventure, L.T. enjoys traveling, hiking, riding his Peloton, and spending time with his wife, daughter and four dogs at their home in central Virginia.

* Sign up for his newsletter to hear the latest goings on and receive some free content ➜ https://ltryan.com/jack-noble-newsletter-signup-1
* Join LT's private readers' group ➜ https://www.facebook.com/groups/1727449564174357
* Follow on Instagram ➜ @ltryanauthor
* Visit the website ➜ https://ltryan.com
* Send an email ➜ contact@ltryan.com
* Find on Goodreads ➜ http://www.goodreads.com/author/show/6151659.L_T_Ryan

***

BIBA PEARCE is a British crime writer and author of the Kenzie Gilmore, Dalton Savage and DCI Rob Miller series.

Biba grew up in post-apartheid Southern Africa. As a child, she lived on the wild eastern coast and explored the sub-tropical forests and surfed in shark-infested waters.

Now a full-time writer, Biba lives in leafy Surrey and when she isn't writing, can be found walking through the countryside or kayaking on the river Thames.

Visit her at bibapearce.com and join her mailing list to be notified about new releases, updates and special subscriber-only deals.

Made in United States
Troutdale, OR
01/18/2024

16993835R00168